"Elsa Sjunnesson effortlessly ___ mythos of *Assassin's Creed* together with history, pagan faith, and Arthurian legend to create a thoroughly engrossing story of one woman's fight to defend her people. Sjunnesson's take on the world of *Assassin's Creed* is thoroughly refreshing, and Niamh is a conflicted, fearless and relatable heroine for the ages."

Karin Tidbeck, Crawford Award winner and World Fantasy Award finalist, author of Jagannath

"*A* gorgeous addition to the *Assassin's Creed* canon, a steely and golden skein in the rich tapestry of this tale that intersects so many other tales. Sjunneson offers a treasure that rewards a careful reader and a dedicated player."

Meg Elison, Locus & Philip K Dick Award-winning author

"A fun read, and amazingly, felt just like playing a chapter of *Assassin's Creed Valhalla*. It is a great extension of the world and readers will love meeting old friends in new ways."

C L Clark, author of The Unbroken

"*Sword of the White Horse* puts readers right back into the game with an inspired, nonstop adventure, featuring dazzling action, a brilliant heroine, and a story as tight and sharp as the edge of a blade. I'd follow Niamh of Argyll anywhere."

Karen Osborne, author of Architects of Memory

ASSASSIN'S CREED

VALHALLA

SWORD *of the* WHITE HORSE

Elsa Sjunneson

ACONYTE

First published by Aconyte Books in 2022

ISBN 978 1 83908 140 8

Ebook ISBN 978 1 83908 141 5

Cover art by Alejandro Colucci

Distributed in North America by Simon & Schuster Inc, New York, USA
Printed in the United States of America
9 8 7 6 5 4 3 2 1

ACONYTE BOOKS

An imprint of Asmodee Entertainment Ltd

Mercury House, Shipstones Business Centre

North Gate, Nottingham NG7 7FN, UK

aconytebooks.com // twitter.com/aconytebooks

For Day, who got me to pick up the blade again. Blind swordswomen stick together.

PROLOGUE

The craggy landscape of home greeted Niamh as she trudged up the hill after the man she would have to betray. The horses had been left behind at Hadrian's Wall, as it was too risky to bring them across the border into Caledonia. The path forward was on foot, something Niamh knew would weaken her companion the longer they had to walk. She had some misgivings about physically tiring the man out, but her loyalties could not be in question.

A part of her wanted to suggest that they steal another pair of horses despite the risk, to keep Hytham from losing speed on the recovery that he had clawed for. But two strangers riding through these parts of Caledonia would be more suspicious than two travelers on foot, and Hytham had driven the horses too hard on the way up, regardless. Niamh didn't know precisely what had happened to him to leave his body in such a weakened state, but it had been enough to keep him bound to Ravensthorpe for a long time even before she'd met him. Because of this, Niamh had tried to convince him to let her go on this journey alone. It would have been easier without his watchful eyes on her, after all, analyzing every action she took, every motion of her head, every thought that he could see cross her face. It hadn't been an easy ride north, and she'd been cautious, had slept as far away from him as she dared, just in case she spoke in her sleep.

Why he'd insisted on going with her this far north with his injuries baffled her. Being rain-soaked and without much in the way of comfort wasn't helpful to healing. There had been wolf attacks, bandits to dodge, and that was just the violence. The chill of the moors had been enough to make *her* knuckles ache when she gripped a sword, and whatever was happening within his knees couldn't have been much better. But he had insisted nonetheless. And now, the cost to her meant being careful, and just a little bit more suspicious of what he could observe than she would have liked. It also meant she would destroy what comradery had built between them.

But if he was tired… if he was distracted… if he wasn't at his best, she might be able to get what she needed out of this trip without notice. At least, not until she had gotten far enough away to hide in the fens, or maybe convince some of the locals to conceal her. If she was lucky and those same locals didn't notice she wasn't quite who they expected or wanted to see, either. This was not going to be an easy trick. But she'd trained for adventures like these, not just with the people she answered to, but as a matter of course in the kind of village she was from. They had always needed people to be stealthy for them, to sneak into rival villages for supplies, or to steal back their weapons.

They continued to scramble across mossy rocks, viewed by red fluffy cows with large horns, the only witnesses to their entrance into her homeland. The cows didn't seem very concerned by their appearance, not like the foxes and wolves that lived further south. The cows simply stared and chewed on grass. They didn't even move.

Niamh wished she could actually go home – to her village, her people. She wished she hadn't gotten in this deep. She wished she could have the kind of peace that the cows had, to just stand and eat and be left to their own devices. The adventures she'd had were wonderful, of course. The chance to see more of the world beyond the shores of her own village, but she had learnt that with adventure came costs. Costs to safety, costs to friendships, and costs to her sanity.

She watched Hytham walk ahead. He'd insisted on taking point for a little while, even though she knew these lands better than anyone.

"Are you quite sure you don't want me to guide us now that we're here?" she called out again, for what had to be the hundredth time.

"No. I know where we're headed now, and I would rather be the one that showed their face first," Hytham responded.

It was then that she saw him make a mistake. One she couldn't let him make because of course it would risk her neck as much as his.

"I wouldn't step there, were I you," she called out across the wilderness, picking up her pace and chasing after him.

Hytham barely paused in his stride. "It's fine, it's just more of this moss we keep walking over."

She internally sighed. People who weren't from these parts of the islands always said that. It was how they ended up mummified in the middle of the moors, their corpses making for excellent fire fodder later on.

"That's a bog, Hytham. You're looking at peat."

The scent told her what she was looking at. Not the ground itself, but the smell of loam and rotting vegetation that she knew heralded spots where one shouldn't put their feet.

Hytham paused, stepping backwards slightly and glancing back at her. "A bog? But there's no water here. Just moss."

She nodded, picking up her pace to get close, just in case he didn't listen to her. She thought he might die as a result of her betrayal, but no one deserved to die because they accidentally stepped into a peat bog that they'd been warned about. That was the kind of death no one, but especially not people she liked, deserved. Maybe Old Mae back at the village deserved it, but she was mean to children, and she drank too much ale to be either sensible or useful. Those people deserved to be in bogs.

Maybe Marcella deserved to be in a bog, if she couldn't find a way to be cooperative. But Hytham? Hytham was funny, and sensible enough to deserve a death that the Morrigan could respect, not one that he'd be made fun of for in the afterlife.

She stepped around him and toed the brown and green substance she knew wasn't safe to bear weight. It was squishy under her foot, not hard. "You can't put your full weight on it, but you can test it out. See?" she said, gesturing for him to try.

He did, and his face paled as he realized what he had almost done. "I see your lands are more complicated than I gave them credit for, and that I was wise to bring you with me instead of coming alone."

He smiled when he spoke, and Niamh felt the guilt welling up inside of her. It was hard to breathe for a moment, or even look at him, though holding his gaze was the most important thing that she could do. Liars did not look away when they spoke.

"I am glad that you allowed me to come, though I wish you had stayed back to spare your body the hardship. These are difficult lands with little sympathy." Niamh found a stick on the ground and used it to poke at the edge of the bog, uncovering its boundary. "If you follow me, I can get us past this to a safer path forward," she said, turning her back to him. She hoped her hunched shoulders wouldn't give away her true intentions, and the doubts that plagued her.

Pulling her hood up over her head, she fought the urge to turn around, to tell him to go back, back to Lunden. To tell him of her plans. To confess. She couldn't, she shouldn't. Instead, she stabbed at the earth, making sure that neither of them fell victim to the bog they had stumbled across, because if there was one thing she wouldn't allow to happen, it was the death of both of them in the most ridiculous way possible.

"You've been a good travel companion," Hytham murmured, after they finally reached the other side of the bog. He leaned against the stick he had gathered, having learned the trick of safety. "But you're quiet. I don't think you were this quiet before."

She sighed. Of course, he had noticed that she found words more difficult as they neared their goal.

"It is strange being back home," she said slowly. "I thought that when I came back this way again, it would be to head to my village to rest, that I might be old and feeble then. Or that perhaps my bones would be carried back to be buried here. I didn't think I'd be..."

How could she find a way to speak the truth without speaking it?

"... on a quest, not with anyone. I didn't think I'd have a purpose here again. Home is complicated. It is the place I most want to be and the place I least want to be at the same time."

Hytham nodded in agreement. He had his own secrets, she could tell. He didn't speak of his past, or where he had come from. Nor did Marcella or anyone else she had met with the Hidden Ones. They all shrouded their origins in mystery, preferring to speak of the present, of their purpose. They lived in a world where what mattered was their mission, and nothing else.

They crested another hill, and far in the distance she spotted smoke rising up out of a valley. A camp. Perhaps the one they were headed to? Even with the trust Hytham had put in her, allowing her to sleep by him, allowing her to lead the way, when it came to their actual destination, Hytham had been cagey. He had not wanted to be precise in what he shared with her.

"Hytham, you're going to need to tell me where we're headed eventually," she told him now, exasperated.

"Just there, over that hill toward the smoke. That's where we're headed." He confirmed her suspicions, and stepped around her, insisting bodily that he be the one to lead them forward, at least for now.

Niamh saw her destiny coming. The choice she had made months ago was now here, and all she could do was be loyal to those she had made promises to, and she had made no promises to Hytham.

ONE

The waves crashed onshore, slamming against the stone-studded beach in the very northern reaches of Caledonia.

Niamh sat on a rock overlooking the surf, surveying the cold water as she meditated, her hands resting gently on her knees and tapping out the rhythm to the song playing in the back of her mind. Beside her sat a sword, battered and battle worn, not too far out of her reach. Her eyes were half closed, focused gently on the horizon, but also on nothing at all as she wandered through the parts of her mind that needed to be set free to connect with the energy of the ocean.

The sun slowly crept up toward the sky, lighting the beach with the golden and orange colors of dawn. Her dark auburn hair, plaited back with ribbon as orange as a fox's tail, stayed well out of her face. A practical solution for a swordfighter. In the back of her mind, even while she focused on the meditation she had set herself, she knew that raiders had been spotted not too far away from her village. If they came upon her, she would have to defend not just herself, but the whole village on her own. Such was her purpose as the witch-warrior of this town.

Thus, the sword, and the awareness of her surroundings, were something she wished she could entirely let go of. It would be easier to connect with the energies of the earth if she could pretend that there were no dangers to her in the world. Her fingers brushed on the deep green wool she wore, cut into a dress that had a slit on the left side for her sword to hang. Niamh of Argyll was the kind of woman who never came unprepared, even to make a morning meditation beside the sea.

As she finished her silent prayer, she inclined her head toward the path she had taken down to the water's edge, drawn by the swift noise of footsteps. Her apprentice ran down the path, her face flushed with exertion, a sight which left Niamh concerned – the girl was never going to make it through her first battle if she didn't work on her endurance. The sword in her left hand shook with every step she took. Her other hand was tightly fisted around some kind of paper missive. Niamh briefly imagined what would happen if the girl tripped, and made a note to work with her on proper speed with a sword. She should be waiting to draw until there was an enemy, after all.

After what felt like forever, the girl finally reached her, and took breaths deep and ragged.

"You can sheath your sword, girl," Niamh said, voice stern as can be. "There are no enemies to fight, no wolves to catch us unawares. Unless you've come to kill me?"

The role of mentor was not one that Niamh was used to, and her reprimand felt odd coming out of her mouth. But the apprentice needed her to be full of displeasure, it seemed. Being impractical with a sword would just get a number of people dead, Niamh herself included, if Birdie wasn't careful.

Lifting herself off the rock, Niamh hopped down, going to meet the girl amid the sea grasses. From the concerned look on her apprentice's face, Niamh could tell someone had read the letter Birdie held out in her off hand for her – the child couldn't read, which was another problem that Niamh would have to solve with education before her apprentice could be sent for further training. No one would leave her care without the ability to read a message.

"What is it?" She tried to sound bored. The girl was overexcited, perhaps thinking she might be included in whatever urgency the letter indicated, most likely envisioning her first quest. Perhaps that was true, if Niamh needed the help, but she was loath to take someone who couldn't think to sheathe her own sword when going at a dead run…

"The Lady seeks your counsel," the girl said formally, stilting the words out of her mouth like she had been practicing them the whole way down to the beach. Spoken with the kind of formal phrasing that might have been given to her by the letter sender, and whoever read it to her.

The Lady. Spoken with the kind of emphasis that meant it could only be one woman who sought Niamh's aid. The only woman who could summon her from anywhere, at any place, at any time, and successfully get her attention.

Except, though she was loath to admit it, Niamh was tired. She wanted to stay here, in her village, and not answer such summons. It felt like she'd been fighting her whole life against those seeking to take, take, take – be it raiders or newcomers arriving on her shores from other lands. She'd rather get comfortable in her home village, do the work of guarding the town from the constant raiders and harm, maybe raise a child or two if the Goddess willed it.

Instead, it seemed the Goddess was calling her down a much less peaceful path. One Niamh had trained for, to be sure, but not a path she had really considered would come for her. And of course, this girl, Birdie, was not ready to go that far south to where the Lady resided or might send them.

Niamh glanced at the paper her apprentice handed her with a shaking hand. After a moment, she realized that Birdie had not one, but two pieces of paper in her grasp. The first was not in a hand that she recognized. A spidery scrawl in a language that was not completely unfamiliar to her, but was more challenging to decipher. She sat down again among the sea grasses and dunes, bringing the paper closer to her face.

Whoever had sent this first missive sought a skilled warrior who went by the name of Nimue. According to the letter, she was skilled with a sword, could creep with the stealth of the fox and the silence of the adder. Whoever wrote this letter was asking someone to meet this Nimue, because she was meant to join their order.

The feeling of exhaustion intensified, as she could see without even needing to read the next page what was going to be asked of her. The Lady was going to ask her to pose as this warrior, to take her place. Somehow, Avalon had intercepted this message. It would never reach Nimue, who would remain blissfully ignorant of this call to action. Niamh would take her place.

Birdie had told her that the Lady was calling. That meant one thing: the Lady wanted her to go not just to the Tor, but to Lunden. The letter from the strangers who sought such stealthy warriors had been clear about their location, and while Avalon wrote in ciphers, the investigation of the provenance of that note was clear. Niamh had avoided visiting the city for every trip south that she had ever taken. The concept of a city made her bones ache. Too many people. Too much noise. Too many things she could never imagine because she had spent so much time in the bogs, and the fens, and the coast. She knew this land, these kinds of people, but to go all the way to Lunden meant she might never return. It was a far enough trip that many made it one way and never came back. So much danger resided in such a voyage that Niamh knew it would take all her skills to arrive there safely.

Staring at the long-suffering piece of parchment that had made that journey to her corner of the world, she folded it away and placed it in the leather pouch at her hip. Her suspicions were confirmed when she looked at the second page.

It was from the Lady herself, in her own hand, written on the lightest parchment Niamh had ever seen, in ink that shimmered from the magic of the isle.

The Lady was asking her to leave her home, to go to

Lunden as Niamh predicted, and to find out who these people were. To do this, she would take the place of this Nimue. Who were these Hidden Ones that needed people for their stealth? Who needed people who could sneak and murder at the same time?

The Lady made it clear that no one should be operating any kind of group such as this without the knowledge or approval of the Women of the Mist. So, she was activating one of their best witch-warriors, the only one she felt could meet the needs of this particular mission. Niamh of Argyll. It helped, the Lady noted, that their names were almost the same. Though Niamh knew she could have changed it for any mission. It was her skills that made her perfect to suit this calling, not her name.

Even through the tiredness, through the dread of the journey that Niamh knew faced her, she also felt the knowledge of her own skill. She was proud of what she could accomplish in the name of Avalon. What she knew she had been trained for, because they had put time, energy, and prayer into her. It had been the focus of her life, to find ways to serve the Goddess through the art of the sword and herb craft. It was what she had been meant to do. So, even though she was ambivalent about the long ride, she couldn't help but feel a spark of pride. She had done enough to be worthy of a quest for the Goddess' own voice.

And thus, she would obey the Lady, and take this perilous mission.

She wished she could take more time beside the water to say goodbye, but her apprentice seemed unable to wait patiently. Birdie's feet shuffled on the sand, digging further into the soft earth. Her fingers danced along the edge of the pommel of her blade, primed to strike though her skills weren't quite up to par. At least the girl was eager, that would take her a long way on this path.

Niamh nodded and stood, folding the second letter into her pouch, and then started up the path toward their small village. She didn't wait for her apprentice to follow, knowing that the girl would take her cue.

Birdie couldn't quite keep up. Niamh's steps were long and fast, and she made progress past the sea grasses and into the sparse woods that surrounded their home with ease. But nonetheless, the girl shouted after her, her words nearly unintelligible with the distance that Niamh had put between them.

The child repeated her request again, and Niamh could hear her steps speeding up. She paused to allow Birdie to step around her, to face her, and to speak to her. She was not entirely impressed with the girl, but she had the right to speak to her mentor and ask questions at any time.

"Are you going to need me to come with you?" Birdie asked, breathless.

Niamh looked at the dirty little girl, frail and scrawny, standing in front of her. She thought about the long ride from Argyll all the way to the southern edge of Mercia, the time spent alone on the road with nobody but a horse. She thought about how helpful it would be to have a second pair of eyes, and as she gazed out into the gloomy sky, she knew that even if she didn't want to bring the child, she needed her apprentice on the road ahead. Perhaps if Niamh were smart enough, quick enough, gifted enough, the child could be sent to Avalon instead of back to a long life of spinning wool. But Birdie hadn't shown that she had the good sense to be useful. It was a hard decision for Niamh because she knew she had Birdie's entire future in her hands.

Lives up here in the north were hard. They were often short, and girls didn't fare as well as boys. Niamh had done well for herself because she had escaped, found a purpose and a blade that served her well.

If the girl could serve a purpose and find her inner strength, perhaps the trip out of Argyll would be well worth it. If it could make Niamh's life a little easier, even if Birdie wasn't quite as smart or as quick as Niamh would hope… Well. She'd give her the chance.

"Saddle up two horses, get us enough food for two days ride south, and don't forget to find yourself a decent weapon. You can't be caught without one once we leave, and that one in your hand isn't sharp as I'd like. See to the blacksmith at once."

"So, I get to go?"

"Yes, Birdie. You get to go."

The eager girl nodded and dashed off without another word. Niamh was left with the two letters, and her thoughts.

She was the hedge-witch of this community. Her goal was to keep watch over the people who had raised her, to heal their wounds, to birth their babies, and when danger was afoot, to protect them through whatever means necessary – whether it was by the blade or by herbal means. She taught children how to make poultices, and she meditated every morning on the beach to attune herself to the energy of the land, knowing who hunted there, who lurked, and who came in peace.

Niamh stared out at the forest and wondered if this time, unlike the last time she left her home, would be the time that she never came back. This forest knew her, and she didn't want to lose her connection to the land that had birthed and raised her. Her family was dead and the only things that remained which had known her for her whole life were these trees and this land.

She had regretted the lack of care she had taken in saying goodbye when she left for Avalon to train when she was young. While on that magical isle, she had missed her home fiercely, and she wanted to honor its impact on her soul more honestly this time around.

She wandered back toward the village and studied it as if with new eyes. The small huts had thatched roofs and the bushes were just starting to get berries hanging off them. Sheep bleated in the distance as the shepherds brought them back into the town. In the distance, the womenfolk were beating out the wool. The smell of cooking in someone's cottage wafted between the huts, and again, she regretted that she would be leaving the people she loved behind. She walked past it all. She had another location that required her attention.

At last, she made it to the spot that she knew she needed to spend the most time at: the cairn just outside town, built to house her mother's bones when she had passed.

Her mother had been the witch-warrior for their village before her, a title passed down. Niamh had thought perhaps one day she would have a daughter and pass the title down once again, but instead she was leaving, her future uncertain. That wasn't how she'd thought things would go. After all, her mother had been the one to send her away initially, insisting that the best thing Niamh could do to serve her people and herself was to learn everything she could from Avalon. To accept the role passed down to her. Like she had done.

Lines from the Lady's letter rang through Niamh's mind.

You are the one with the best skills we have to assess the situation. The Goddess has spoken, and it is your fate that you should walk this path. We choose you as our spy.

A spy. She'd never really thought of herself as having those kinds of skills, skills of a warrior and a witch, but of a spy? She supposed the skills were transferable, but it would be a new challenge for her. She was ready for it.

She remembered her first raid. The Northmen had come to the coastal shore and they had tried to take everything that their village had... not that there was much for them to take this far north. Niamh had crept through the chaos of the fight and made her way to the longship they had brought to their shore. She sank it, leaving them with no choice but to run through the moors back to their own Danish settlement, which was settled on stolen land to the west. It had left them without food or new furs.

But that hadn't been the only time Niamh had been clever. Her hands brushed over the rough stones of her mother's cairn, and she thought back even earlier, to her time at Avalon. Her mother had warned her, when she left, that it would take more than just stubbornness to become a priestess. It would take bravery.

One of the final tasks of the women who studied on the isle shrouded in mist was to take a walk. The walk was not a stroll through a meadow filled with sheep, nor was it a walk along a peaceful shore or a river's edge. The walk was in the dark on the coast, to the cave that was rumored to belong to Merlin. At the cave, every person who wished to serve the God and the Goddess must ask for the blessing to tread the path of the witch-warrior.

Niamh had walked in near darkness by the shore. Her feet were bare, her hair unbound. She used only her hearing to understand where she was in space, because the sky was so dark. Somehow, no stars shone, and the moon was at its darkest phase. Even now, as she stood in the forest of her home, she could feel the frozen waters that licked her ankles. She knew that one wrong step would mean her death then, and she had accepted the cost. She had accepted the consequences to follow this calling to the end.

When she had reached the cave, which was filled with round stones worn smooth by the ocean, she stripped off her robe and waded deep into the frozen waters that flooded it. She dipped beneath the salty water and came back up, asking for the blessing of the waters. The bravery it took to swim into that cave was significant, because she knew that at any moment, if the waters willed it, she would drown, or freeze, or be bashed against the rock wall by the surf and be lost.

Yet, none of these memories made her a good spy. She was a good priestess, a good warrior. She had helped birth babies safely in conditions that raised the hair of many a midwife, but these were not the traits of someone who could lie and sneak and tell untruths to get what the Lady needed.

But if the Lady wanted her to, if the Goddess wanted her to, perhaps they both saw something in her that Niamh did not. If this was the calling that she was meant to heed, then perhaps she was truly who they thought she was. Sometimes, it was necessary to let the people who knew you best show you who you could be. She had trusted the Lady before, when she took her walk to the cave, and she had been told she was ready for it, even if she didn't quite believe it.

Following the path to Lunden would be just as dangerous as the path to Merlin's Cave.

Niamh pulled the two pieces of paper out of her leather pouch and examined them. The Lady had been clear and direct about what she needed from Niamh. The expectations were clear, and it didn't escape Niamh's notice that this was not a request. It was an order.

The other letter was odd. Worded more like a puzzle than anything else. She mouthed the strange words, trying to see what they sounded like out loud.

We who hide in the shadows seek the trust of Nimue, who hails from the islands north of Caledonia. We know you are as cunning as the fox and as silent as the adder. That you have within you the fierceness of the wolf and the speed of the rabbit are of great assistance as well.

*We know why you have those skills. If you would
like to hone them further, to know who you are better,
come to the Hawk's Nest by the Tamesis. Ascend our
ladder and tell us what you know of the ways to walk
with shadows and darkness.*

What did it mean to walk with shadows? Niamh wondered. She had certainly done her time studying the rites of the Morrigan and taking lives with respect. She was good at understanding the shadow world, but that was not quite the same thing as walking with shadows. She was curious what that could mean. She also wondered what kind of past could make someone more suited to it.

Reading the call was like reading her own traditions as written by someone who only understood them on the surface. She could see that whoever wrote this knew her people believed in understanding the energy of the creatures around them, and that they respected them. But she didn't believe that she could take on the spirit of any creature, only to learn from them as she did from the other energies of the forest.

But this wasn't an ask of bad people, necessarily. They may work from the shadows to good purposes. She knew that she had been trained by people who believed that sometimes it was necessary to do difficult things in order to protect the people who looked to them for guidance and support. She knew that she had been educated well, that she could teach these strangers to understand her people better if she were able to form an alliance with them.

Glancing down at the Lady's letter once last time she read the final lines again.

Even as you give them your trust, you must still pretend to be this other woman and you should not yet tell them who you represent. Give them the tale of your origins, not that you are a Woman of the Mist. They may not know of us, or if they do, they may trust you less because you are one of us. Use your judgment, we trust it, but we believe they will want to keep you away if they know you are backed by our community.

She would have to pretend she was someone that she was not. She would have to deny her abilities, to some extent. It was clear that whoever these people in the Hawk's Nest were, they were not entirely friends. But they could be, if she had the sense to bring them around.

The cairn was small, about as long as her mother had been in life, barely taller than Niamh, and wide enough to keep her mother's body protected from the crows and other beasts that would come to feast.

Niamh's hands remembered building it, each rough-hewn stone had passed through her grip, even if briefly, as she had had help in constructing it. Now, the stones had been worn smooth over time, the years had made their edges softer than they had been when the cairn was built. It had been ages since she had come here to visit, not out of lack of want, but out of time. Her duties to the village had kept her busy these few years since she had returned from Avalon. There was always a pregnant woman to tend to, or a sick child. A pack of wolves that needed to be sent away, or a watch to help with. It had not been a quiet time to pass in these woods by the sea. Little time for mourning of her mother, who would have expected her to be attentive to her people since, after all, Niamh had taken on her role as witch-warrior of the village.

Niamh closed her eyes tight, remembering the final recollection she had of her mother.

While she had been preparing to leave for Avalon, her mother had been ill. Her body had run hot, and there had been nothing to cool her skin or stop the sweat from rolling down her brow, no matter what she tried. No herbal remedy, nothing had stuck. Niamh had fought with her about leaving, but her mother had instructed that Niamh could only wait until after her body was under a cairn. She would be expected to arrive at Avalon as soon as she was done burying her.

Niamh had sat vigil with the women of her community, her mother laid in a bed of reeds, under furs and blankets brought to keep her warm even as she burned from the inside. She held her mother's hand as she passed through the veil, and they built her cairn fast enough that she could leave without time to spare.

The ride to Avalon had been lonely, quiet and meditative. She had felt the role pass from her mother to her own soul, and even as she mourned the loss of the only person in her family, she knew that she carried her mother's spirit inside of her.

Now, her thoughts became less noisy, and she realized that it was settling into darkness, the sun going to bed beyond the sea. She had spent the day at this site, mulling over these thoughts and trying to find her place.

Even now, as the sun was setting beyond the hills, she knew her mother's spirit would guide her as she traveled south and heeded the orders of the Women of the Mist.

Behind her, she could hear the drums in the distance calling her to one last dance before she left. The heather and the scent of the sea whispered to her, and the road lay ahead as soon as she awoke.

TWO

Niamh and Birdie left the village at first light. Unlike the rest of the town upon hearing of her departure, Niamh hadn't drunk too much ale, and instead had watched the dancing and joined in for a few rounds, even though she knew that she wasn't just a villager. She hadn't been for a long time. Her horse – a beautiful brown boy who she had brought back from Avalon – snorted gently in her face while she got him saddled up and ready for the long ride to the south.

Quietly beside her, Birdie went through their saddlebags and made sure that they had enough food and waterskins to last them. Niamh had been clear this wasn't the kind of ride where she wanted to stop at every village and ask for assistance. She wanted to make it to Lunden with as few witnesses as possible. After all, these strangers wanted her to work with the shadows. She would keep to them as best she could.

Niamh didn't look back when she finally mounted

Mathan and guided him down the path out of their home. She steeled herself. She couldn't mourn too much. Even though she hadn't wanted to leave, there was a strong possibility that the Goddess would ask her to use the knowledge she had gained as a witch-warrior for more than hedge-witchery. Even if it took time, witch-warriors always went on adventures, eventually.

Birdie did not ride quickly. She hadn't left the village for more than a day's ride in her life. Niamh passed her, going around her apprentice and leading the way, knowing that Birdie wondered in her heart if she would ever make it back here, to her home.

Niamh wasn't able to reassure her, or to give her a notion of the answer. No one knew what a quest like this would entail. Only the Goddess, and she wasn't speaking to them about it.

They had a long ride ahead of them. It was the kind of ride that chafed your thighs and wore out your horse. Niamh would usually have traded horses midway through, choosing to borrow another one of Epona's herd, the name of the herd that was kept for Avalon, tended by their followers all across the island, for the sake of the beast, but she'd gotten a sense of urgency from the letters. The Lady was worried. There were new people on this island, and they had not made their intentions as clear as they could be.

Birdie picked up speed to stay close behind her, stubborn to the last. She had dressed in clothes similar to Niamh's, practical breeches under a kirtle that could be pulled up over her hips when she rode. As instructed, she had found herself a sword that was in better condition than the one she had been waving about on the beach.

But it was clear from the first day's ride that Birdie was not used to the pace of a long journey. Niamh could sense the ache in Birdie's hips from the way that she slid off her horse at night, and the bone tiredness of riding for so many miles at such a pace. Niamh had gotten used to it, she had done long rides like this before, but she remembered that it was a shock to the system when you first experienced it. Her bones had ached for days after her first ride to Avalon.

Later, they rode past villages full of Picts, and Birdie complained about being unable to ask them for assistance or comfort. Niamh rolled her eyes and pushed onwards, knowing there was nothing to be gained by visiting their neighbors. If it was the wrong village, they would end up as prisoners, or worse.

There was nothing Niamh could do to help Birdie's sore muscles or her need for comfort on the road. They kept moving with the swiftness that Niamh felt was necessary. When they reached the rock wall that had been constructed to keep them at bay, Niamh stopped.

"This is the line between Caledonia and Mercia," she said, turning to Birdie with a stern expression. She remembered the first time she had crossed Hadrian's Wall, knowing that it had been built to keep people like herself behind it. It was a warning. *Do not pass, you are not welcome here.*

"Once you go past this wall, there is no turning back," Niamh said, finally. "At least, not with me at your side." The revision was added hastily, but with the knowledge that it was necessary. Birdie might decide halfway to Lunden that she wasn't cut out for this kind of adventure, and if she wasn't, Niamh couldn't lead her back home. She had a job to do.

Birdie swallowed audibly as she glanced behind them, taking in the land that she knew accepted her. Niamh could see the girl weighing her choices, trying to decide if she really had the stomach to continue.

To her surprise, even though Birdie seemed a little pale and out of sorts, the girl nodded.

"Yes. All right. I'll follow."

It was all the invitation that Niamh would wait for. She began to lead them along the Caledonian side of the wall, searching for a hole wide enough to allow for their horses to pass. It took several hours of trudging, but while they walked Niamh had the opportunity to think.

Leaving Caledonia had always been difficult for her. She loved the ways that she had been raised to follow the seasons, to honor the gods and goddesses, and to pay attention to the energy that surrounded her. She was not so sure how the pagans in the south handled their rituals, but she was sure she would get along with them in the end.

It was the others that worried her. The Christians who wanted to change the practices of these islands wholesale. The Danes who came with their own magic and their own peculiar gods. New beliefs and new deities mixed and matched with the old ways, leaving Niamh uncertain. While the old ways she'd known weren't confined to small villages, those practitioners living in towns and cities were being actively hunted down by invaders.

Here, in Caledonia, at least it felt like things were far

enough apart that she and her people could mind their own ways, for the most part. They could forget that change gripped the south, filling it full of myths and stories unheard of before.

Finally, they found a hole in the wall and pushed through. Niamh glanced around, wary that a guard might attack or call them out, but no such warning came. She let out a deep breath and together she and Birdie rode into Mercia.

These northlands weren't so different from those in Caledonia because the geography didn't change very much at first. After they had gotten far enough away from the wall, which was often a place of known conflict, Niamh found them a river to fish.

Birdie tended to the fire while Niamh secured them food, and they ate and drank quietly. Birdie's nervousness peppered the air still.

"It's all right to be afraid," Niamh said after they had eaten. She was nervous herself. "Fear tells us things we need to hear. I was afraid when I first left Argyll. I was afraid when I first went to Avalon. But the fear cannot consume you, and I see you fighting it."

Birdie stared at her, chewing around the last remains of the fish.

"Things have changed much on these islands…" Niamh continued, looking around. "We'll ride past settlements full of Danes, people who came here from another land – a colder one than ours. And yes, some of them are our enemies, but not all. There are Saxons, too. And Normans, and Picts… and other clans than ours. There will be pagans who treat with our gods and goddesses differently."

She recalled the first time she had seen the midsummer celebrations observed at a settlement that had combined with Danes. "But none of those things are bad as long as the old ways are respected. As long as people like us can be left in peace."

Birdie continued to stare at her. Niamh wished that she would learn to speak more quickly, as she knew that the less quick-witted people in the world had a harder time of it.

"You must learn to be quicker with your voice than you are now," she said, interrupting the silence yet again. "You'll meet people who expect an answer and won't take kindly to your silence."

Birdie thought long and hard before speaking, but eventually, once the sun had set, she did so.

"I do not know if I am as brave as you are, Niamh. But I will try. I want to see more than our village, and I want to be able to serve our people in the same way you do now. I know that you don't have someone to inherit your position, and I hope I can do it when you are finished."

Niamh looked at her with narrowed eyes. "If you want to be like me, and to serve Avalon, you will have to go wherever they ask, no matter what."

"I know that, and I believe that I will learn."

Niamh wasn't sure that she believed this girl, scrawny and out of shape as she was, could do it. But she was willing to let her try.

That was more than enough.

They rode further into Mercia, leaving the cold and damp highlands behind, abandoning the peat bogs and the scent of rain, and finding themselves in forests that teemed with wildlife – wolves, foxes, even a bear or two.

At one point, Niamh knew that they passed by Dane settlements, and she could not restrain her feeling of resentment toward them. They had done so much harm to her people, so much violence. And she knew that it wasn't safe for her to stop in those villages, because if any of them had raided her own village, they would know who she was. They would know she had fought them, had once sunk their ship and left them stranded to be slaughtered while fleeing for their home. She had no forgiveness for them. There had been so many people she had fought on the battlefield, and it was important that she not be seen by those former foes. She did not want any unwelcome attention while on her quest to the Hawk's Nest.

Niamh found a meadow amid the dense trees that looked as though someone had made their camp in the same spot, but long enough ago that they had gone their separate ways. It was clear and big enough to host a fire without a danger to the forest at large.

"I think you've been learning enough to do a bit of a scouting tonight," Niamh said to Birdie, indicating that she would lay the fire and make their evening meal. Birdie's face lit up with the opportunity, and she eagerly set off into the woods to check for predators of both the human and animal variety.

When she had disappeared from sight, Niamh cast her eyes around the meadow anyway, and spotted something that felt out of place. Freshly ground out ashes at the edge of the clearing. It wasn't anything sinister, but it meant someone had slept here much more recently than she had first thought. But she recalled that few people liked to rest in the woods for long. While they might say it was because of the wolves, she knew it was because of the woods themselves. She could feel their hostility toward humans.

When Birdie returned, she arrived through the trees behind Niamh, as loud as a bear.

"You have to learn to soften your steps, girl," Niamh said, frustrated with the lack of care the girl took to not draw attention. It would be a problem someday.

Birdie looked at her, shamefaced. Obviously, it was not the tone of voice she had hoped to hear from her mentor.

"Things seem clear," she said, not promising a thing regarding her performance.

"Very well. We'll rest here for the night and leave these woods behind in the morning."

"They're creepy," Birdie said, wrapping her arms around herself unintentionally.

"They're angry with us for trespassing. These woods aren't meant for people," Niamh corrected her, looking around at the tall pines. "I'll take the first shift..." she began to offer, but Birdie shook her head vehemently.

"Lady, you've taken first shift every night. Let me do it. You need your rest too."

It was true that she who took first shift took the third, and that meant less sleep before riding another long day forward.

"Very well," Niamh said reluctantly, before turning over onto her travel fur on the ground and wrapping herself up with her hood over her eyes. She knew she had to trust

Birdie at some point, and showing she had faith was a way for Birdie to find confidence in herself. She dropped off to sleep with very little trouble, leaving Birdie to keep watch over her while she slept.

When Niamh woke, the sun was shining. Yet, she did not wake to the gentle hands of Birdie, asking her to awaken to continue their journey just before dawn. She woke to a sky full of birds in flight and blue tinted clouds overhead. It was a beautiful, if late, morning, and Birdie was nowhere to be seen.

Niamh bolted upright. The girl wouldn't have abandoned her. She looked around and found both horses still tied to a tree, glancing with bored eyes around the meadow before continuing to munch their fill on the grass in front of them. Niamh threw her furs off and leapt to her feet.

Birdie might have been untrained, and she might have been ill-suited for the road, but she was not the kind of girl who would leave a woman alone in the woods to fend for herself exposed in her sleep. Niamh knew her better than that. Niamh had taught her better than that.

The only thing that explained what had happened was that Niamh's apprentice had been taken. Niamh didn't like the implications: first, that someone had been able to sneak into her camp quietly enough to avoid awakening her, second that Birdie hadn't thought to call out, and third that they hadn't taken the horses.

None of it added up to smart enemies or a good situation for her apprentice.

Grabbing her sword and unsheathing it, Niamh searched

for evidence and spotted footprints leading into the forest, away from the camp. First Birdie's, then two other sets, before Birdie's disappeared. The girl must have gone out on a patrol when she was too tired to pay attention to her surroundings, or perhaps Birdie had heard someone in the woods and gone off to investigate and found herself up against more foes than she could face alone.

Niamh worked to keep her weight balanced, leaving the quietest steps that she could even if she was quick. She listened to the forest. Behind her, the birds sang and the cry of some wild creature could be heard in the distance, but ahead of her there was nothing but an uncanny silence. She turned around, facing where the distressed animals were calling, and began to hunt through the forest.

She slid behind trees, danced through shadows, and followed the sound of animals calling out the movement of other people. Soon enough, she heard the sound of men's voices cutting through the forest. Niamh sank down to hide and crept forward.

"Really, we don't have anything, two horses and some food. But we're just from the northlands. We don't even have coin." Birdie's voice sounded tinny in the distance, threaded with a certain type of terror that Niamh knew would send her home. She bit her lip in concern.

It wouldn't even be Niamh's decision. Birdie would ask her to go home as soon as she had been rescued. Niamh knew this because she had seen apprentices fail in this manner before. It wasn't shameful. Some people just weren't ready to be out in the world with their own wits and a sword. Birdie seemed like she was likely to be one of them.

Ducking into a patch of bushes, Niamh crept closer, dodging brambles that clawed at her clothes, and trying not to disturb a rabbit with her babies hiding under another bush.

"I just want to go home," Birdie wailed.

Niamh snuck closer, able to see now that there were three men, ill fed and ill dressed, surrounding the poor girl. They were filthy and were not like people who lived in villages and kept the peace, but people who found the weakest travelers they could and took no pity in stripping those travelers of what little they owned.

One man held a rusty looking knife to Birdie's throat, while another loomed over her, and a third kept watch. Niamh stilled as his gaze swept over where she hid. She wished she could remind Birdie that she had a dagger on her, that she had a way to fight back, but the whites of her eyes were showing, her lower lip quivered in fear, and it was clear that the girl would not find her way to sense before she got hurt, or before Niamh needed to intervene.

"Just tell me where your camp is," the tallest one with the knife growled. "You stumbled on us and it seems it's only fair you tell us where you came from."

"No. Look, you don't want to go there anyway – she's dangerous. Just let me go. Just let me go home. I promise. I'll give you whatever I have on me… just let my hands go."

The men loomed over Birdie, violence apparent in their eyes. If her apprentice didn't give them what they wanted, she knew that they would try to take it from her by force. That wasn't the kind of mentor that Niamh wanted to be.

She didn't want to ask this girl to experience any more terror than she had to. It was time to act.

With sword drawn, Niamh stood into their periphery. She rose up out of the bushes silently and glowered in the direction of the men who kept her apprentice captive.

"She's right, you don't want to deal with me. Let the girl go and I'll let you go with your lives."

Niamh hadn't felt a lot of warmth toward the girl – after all, Birdie wasn't practiced, or ready, and Niamh was having a difficult time molding her into what she thought a witch-warrior should be. The girl was clumsy, inattentive, with a blind outlook on her surroundings. Yet, Niamh couldn't help but feel a pang of fear. If she didn't negotiate this moment correctly, Birdie would die. She knew that. She didn't think that Birdie should lose her life for having made the rather brave decision to leave the village before she was ready. And perhaps some of Birdie's failings fell on Niamh – she who was supposed to mentor and train, but also nurture. So even though Niamh had been, at best, a reluctant mentor, she was unwilling to let the girl die on her watch.

"I know how to use this weapon," Niamh threatened, taking a step closer. "I know how to make you feel pain. I know how to make you meet the Lady of Crows. You don't want any of those things, so leave the girl with the blood left in her veins and you'll leave unscathed too."

Birdie's face drained of blood. She was already terrified, but seeing Niamh in full form, as a woman who knew exactly what to say to make these men regret their choices, seemed to be even more frightening than her attackers themselves.

Usually, Niamh would have killed them outright, but she could see that Birdie could not handle the experience of death this close to her, that the wash of blood over her body would destroy the girl as much as this encounter would. There would be no going back for her – not back to the village – if that happened.

In the woods, the birds trilled and the fox yelped and the men stared with widened eyes as they weighed their choices. The silence lengthened as they took in her stance, the heft of her sword, and the numerous arrows that could be counted in the quiver that was slung across her back alongside her bow.

"These woods don't like any of us being here," she said, and it was true. She could feel the trees watching them with disapproval. "Bad things will happen to all of us if we linger too long here."

Even as she spoke, her eyes roved over her adversaries. Niamh was smaller than they were, and there were more of them. These men saw odds in numbers, not in skill. Niamh had known that it wouldn't really be up to her what happened next. She knew that the way she held a sword was intimidating, but if they weren't smart enough to notice her skills, this would end in disaster no matter what she did.

It was the tall man with the bad teeth who struck first. His axe dropped down from above his head, hefted with strong arms that knew what they were doing – even if it was with little finesse. Niamh slid to the side, darting out of the way – she assumed her own sword wouldn't survive that attack.

Birdie squeaked in fear. Niamh hissed at her, a wordless

sound indicating that she should get out of the way as quickly as possible.

The second tallest man, who had no hair and whose scalp shone brightly under the sun, struck forward, leaving one man to tend to Birdie.

"Get your knife, girl!" Niamh shouted, but she didn't have time to engage the girl in conversation, to remind her where it was. Her cry would have to be enough.

After she spoke, she lunged, bringing her sword out and around to the side of the bald man, cutting into his right side as he swung to hit her head. Before his sword could connect with her body, she flung herself forward, rolling into him with a shove of the shoulder, landing him in the dirt, screaming at the bite of a sword in his side.

The smallest man still held a dagger at Birdie's throat – though he, like her own apprentice, didn't seem to have the blood to commit to the fight. He stared at Niamh, daring her to move any closer, and smirked.

She turned around swiftly, raising her sword to barely block the axe that was dropping down upon her head from the first attacker. She felt the blow through her whole body, screaming with the pain that ran down her spine like lightning. Miraculously, her sword only quivered upon impact.

Instead of giving in to the pain, she whipped her blade around, while his axe was still in motion to strike again, and drove straight for his belly, wounding him badly enough that the axe dropped from his hand into the dirt. She turned around and looked at the last man, the one who still held a dagger to Birdie's throat.

He was clearly unprepared for this interaction. The dagger dropped from his hand as soon as she made eye contact with him, and she raised her blood-soaked blade.

He ran into the forest, making enough noise to attract every predator for miles, if they didn't come to scent the blood of his compatriots first.

Birdie didn't seem to notice that she was free. She stood stock still in the place where she had been held, staring at Niamh, her mind clearly not connecting with reality. When it finally did connect, however, she rushed forward to Niamh, throwing her arms around the woman.

They stood in the middle of the forest, Birdie with her arms wrapped around Niamh for comfort, and Niamh scanning for the men to return and catch them in a vulnerable position from which she could neither defend nor attack. Finally, she withdrew, and looked her apprentice deep in the eyes.

Before Birdie could speak, Niamh cut in. "The kindest thing I can do for you, my girl, is to let you go home. You're not ready for the road, for bandits or whoever else might be in my path. Your best choice is to go and remember that you are not quite ready to see the wider world. Go home and tell them you saw me halfway, and I sent you back. Decide what you like, but I swear to you, someday you will be ready."

Birdie looked as though she was about to cry, but swallowed back her emotions and took a deep breath to calm herself. "I do not think I am suited for violence, lady." The words did not come easily to the girl, who clearly saw it as defeat.

But Niamh did not see it that way – she saw it as a knowing of self – that the girl understood she was not meant for this life.

"Get home safely, Birdie. Tell our people that I will send a new witch-warrior to them from Avalon if I can, and if I cannot, I will come back myself when my quest is done."

She couldn't promise that she would come back, of course. But she could promise that her home would not be without a defender for long. That, at least, could be done. She would write to the Lady herself to ask for it if she had to.

In the morning when Birdie struck out on her own, Niamh asked the Goddess to protect the girl – she wanted her to be able to go back to her quiet life, the one that she was meant for. Not the life that Niamh clearly deserved, where she could fight, and where she found danger enthralling rather than frightening.

She mounted her own horse, and made her way out of the forest that felt to her like it wanted nothing to do with humans, and made her way toward Lunden.

THREE

Niamh had never seen anything like Lunden before. Her world had been so small – even the place where she had trained with the Women of the Mist was small with hundreds of women in one place, to be sure, but on an island in the center of a misty lake. Far away from… this.

This was a stinky, dirty, unkempt place with roads that had been trod by too many feet. The people were loud, and they spoke languages she didn't know and they wore clothes she didn't recognize. Niamh was not sure she wanted to be here, let alone wanted to meet these new people at the Hawk's Nest or work with them. But she found her confidence and followed the instructions on the letter down one street full of merchants, a busy marketplace, a gathering of houses, and finally down another alleyway into an area that was a collection of mostly empty buildings. She stabled her horse, Mathan, close by to where the letter told her to go. She hoped it wasn't wrong, or else she'd be losing her best and only horse in the middle of this awful city – it felt that easy to get turned around here. It looked as though some of the buildings were filled with wares owned by merchants, or else were tasked with the storage of boats, but it was not an active neighborhood and had a deserted feel about it. She made her way through a few streets, not seeing a single solitary soul, and finally approached a doorway that was only marked with an eagle's head in profile.

She pushed the door open, a pit forming in her stomach. Perhaps this was a trap. It could be they had lured this Nimue here to kill her. Maybe she was being brought here to be interrogated. Doubts filled her mind. She should have stayed home, where her mother had been laid to rest. She should have borne children to a man who would keep her comfortable. Instead, she was here.

She could hear voices up above her, speaking in a hushed tone. She crept up the stairs, her hand wandering gently to the pommel of the sword at her hip. A silent prayer passed her lips, asking the Goddess for protection. Asking anyone who would listen to keep her safe as she ascended the stairs to meet the stranger who had summoned her to a secret place.

Coming through the door, she saw two people huddled over a small table in a corner, a wall of armaments not far beyond, covered in swords and other tools of battle. A set of bows, each more powerful in strength, hung next to arrows designed to puncture armor and boots. None of these weapons seemed designed for the task of hunting animals, each one was built to hunt a person.

The sight stopped her, and the pit in her stomach widened. These people were the ones who wanted to do harm.

The man and woman who were talking noticed her. Their faces filled with scrutiny, trying to figure out not just who she was, but also which language to use and what tone to take to address her.

"I got your letter," Niamh finally said, hoping she had begun the right way. "I followed the instructions and wanted to see if I fit what it is you're looking for."

The man was bearded. He wore a light-colored tunic with a hood, and a leather harness that carried weapons. He looked very different from anyone she had ever met before, with black hair and dark brown eyes, and a sloping nose. Across from him was a young woman with long black hair that had been bound up in braids. She wore a set of clothing that looked as though it had come from Rome, though the fabrics were distinctly Breton. So – a Roman woman who had overstayed her welcome.

"She holds a sword well, at least," the woman muttered to her companion. The disdain in her voice was plain enough to Niamh. This woman was less excited about her arrival than the man was. "Perhaps your gambit paid off, Hytham."

The man – Hytham – stood. "You got our letter." He sounded excited. "Yes. We were looking for you. It's Nimue, isn't it?"

Here, she had to be careful. The name was so close she could fake it, but she had to pass it off as best as she could.

"It's Niamh, actually." She spoke as breezily as she

could, hoping they would take it for a common mistake.

"I'm unfamiliar with Caledonian names," the man said, acknowledging the error. "I'm sorry."

Niamh knew she couldn't say exactly who had sent her, where she had come from, except that she was Caledonian. Even that was risky. Not everyone liked the Picts, or others from her region. Not everyone from the south knew the difference, either. That was a help. But of course, she would have to pretend to be this other woman… a woman she knew nothing about.

"I'm Niamh of Argyll." She repeated herself, remembering what the Lady had told her to reveal and what to conceal. It bothered her that she could not say more. She was proud of who she was and where she came from. But she would have to figure out why this Nimue was being invited to come and train.

"I'm Hytham. I come most recently from Constantinople but have spent much of my recent time in Ravensthorpe. Do you know of it?"

Niamh shook her head. She had never left the islands. She'd heard of such places, like Constantinople, but not enough to discuss them in depth.

"Can I ask why I'm here?" she began, hoping to get more information. She could barely talk to this man without details.

"You are here because one of your ancestors was a part of our community. We train people in the ways of their ancestors so that they can carry on the work that came before them. We believe, based on what we have heard about you, that you would do well in this work." He watched her carefully, as though he were hoping that she would have a reaction to his words.

Niamh liked his voice. It was pleasant to listen to, unlike some of the other accents she had heard from people who had come from foreign lands. But she had no particular response to the revelation since it was not her actual ancestors he was speaking of.

The black-haired woman still sat at the table. "And I am Marcella. Of Rome. I am the head of the Lunden Bureau. You will ultimately have to satisfy me." Marcella's voice was harsh. Niamh thought it had more to do with the woman's personality than her actual voice.

She glanced out the window over the river – the Tamesis, she thought – and fumbled with her story. Give her a rabbit to track or raiders to kill any day. She was not trained in spy craft. She didn't think it was wise to mention Avalon until she had a sense of whether these Hidden Ones knew about them – and even then, opinions varied. Some people felt the Women of the Mist were trouble, stealing women from their proper roles as wives and mothers. The Christians thought they were witches. Which, to be fair… they were, but the church had issues with witches. She didn't know if Hytham or Marcella were Christian, or pagan, or something else she'd never heard of. Best to be vague. And yet truthful at the same time.

"I was trained by the women of my village in herb craft, but mostly I picked up the use of the sword because of the Viking raids. I study the seasons and I follow the old ways because it is what I was taught was good for the land."

"Interesting. You're essentially self-taught." Marcella

turned back to her drink. "Hytham's little experiment to reach others was all his, and I admit, I've been curious to see if he dredged anything up. But know this: if you do stay, you report to me, not to him."

"Self-taught isn't necessarily unwelcome, Marcella," Hytham replied, eyes narrowed, dodging the implication that he wasn't good enough to tell people coming out of this organization what to do and where to go.

"I'm trained well enough to keep myself and my people safe," Niamh said, feeling her cheeks redden and wanting to defend herself. She was not some self-taught swordswoman. Avalon had trained and forged her. But she would have to suffer Marcella's perceptions to keep her true intentions quiet. "The Romans, the Danes… some of our Pict neighbors… there's not enough food to go around and not enough warmth. We end up fighting over everything in the dead of winter sometimes." It was true enough that Niamh had been required to fight for what kept her and her people alive. Leaving out how she got there was just rational, of course.

"Who doesn't have issues with the Romans?" Hytham snorted, picking up a flagon and sipping from it. Marcella flinched. Niamh reflected that it was useful for her to know that they didn't entirely get along.

"Have you ever been in a skirmish?" Marcella asked.

Of course she'd been in skirmishes. She carried a sword, after all. She lived in Caledonia. No one lived where she did and managed to come out of it without a little battle experience. The last few years had been hard on everyone. "Many," Niamh replied, knowing that Marcella was going to be difficult to work with, and feeling too travel-weary to stay sharp in her presence. "I've also ridden a long way – I've been sleeping in the forest and that's not quite as restful as it could be. If you've got some reeds for me to rest in, and a bit of food, I'd be happy to answer more of your questions in the morning." The long ride had worn her raw, and she wasn't going to make the best decisions under these circumstances, especially not with Marcella eyeing her with the same attitude with which one usually watched an adder.

"There's a bed up in the loft, and we've food enough to share," Hytham said, cutting off Marcella before she could speak. Niamh sensed the woman was stricter about who she allowed to sleep in this place than he. Niamh gave him a tired, grateful smile. Marcella seemed displeased, and Niamh wondered if the discord between the two strangers would cause her trouble with her quest. Understanding there was tension already within this organization was something to make note of.

Niamh ate her fill and drank, and then was directed to clamber up a steep and narrow ladder toward a loft. The reeds were clean and the window looked out on the river, where she could hear people paddling past. The drifting music of a tavern was not too far, and it was much noisier than the village she had left.

She missed home. The quiet of the ocean, the quiet of her people. Their language was harsher here, less beautiful than hers.

But the exhaustion of the ride south overtook her as she repeated the story she would tell. A hedge-witch – to cover that she knew how to use herbs, birth babies and weave spells. Trained under a sword master – who traveled so that she could never know his name. And enough raiding parties to know that she knew her way around a blade with confidence. Soon, she would gather all the information she could on these Hidden Ones and understand their true purpose in coming to these lands and spreading their mission. Whatever it may be.

She drifted to sleep knowing that she had made it this far, and the Goddess would smile on her obedience.

FOUR

In the morning, Niamh wandered the foreign streets of Lunden without supervision. She had woken before Marcella and Hytham, and wanted to spend some time orienting herself to the city. It was a strange place to be, but she knew that in order to survive the task she had been given, she would have to become comfortable quickly with this kind of chaos. She immersed herself in the busy streets, breathing all the horrible smells that it had to offer. The Tamesis was a short walk from the bureau, and Niamh wanted to see what she could find out about this place that was so connected to the rest of the world.

Her body tensed at every large crowd that she passed, unused to seeing so many people in one place. She had especially never seen so many men – their voices deep, rough, and speaking in multiple languages she had never heard before. She had not spent much time in the company of men outside of her village. She didn't trust them. Hytham seemed all right – he was not as intense as some of these others that lurked on the streets of Lunden.

It felt overwhelming to hear so many new languages, to see so many people, to experience so many new smells. Like any good warrior, though, she knew she had to understand her environment. It was true of the battlefield, and it was true of this city, too. So instead of turning back to the comfort of her reeds like she wanted to, she forced herself to continue her explorations.

She wandered the docks, listening carefully to the voices of the men who disembarked from the ships. They dressed in furs and had braids and feathers and long ships beset with faces. She kept her distance, recognizing them as Viking warriors. She had no interest in exchanging friendly words with the likes of them – people from another country who wanted to settle these islands for their own profit.

Finally, she left the docks for the fresh banks of the Tamesis, wandering past women gathering water for their homes, and people of all genders making sacrifices in the water. A young woman, not much more than a year or two older than Niamh herself, lifted a sword from the water, her eyes closed, reverently asking for assistance from the Goddess – the Morrigan, Niamh thought, closing her eyes and adding to the request.

She continued navigating the city, finding ruined structures beyond the populace, and as she left the crowds, the smells of humanity, and the docks full of strange people who did not seem to come in kindness to the shores of her homeland, she began to breathe easy again.

It would be difficult to pretend to be someone else

while on this mission, but now that she had seen how big Lunden was – how overrun with strange people who wanted something from this country – she knew that even though it was hard, she was going to do it. There were so many dangers here, so many ways to be caught unawares. If people knew who she was – who she worked for – there were many enemies that she would have to fight. The Women of the Mist were legendary, but not all the myths were kind. It wasn't safe to be a witch-warrior here, and she could see why as she made her way along the Tamesis.

But if she was going to fool all of them and not let them see her for what she was, it was going to mean she had to be focused on her task. She settled herself on the bank of the river, lidding her eyes, but not fully closing them, because she wasn't unthinking. She plunged her hands into the cold water, coming up with a rock, smooth and worn. She smiled. She had something that would feel like home now. Something that would keep her grounded to the land that she wanted to protect.

Opening her eyes after her meditation, she saw ravens circling overhead, and a fox staring at her from not far away. The gods had heard her requests; they had seen her asking. She knew that she would be protected even as she took on this dangerous task of infiltrating this strange organization. Rising from the bank as dusk approached, she headed back to the bureau, where Hytham and Marcella waited.

Marcella sat on the front steps of the bureau with folded arms and a distrustful expression on her face. The bustle of Lunden was still unsettling to Niamh, but she tried to keep her shoulders relaxed as she walked toward the difficult woman. She had worked with such women before, after all, Avalon was full of them. Old priestesses who demanded that every ritual be done the same way it had been done for the last five hundred years. But the hostility that Marcella exuded towards Niamh was new, and she didn't like it.

"What should make me trust you?" Marcella demanded when Niamh reached the front step.

The woman was piercing. She could see through people, Niamh thought. She hoped her observation was wrong, because if Marcella was able to see through people, Niamh's thin disguise was already useless. Niamh didn't think Marcella paid much attention to the energies of those who surrounded her. She was more practical than that, less in tune with the world that she could feel, but sharply connected to what she could see and hear.

If Niamh had to guess, these were survival mechanisms that Marcella had had to learn to survive where she came from – and that was far away. To get to these isles, she must have traveled a long way in the company of unsafe people – there was no telling what Marcella considered a threat and what she considered reliable behavior. Niamh imagined that perhaps if she tried to bond with Marcella, to show her that they weren't so different, that might put her suspicious mind at ease.

"I'm a poor girl from the northlands who rode here because you asked for good fighters who knew how to be stealthy and cunning. There wasn't much left for me up in my homeland but to marry and have bairns, so instead I decided to come here, answer your mysterious call, and lend my sword to whatever cause would have me. I wanted to forge my own path." Niamh shrugged her shoulders, hoping her explanation was enough.

Marcella's face remained expressionless, but her eyes searched Niamh for any hint of a lie. Niamh fought her own instincts to shy away from such an observation, or to glance away when Marcella locked eyes with her. Marcella's disapproval, disbelief, and suspicion washed over her.

"I can't take you at your word," Marcella finally said. "Not that we can send someone to your village to ask questions, but I can at least test you in the skills you claim to have. Then, perhaps your true abilities will become known."

Of course there would be a test. What could Niamh have expected except that they would ask her to do something to prove her worth? She wondered if this was how Birdie felt under Niamh's care, always scrutinized, constantly being flagged. Perhaps she should've been kinder to the young girl.

What kind of a test it would be, she couldn't say, but she'd find out shortly, she imagined. Even at Avalon, there were tests for entry. New women weren't just welcomed with open arms, they had to show that they were capable of following the instructions of the Lady, and of her priestesses. They had to show that they could at least lift a sword, too. The tests she had passed at Avalon were very different, she thought, than what Marcella would ask of her.

"Well, we have a few targets I think I could suggest," Hytham's voice cut in, inserting a friendly tone into what was a tense conversation. He emerged from the inside of the Hawk's Nest and closed the door behind him. His accent was soft when he spoke her language, but clearly not to be misunderstood. There was something about him that was sharpened until his mind gleamed.

Hytham's mind was what Niamh really had to watch out for. He would scrutinize her within an inch of her life – and she did not want to be proved wanting. But he didn't seem to be approaching her with any hint of hostility. That was a surprise to Niamh. She would not have been able to muster the friendliness that he did. She'd barely been able to do so for her own mentee.

"A few targets, but only one that I think she'll find compelling," Marcella contemplated, prodding Hytham in the correct direction. "The best people to carry out missions are those who have a reason for fulfilling them. If I'm right…" Marcella trained her sharp eyes on Niamh again, "… as a follower of the gods and goddesses that they worship up North, what he's done won't sit well with her."

Trepidation filled Niamh. She had to be patient, even though she was curious who this mysterious "he" was. She couldn't blurt out that she'd do whatever they asked – even if she knew that was her duty – because appearing too eager would also be a sign that she was not to be trusted. She held her tongue and stared. Waiting.

"Before that, I'd like to take you on a bit of a tour," Hytham said to Niamh. He opened the door and gestured for her to follow, bypassing Marcella and leading her up through the stairwell into the bureau. Upstairs, he stopped to look out the open window which overlooked a dark alley.

Without another word, Hytham dropped out of the window and into the darkness. Niamh gasped at his sudden disappearance. Was this the test? Or perhaps just the way that Hytham liked to go about things? Perhaps one of the reasons the letter talked about shadows was because he plunged into them with nary a hint of fear or concern.

Instead of asking questions, however, Niamh leapt through the window after him, going into a free fall out the window.

Dropping through the air like a stone, she landed in a cloud of dust with her feet firmly planted in the haystack underneath the window. An odd choice, but it made for a good landing place out of sight. Canting her head, she listened, and felt a wave of anticipation wash over her. Was Hytham... hiding from her? She couldn't help a small smile from crossing her face – this was an interesting test, to be sure. One she would master.

The sound of Hytham running down the alley was quiet. He was practiced in walking stealthily, like one of the big cats that stalked the moors in the highlands. This intrigued her even more. Where had he learned such an ability?

She darted out of the haystack, following the subtle sound of his feet, and charged forward looking for him. She followed the graceful steps down a narrow alleyway, strolling casually past passersby, pretending that she knew where she was going, but instead was only barely holding on to the soft shuffle of Hytham's walk. When she came to a crowd, she sped up, and caught sight of his hooded figure. She followed more closely behind him, and figured this was clearly a game for him. But for her, it was the first knot on a lifeline to get what she needed.

Hytham scaled a wall up the side of a building ahead

of her. Niamh followed, hands grasping at the roughened stone to keep her at pace and catching up to him as he reached the rooftop. Even so, she was winded.

"You sure are fleet of foot," he said, smiling a little at the corners of his mouth. "But are you clever?" He nodded to the city, indicating that he expected something of her.

She didn't know what he wanted, but perhaps it could be good to show him what she could do from the other side. After all, she had her own tricks up her sleeve she could impress with. She merely smiled at him and leapt off the rooftop, plunging into the busy streets.

First, she glanced around to find Marcella, under the assumption the woman was following her, possibly with the intent to attack her while she was unawares, but the Roman was nowhere to be found. Then, Niamh focused on the problem at hand: she wanted to disappear to make him find her. Hytham seemed knowledgeable and practiced at hunting people in a city – the sort of a place that Niamh had never been before. But she thought of it like a different kind of forest. The energy was similar, but the trees were buildings, and instead of foxes, or boar, or wolves, or even the dread bear, there were people, carts, horses, and all manner of obstacles that she could use to her advantage.

Dropping her head to her chest she asked the Goddess for guidance, for the instincts of the wolf and the rabbit, of the hawk and the bear. And before Hytham could follow her right away, she took off swiftly.

Her heart pounded loudly as she ran through the alley out into the open street. She blended in with a group of nuns crossing the way, following them directly into their cloistered walls. She swiped a headwrap hanging from a nearby hook and draped the cloth over her head, hoping to pass as one of the nuns. She had to slow her heart and her breath, trying to seem as contemplative and prayerful as the women she walked with. Niamh glimpsed Hytham standing in the distance, staring right at her, but without recognition.

One of the nuns glanced at her, removing her hands from a position of prayer to indicate her sword briefly. Niamh's eyes grew wide, and she raised one finger to her lips. But the young nun just smiled and nodded, keeping her silence as they filed into the church together.

"Are you a warrior, then?" the young woman asked, speaking in Niamh's native language. Niamh was surprised to hear it so far south but kept still and calm as they walked together among the nunnery halls. Hytham disappeared from her sight.

"I am," she replied, reaching out to take the hand of this nun. For a moment they merely stood together under the arch of the church doorway and kept each other close. Niamh marveled at finding someone who knew her tongue in this Christian place.

"Are you one of the women warriors they speak of? I remember knowing of them back in Caledonia," the nun continued. "They were always kind, even to women who didn't follow their faith."

Niamh had to think about it for a moment, but then she nodded decisively. She did not know if this nun had been taken from her homeland and raised within these church walls, or if she had joined the ranks willingly. Either way, she did not want to deny herself to this woman if she needed help getting back to Caledonia. "I am a witch-warrior, yes."

"Good. I could use your help. I remember that women like you were good to us in times of peril." The nun's eyes darted back and forth, looking to be sure no one overheard their conversation, and shuffled Niamh along with the group towards a prayer room. "There's a nunnery to the north. We don't understand what's happening to them, but the reports indicate the women there aren't safe. The church blames the pagans, but..." the nun broke off, seemingly conflicted, "... I know the pagans. I know them because I'm from a village full of them, that followed the old ways."

Niamh filed into a pew with the women, their voices hushed and furtive.

"Why did you leave the old way?" Niamh asked, wanting to focus on the danger to the women in the north, but also desperate to understand why this woman had chosen to leave a path that had been kind to her, for one that seemed less kind.

The nun hesitated. It was clear that she chose her next words carefully. "It was too dangerous after the Vikings came. I didn't have a husband and I didn't want to stay where I was vulnerable... so I left the village. This was the safest place to go. This place, these women, have been good to me."

That, Niamh could understand. Some villages were less safe than others, even under the protection of the Goddess. This woman probably didn't have the same kind of safety that Niamh's village had been able to provide. It frustrated her that Avalon might have had the chance to better protect this woman's village and would have kept such a bright mind under their purvey, instead of losing her to the church.

"Do you know where the nunnery is?" Niamh asked, changing the subject, but she received a shake of the head, and a book shoved into her hands. Not that she could read it, as it was in a language she was unfamiliar with. She held the heavy book open and kept her face turned toward the altar at the front of the church.

"I think it's got something to do with another order. They call themselves the Order of the Ancients. Bad things happen to people who oppose them. When I saw you, I thought you might be the answer to my prayers. You look like a woman who can do something about this because I don't think anyone else will be thinking of how this affects the nuns or their future."

Niamh understood. If the nun was from anywhere near where she came from, she would not have the same aversion to the old ways that so many from the south did. And she would be seen as the kind of person who could keep other women safe. No matter their faiths, she was bound to take care of all women, because they often had no other protectors.

"The Goddess must have sent me," she murmured.

The nun smiled. "Or perhaps another deity."

While the nuns began their prayers, their soft voices rising and falling, hands delicately turning the pages on their books, Niamh set her book down and crept out of the pew, slipping out the side door. She did not want to associate herself with these Christian practices, exposing herself to their holy waters or prayers that made her uncomfortable in her own skin.

She had seen Christians come north. They had tried to press all her people into their god's service, and she remembered how they would start with kind words, and then move to rougher ones, words that made it seem as though it was not an option to believe in their gods, and she did not choose to follow them. She chose to follow the gods and goddesses who had raised and trained her, who gave her fleet feet and a wise head. She didn't care to change her beliefs based on threats either, and it always seemed to come down to them.

Behind her, the nuns bowed their heads as one as Niamh slipped out an open window to the other side of the building from where she had left Hytham, and made her way back toward the Tamesis, their chants following her closely. Keeping alert, she continued to sneak away from the church, listening for any footsteps that dogged her path. She moved as she did when she was young, outrunning the wolves in the forests and moors near her home, or more recently, the Vikings. She had become an expert at hiding in the shadows to protect herself and the people around her. This was one of the reasons why the Lady had sent her on this particular adventure. Now, she would prove that to Hytham. Perhaps, if she bested him, he would see the value in her skills. No doubt he was a heartbeat away from finding her.

When she reached the Tamesis, she looked for a spot

to hide and found a tall willow bending over the river's edge. She climbed up into it like an owl, and hid among the drooping arms of the tree, and watched, willing herself to become part of the tree. Eventually, she spotted Hytham creeping along a bridge not too far from her, following a group of drunks that masked his movement and kept the focus on the loud men screaming for more ale. He looked at ease, but alert, looking for someone to capture: specifically, he was looking for Niamh.

There was a pack of children that chose that moment to rush the bottom of the willow. Niamh froze, hoping that none of them would look up. To her delight, they settled underneath the tree, shouting excitedly at one another about the spoils of their pickpocketing exploits throughout the city.

She knew that if she fled her location, she would be caught. The children would look up, or Hytham would notice her. She hunkered down in the gently swaying branches and watched as he scanned for her. He was thorough, but he didn't approach her tree. He checked a well, he checked another tree, he checked the graveyard not too far away, but the tree in which she sat, in which she breathed as little as possible, was left to the feral children who had taken up residence. Though they were a threat, they could also be an asset if they never turned their heads up to glance at the branches.

Finally, Hytham stopped and waited by the river's edge. A ghost of a smile played across his face. Her heart dropped. She could see that he was waiting her out, that he probably knew where she was after all. After what felt like an hour, her legs began to cramp. The children, having parceled out their winnings from their day of thievery, dispatched, and still Hytham waited. But she didn't want to give herself up. She wanted to wait until he left, and then meet him back at the bureau. That would prove her skills to him in a way that nothing else would.

She felt desperate to prove her worth, much as she had wanted to in her early days training at Avalon.

At that moment, though, Hytham began to walk straight for the tree with a deliberate stride that told her she had been caught. At first, she considered running, about dropping out of the tree and dashing for somewhere else to hide. But there was nowhere that would serve her, at least, not anywhere that would also be a decent enough hiding spot to fool Hytham. What things he could teach her, she marveled.

Instead, she stayed in her spot, feeling the ache and burn in her thighs and upper arms. She let Hytham stand under the tree while she kept her breaths quiet and slow. And eventually he looked up, his dark brown eyes full of mirth.

Niamh dropped down from her perch with some disappointment. She had hoped that he would walk away, but it was not to be.

"What can you do better to hide yourself from those whom you are hiding from?" he asked, gesturing for her to follow him as he walked back towards the bureau where Marcella was no doubt waiting to hear about her failure. She felt disappointed, knowing that she could have done better. She wondered if Birdie had felt as such when under her tutelage.

"Soften my steps more?" Niamh guessed, thinking back to the sound that her feet made on the dirt road, and the clouds of dust that she kicked up when she ran. The texture of the earth was certainly hard packed, not the soft dirt of a village road that saw little use or horse traffic. The difference meant that her steps were louder on the hard packed earth, like inside a church and its stone floors.

"You certainly left evidence of your escape in your tracks." He gestured above their heads to the laundry ropes and rooftops of the city. "Use alternate pathways where you can. Find trees, as you did, rooftops, crawl underneath bridges and hide under boats. Use the environment entirely hidden from view, rather than using plain sight to hide your true intentions. The nuns were a nice trick, though."

Niamh found this fascinating. She had always thought about the stillness of the fox, or the snake, who could blend into the forest. But being like the birds in the trees... the creatures never spotted until they were startled out of their nests, made sense to her. She nodded.

"Thank you." She had learned to always be grateful to her teachers, like the woman on Avalon who guided her to learn the poultice and the sword as well as she could.

This time, as she walked through Lunden with Hytham, she kept an eye out for places to hide, and where she could walk that did not make her feel quite so exposed to the relatively large swaths of humanity that kept pace with her in the street. The marketplace was much bigger than any she had visited before. The merchants sold all sorts of things she could not get back at home – decadent and unrecognized furs, colorful ribbons, dyed clothes of vibrant colors. The closest to this that she had seen was in Oxenfordscire, but even that market didn't match this one. The shouting of the merchants and the haggling of the customers filled her ears. Her curiosity was piqued, instead of just her fear, and now she was ready to learn.

But as soon as they had entered the market, they were leaving again. Hytham cut through the streets quickly, not stopping to eye any wares. He broke through a side alley which led them quickly back to the bureau.

And, Niamh thought sourly, Marcella's judgment.

Hytham led the way, ascending the ladder ahead of her. She felt comfortable letting him lead, because she didn't think Marcella was going to warm to her. If she and Marcella were left alone, she wouldn't put it past Marcella to kill her for her convenience.

When Niamh popped her head up through the floor to the main sitting area, she was greeted by Marcella sitting and facing the entrance with her arms folded in disapproval, yet again. This was beginning to look a lot like a pattern. Niamh waited to speak until she was addressed, as it was the same coping mechanism she used with the older priestesses. One of the best methods of dealing with them, in her experience, was to make them feel a bit less in power than they were. Throw them off their pedestal, as it were. She had a plan.

"Well?" Marcella said, directing the question to Hytham.

"She's as skilled as she claims." He nodded in Niamh's

direction. "I think we should fill her in on what it is we do here."

"I have a question, before you tell me anything," Niamh cut in, causing both Hytham and Marcella to stare at her in surprise. Niamh was frustrated that she needed to speak about this now, but she had to put the safety of women in danger ahead of even her own quest. "I met a nun who asked for my help today. I don't usually work with Christians, but she was clearly from Caledonia... and the victims are women."

Marcella nodded, gesturing for Niamh to continue. She looked bored, but her eyes fixated on Niamh, which gave her a clue that Marcella was play-acting her disinterest.

"She mentioned some people that I've never heard of before." Niamh took a deep breath. "She called them the Order of the Ancients."

Both Hytham and Marcella flinched, their bodies recoiling from the name. Marcella's eyes flared, but Hytham seemed angry. Not a popular group, which was all Niamh really needed to know. Their reaction surprised her. She'd meant to bring this problem to them, to show her trust in asking for their guidance on how to proceed, and that she was willing to help others.

"The Order of the Ancients and the Hidden Ones have been fighting for... a long time," Hytham began, his voice taking on the tone of someone sharing a story that they knew well, and that they believed needed telling.

"How long?" Niamh asked, intrigued.

"Longer than you've been alive, certainly. Longer than I." Marcella relaxed, unfolding her arms just a little.

"The Order of the Ancients is why we are here," Hytham insisted. "They're everywhere in the world, trying to take hold of the power that controls the workings of society. They want to make decisions for everyone, not just the people who choose to follow them."

Niamh didn't like the sound of that. People who wanted to control others didn't tend to work well with witch-warriors, as the witch-warriors were given dispensation to do whatever they thought necessary for the safety of their community.

She also thought it sounded a lot like the Church that seemed to desire power, and they too had been trying to make people who followed the old ways conform to new practices. Ones that didn't feel right to her when they were not in line with the land.

"Tell me more," Niamh asked.

Marcella and Hytham exchanged a glance, but Marcella nodded, as if granting her permission. Hytham launched into a tale that left Niamh overwhelmed and full of awe. She had no idea such organizations existed and that they didn't just expand across the islands, but the whole world.

"Are you asking me to help you fight them?" Niamh asked, once Hytham had finished his telling of the Order and after chewing on the details they had given her. "Is that why you sent that letter?"

This seemed to be in line with what the Lady was asking, but more and more it seemed that the Hidden Ones weren't the real foes at all. The Women of the Mist didn't like people who made grabs for power on this island, either. They had stopped men who had a greedy eye on control before, and they would do it again. Men like Mordred and his fellow Descendants of the Round Table. She remembered that they had learned all about his attempt to take over Avalon, and it sounded similar to the ways in which the Order of the Ancients operated. She was familiar with people like this, and she didn't like them much. Perhaps these Hidden Ones were more like the Women of the Mist than the Lady had previously thought.

"That is why I sent out the letter, yes. We are bringing in new talents, people who have the bloodline, to fight them. We also need to know more about the people here, those who would ally with us, or who would be allied with the Order of the Ancients. They will break whatever power structures don't serve them in order to make their cause successful." Hytham walked over to his desk and produced a piece of parchment covered in names and titles and locations.

"These are our suspected members of the Order," he said, showing it to her. Marcella looked ready to intercept, to take the paper away, but Hytham was too quick, and once Niamh laid eyes on the information, Marcella couldn't object. "They are all in positions of power. Some in the church, some are kings, some are merchants of high standing. All can cause enough trouble for us if they catch that we are here. That's why we need people like you."

"Or, you precisely, since no one else has heeded the call," Marcella said. "But can you work independently from us? Now that you know who we are, are you ready to be given some real work to prove yourself?"

This was what she had been asked to do. Infiltrate. And

while their goals didn't seem terrible, she was sure she was missing something. The Lady wouldn't have embedded her within this organization if she didn't have concerns about their true vision.

But perhaps the Lady had never heard of the Order of the Ancients either. No matter what, Niamh needed more information. She needed to understand further how deep this rivalry went.

So why was she frightened by the possibility of doing something unknown for the Hidden Ones?

"First, I have to ask, are you a follower of Christ?" Hytham asked, and Niamh wasn't prepared enough to give a more subtle answer. She shuddered, shaking her head, and pushed the list of suspected Order of the Ancients members aside. None of them stood out to her anyway.

"Would have been better if she had been, more unlikely that way," Marcella replied, shaking her head. Niamh frowned, not understanding Marcella's comment.

"Regardless. There's a priest, in Oxenfordscire." Hytham pointed to a name on the list. "We know that he's connected to the Order of the Ancients, and that he's been spreading misinformation about us, the Hidden Ones. He's also been knocking down those sacred rock piles of yours," Hytham continued. "If we thought he'd have useful information for us, I'd say bring him here, but as it is..."

"Kill him," Marcella said finally.

Niamh was shocked to hear that command given so brazenly, but she didn't let it show, keeping her hands folded inside her cloak. She had been required to take lives before, but on the battlefield, when her own life was in danger. Not deliberately when there was nothing to stop her and no threat to her life. But this is what they'd asked for, in the letter. They needed people who could stealthily kill.

"Can you do it, or are you too afraid?" Marcella said, reading Niamh's face correctly. "Now that you know what the Order stands for, can you do what we ask of you?"

"Has he... I mean to say, knocking down a cairn is evil. It is a disrespectful act. But I wouldn't kill someone for that. Banishment, surely, but not murder."

"Niamh, we are at war with the Order of the Ancients. If they knew that you were helping us, they would not hesitate to kill you, for even a second. He would destroy every remnant you believe in without blinking. You must accept that his death is necessary to protect your people and ourselves. If we thought the Order of the Ancients would be silenced with a word, don't you think we would have done it?" asked Hytham.

Hytham's expression begged Niamh to understand. While she heard in his voice that he was open to other methods, Marcella was bloodthirsty and wasn't open to alternative routes. This unnerved her. After all, if she revealed she was with the Women of the Mist, they might become more suspicious of her. If they seemed ready to kill anyone who wasn't *them*, they probably wouldn't want to be working with someone from another organization.

"Do you think you're ready to go and do something for us that will matter to the Hidden Ones?" Hytham asked.

Niamh didn't want to say yes, but she knew it was the only answer that allowed her to continue her quest. She had to earn the Hidden Ones' trust for Avalon's sake.

"I am. Where am I going?"

"Closer to the west coast than we are now, past Oxenfordscire," Marcella instructed. "The priest is doing a number of things against us. Spreading rumors and lies, ruling the area with an iron fist clad as religion. You will go and find out what you can, and then kill him before he can continue to further his own mission."

Niamh was surprised. Marcella seemed to trust her about as much as she trusted a bear just before snowfall – but neither she nor Hytham seemed ready to come with her on this journey.

"I won't have supervision?" she asked warily.

"Marcella cannot travel outside of Lunden just now. There is a man who is looking for her. He works with the Order and until he is… no longer active, her presence places us all at risk," Hytham said, avoiding explaining his own absence.

Marcella's frown deepened. "And Hytham is not available. This is an excellent test of your skills," she said, looking Niamh up and down. "We shall see what you're truly capable of."

Being alone was, all things considered, a boon to Niamh. She could proceed to her target first, gather all the information that she could, and then report to the Lady in Avalon on her way back. Oxenfordscire was not far from Tor, and it would help her to know what the Lady expected from her in terms of next steps. She could report on the Order of the Ancients and the Hidden Ones and obtain new orders.

Yes. The Hidden Ones allowing her some autonomy

was good. But she couldn't trust that they wouldn't send spies. She didn't think that Marcella and Hytham were operating alone, though she didn't know who allied with them yet.

"What is this man's name?" Niamh asked. Now that she was confident in her decision to do what they asked, she would need all the information she could gather at her disposal. Marcella and Hytham certainly knew more than they were telling her.

"Father Deoric. He serves a small village near Cote. You'll need to be careful, because he knows enough about us to be on the lookout for anyone who isn't a part of his flock – and he hates the Celts more than he hates Vikings, so he might peg you as one and automatically be suspicious. You look and dress like a Celt. You could change that, I suppose. Not the way you look, but put on a less obvious cloak." Marcella's instructions were crisp, her eyes sharp. Niamh felt like she wasn't just being given instructions but observed for her reactions. She gave Marcella a cool stare and nodded quietly, as she had done when she was taught at Avalon.

"It's about a two day ride from here. I should be back by week's end," Niamh said, not wanting to take longer than she had to. "But if I am delayed, I will send a message."

She wasn't sure how she would get a message back to Lunden, without Birdie or any other methods, but she'd find a way. She could bribe a wayward child, and she could perhaps even make a detour if Hytham didn't come to check up on her. Or follow her in secret. She now understood the depths of his skills.

She would have to be cautious about how she traveled. She would have to learn from what he told her, so that if she went through the mist, she would not betray her own secrets.

FIVE

Niamh awoke ready to face her first journey on behalf of the Hidden Ones.

She did not expect that either Marcella or Hytham would be awake to see her off – after all, the sun was only barely beginning to rise. Streaks of pink and orange cut across the dark sky. Dropping down the ladder, she was surprised to see Hytham waiting for her in the common area of the bureau. He had packed a saddlebag full of food for her and was filling a skin with wine as she came down.

"I could have prepared this on my own," she said, hoping to convey not ungratefulness, but that she possessed the capability to care for herself.

"Since I cannot go with you, providing you with supplies seemed like the least I can do." Hytham looked regretful.

"Why are you stuck here?" Niamh pressed.

Hytham sighed, clearly uncomfortable. The sun cut across his face from the window, showing light marks of stress and worry around his mouth and eyes.

"It's not just Marcella," he said. "I was injured... and I am still healing. I try not to take more than one long journey in a month if I can help it, and as much as Father Deoric is trouble, he is a small enough issue that we could skirt around dealing with him, or bide our time until things became too difficult to overlook. But now we have you."

Now Niamh understood. She could see that, in fact, this was one of the reasons Hytham had put out a call. Because with Marcella being hunted by a man from her past, and Hytham unable to travel as often as he would like, they would need people willing to fight and serve for the Hidden Ones. Niamh was a means to support their cause, not just a lucky accident or a secret probing into the underworld of Avalon. That explained the why of the letter. Hytham and Marcella didn't have the means to find more suitable candidates. They had to take whoever they could get.

"I did have a question for you, Niamh. While Marcella is asleep." Hytham's voice quieted. "I hope it is not a disrespectful one. There is a group of women that I've heard of. The Ladies of the Mist or something like that. They seem to hold a lot of power in these islands... a lot of bodies, too."

Niamh was glad that she had turned away from Hytham so that she could keep her expression to herself. She would have to be careful here. After all, admitting she knew anything was too much.

"If you hear a scrap of news about them while you're on the road, do let us know. We don't know anything about them yet, except of their existence and that it seems they wield a great deal of unstated power. We'd like to know more. Are they allies? Are they enemies?" Hytham said.

Niamh restrained the inclination to reassure Hytham that in fact, they were potential friends. That it could be easy for them to work together. But, until she had seen more of the Hidden Ones and their goals, she couldn't guarantee that alliance. And she needed to report to the Lady before she could reveal herself or make promises on Avalon's behalf.

"I will," she said. "Thank you for the saddlebag."

Niamh descended the steps of the bureau and the near empty streets to the stables where Mathan was happily chewing on hay and resting. She saddled him up and got them on the road.

Lunden was certainly quieter in the early dawn. The smells of filth and the Tamesis still hung heavy in the air, reminding her of how much she missed the country. Soon enough, she would be back in the open space she craved. After all, Lunden, while large, was never too far from the wilds of the islands.

She liked the quiet, the whinny of the horse, the quiet clop of his hooves on the soil that had been pounded down by horses before them. She rode past small villages and farms with thatched roofs, the inhabitants just beginning their day, and then rode past cairns and standing stones. Beyond them, the eyes of the wolves lingered on her, and Niamh asked the gods to protect her from them, praying that they find other prey appropriate to the task of feeding them, rather than Niamh's bones and flesh.

After most of a day's ride, she came to a crossroads planted in the middle of the encroaching forest. She had been here many times before, between Avalon and home, when she had been sent on missions during her training. The last time she had been here it had been on her way home, after her dedication to the Goddess.

The right fork led to Avalon and would take her down winding paths and forests to the shores of a lake. There, she would be enchanted by the isle's natural magic and feeling of security. However, there would be no riding toward Avalon until she finished her business on Cote for the Hidden Ones. It made her ache. She missed the rolling green moss that covered the isle and cushioned the falls of young women learning to fight with the blade.

She turned to take the left fork and rode into an unknown forest. The woods became darker, the trees grew thicker together, letting less sunlight stream through their branches. It formed a kind of tunnel, which she rode through until the light formed a spot at the far end, leading out into the bright open fields of Oxenfordscire.

She knew she approached the village of Cote when the farms looked closer together. Instead of cottages shoved out into the woods, inhabited by people who chose to live on their own instead of in a community, she saw people who worked together to build a space. It wasn't like the community that she was used to, though. Unlike her own village, which centered around a common area for bonfires and shared meals, this larger community was built around a church.

But this community was like hers in some ways too.

Children ran in a pack, all of them chasing after a group of chickens that also ran wild. Their mothers were likely dispersed throughout the village, tending to animals, smaller babies, and meals for as many as they could feed. She didn't see as many men – more than likely, they were all out in the fields harvesting their crops. With the exception of warriors or churchmen – and the man she sought, who worked in the small, simple church that she rode past.

Overhearing snippets from the women as they tended to their chores, she understood that the language was different enough that she would be required to listen more than she spoke. If she could keep her questions to a minimum, she would be less suspicious.

Unlike the women from her village, the women here all wore kerchiefs, and no one seemed dressed in trousers. She would need to change her attire to blend in, and certainly not show any indication that she was a Woman of the Mist.

Niamh hunted for a place to hide her horse and change her identity. Leaving the main village area and skirting past the churchyard and burial spaces, she began to look for somewhere safe that no one would go. A small cottage that at first looked abandoned might have been good, but evidence suggested that the residents were merely out working the fields. She pressed on, getting further from the village than she would have liked to be on foot, eventually spotting a barn far off in the distance. It looked to be in severe disrepair, and had no animals left in it, nor anyone to tend it. The small living hut that was associated with it was half undone, burned by fire or destroyed by invaders, she assumed. Perhaps Caledonia was not the only place that had problems with Vikings.

She entered the barn and glanced at the owl's nest resting in the ceiling. Changing out her leather and breeches for a dress, Niamh covered her auburn hair in the village's accepted style. But these small changes would not be enough, she thought. Reluctantly, she laid her bow and quiver in a hiding spot in the rafters. By her observation, women didn't carry weapons here. Though she could get away with a sword under her cloak, the long-range weapon marked her as an outsider in a way that she could not afford.

Once she had garbed herself appropriately, she wandered out into the village. The womenfolk chased children and the men tended to the fields, and the children made trouble. It felt similar enough to home that she didn't feel as though she was out of place, as long as she remembered to think in the language of Mercia. She couldn't help but smile fondly.

Making her way up to the church, she uttered a silent prayer to the Goddess asking for protection before she crossed the threshold. If the priest was to be anywhere, it would be inside a house of worship.

Inside, she found a long room full of candles, with a giant cross hanging on one end of the far wall, surrounded by pews. A few men and women gathered in the seats, their heads bowed in prayer, their mouths moving silently. Niamh slid into one of the empty, rough-hewn pews, and waited for the service to start. She hoped she didn't stand out – but relaxed as more workers, mothers, and children entered.

She was uncomfortable in this church, in this pew. Her place of worship was outside in the woods and the meadows, not behind these closed wooden doors. It wasn't just her beliefs that made her uncomfortable – certainly strangers were welcomed inside the doors of churches as the Christians were always seeking new members of their faith. But if she was caught as a professed practitioner of the old ways... Niamh shuddered. Cold fear ran through her veins.

If they figured out who she was, and she refused to profess her belief in their god, they would either force her to convert, or lock her away until she changed her mind. If she was lucky, they would run her out of town, but she didn't think this was that kind of place. Everyone here seemed to believe in the way of Christ.

Soon, Father Deoric walked in and began the prayers that his Christian congregation expected. Niamh studied him with a critical eye, pretending to mouth the songs and prayers. A middle-aged man with thinning brown hair, Deoric then chose to recite everything in the language that the church provided its text in and expected those who didn't speak the language to sit in worshipful silence until the part of rote recitation. But, that could have been because he didn't sound like he came from Mercia. By the way he spoke the language when forced, it seemed as if he constantly paused to remember the words. No warmth emanated from him towards his flock, not even when he called them forward to drink from the communal cup.

Niamh cocked her head to the side, comparing his

treatment of others to what she'd experienced on Avalon when she led the summer rituals as part of her training, and then the many village ceremonies as the resident witch-warrior. Her first impression was that Deoric was a hard man, not a kind one. He gave no one else time to speak of their troubles at the end of the service either, lumbering off through heavy curtains back to his own place of rest.

But did that mean he should be murdered?

Once the service ended and the parishioners filed out, off to their afternoon tasks, Niamh walked out of the town and into the countryside, searching for evidence of the cairns that Hytham reported had been destroyed. If there were cairns, there very well had to be pagans who kept them. After all, she knew from observation and experience that some men who followed Christ left no space for her people to thrive if they chose to live in Christian villages.

As she explored, she discovered the houses thinned out, indicating some families chose not to live in the shadow of the church or market square. Soon, she identified markers of the old ways on some of the residences. One in particular had a bowl of fresh cream out on the front stoop with a hefty hunk of bread next to it for good measure. Someone seeking the good favor of the fae. Someone that she wanted to speak with.

Niamh removed her kerchief as she approached the building, showing her braided hair. So far, she had seen little evidence of the cairn destruction and wondered if Deoric had used the rocks to build other things, a desecration that made Niamh's heart sink. Or perhaps they were further out than she anticipated. She hoped to find another explanation regarding the cairn destruction and how it linked to the priest. Perhaps this home would have some clues for her.

"Greetings," she called out, peering into the dark cottage. "I see you have the blessing of the Goddess on your doorpost instead of the blessing of the Christ, and you keep company with the fae. I hope I might speak with you."

From inside the hut, a brittle voice came out. "Show me that you are one of us, and I will speak with you, otherwise I'll gut you like I would any wolf at my door."

The voice sounded worn, as though it had seen and heard too many cruel things. The voice of a person who lived somewhere they were not welcome, Niamh thought. While she had never lived somewhere like that, being in the church service had given her a sense of what it felt like not to belong.

In response, Niamh folded her right sleeve up, showing the lunar cycle tattooed in deep blue ink around her upper arm. A symbol of the Goddess, and a mark of Avalon that would name her to anyone who would ask. So far, she had kept it hidden from Hytham and Marcella.

"Priestess, I beg your mercy," the voice said. "The community here is less kind to us followers of the Lady than some other places I have lived."

A woman emerged from the shadows. She wore a crescent moon necklace around her neck, and her red hair was bound in a complicated braid around the crown of her head. She had bright blue eyes, and a dagger at her hip, clearly shown. She wore a blue shift dress, not unlike the ones that the priestesses wore on the isle, though she didn't show a tattoo back to Niamh.

"No mercy needed, I'm here in disguise myself. I'm here about Father Deoric," Niamh said with a kind smile. "My name is Niamh."

"Wisweth," the woman said as an introduction and ushered Niamh inside, indicating a chair for her to sit. The two sat down, facing one another. Inside the hut, Niamh felt safe from what dangers resided on the outside, and what dangers Father Deoric perpetuated.

"He's only been here about three months. The last priest wasn't a bad man. He was a follower of Christ, to be sure, but he didn't ask that those of us who follow another path stop. He didn't see us as a poison, but Deoric says he's planning to burn out the heart of paganism in our town. He wants it to be a Christ-centered community, and the only way he knows how to do that is by getting rid of the people who were already here. To him, people only have the illusion of power, making them yearn to follow and serve certain leaders. This is his way of ensuring people serve their purpose – to follow one god and him."

Niamh sighed in quiet frustration. She had heard about priests like this, who visited from town to town and made it conform only to what they believed was right and true, not allowing the residents to follow their consciences.

"I hear he's knocking down cairns," she said, playing her hand more, hoping to hear what she needed.

"Yes. He took down my husband's cairn only a few days ago." The woman looked shaken. "I built the cairn myself, with the help of some local women who also follow the

Goddess. He had been my companion all my life… and his passing has been difficult. Knowing that his spirit lies not far from me was a comfort. I could visit him when I needed to, but now…" The woman fought back tears, looking ashamed to be crying in front of a stranger.

Niamh's body went cold with rage. As she had told Hytham and Marcella, disrespecting the dead was the worst of all possible choices to make, but it did not mean she had the right to murder Deoric for such a transgression. At Avalon, they learned that angering the Morrigan by disturbing the bones of the dead was the surest way to end up with an unhappy death – a fate imposed by the goddesses. Yet, Niamh had a responsibility as a witch-warrior of Avalon to deal with this problem. Now this woman was one of her charges. It wasn't just the Hidden Ones that mattered. This was a more personal matter than she had given it credit for and she realized how deeply it affected her.

"Very well. That makes my path clear," Niamh said, knowing that the Hidden Ones had a point to remove this father from this world. "Thank you for your honesty, sister. I will make this right."

Wisweth smiled and stood. "If you have the time, I'd like to share a meal with you." She turned to her hearth and began to stoke the flames for a cookfire. "I do not often have company, and I am honored by yours."

Niamh nodded in agreement. This would be the only meal she would have for quite some time with someone who knew her true nature as a witch-warrior. The food was simple, but well cooked, and the cottage kept her dry and safe.

When full dark had come, Niamh pulled her cloak tighter and walked out into the mists rolling off the moor. She was going to investigate the cairn and find out what Father Deoric had done to the resting place of Wisweth's husband.

SIX

Niamh found the cairn easily with Wisweth's guidance. The stones had all been knocked down and burned with a fire intended to cleanse the energy of the soil. The priest had done this – she was sure Wisweth did not lie about that – because a cross had been left sticking out of the ground, alongside the bones of the man whose grave had been destroyed. Niamh sensed the space was angry with such destruction, and if she focused, she could feel Wisweth's husband's spirit, too. This desecration was the act of a careless person who did not respect the practices of people who did not share his faith. Seeing it put everything in a new, terrible, perspective.

Niamh had to focus, but she was so angry, she couldn't imagine what would possess anyone to do this – to desecrate a grave that had been so carefully constructed for someone to be sent to the next world. She didn't understand why the priest was so sure that his god would do better by the dead, especially if those dead had never known him. This was the kind of act that bad and petty men undertook, not righteous men who led faithful people. To be honest, she couldn't believe that anyone who had any semblance of faith could have done this.

Niamh ripped the cross out of the ground and then knelt, her hands reaching for stone after stone, reconstructing the cairn – unsealed, unsecured, entirely in shambles, but enough to cover the man's bones disturbed from his peaceful rest. She fumed, but her anger was now laced with pain. She could only imagine how she would feel if her mother's cairn had been desecrated in this way. The least she could do was reconstruct it and bless it, so that Wisweth could find some semblance of closure.

As she did so, she knew down to her marrow that Father Deoric was not here to preach his own faith, but to violently erase the practices that had come before him. He could not be allowed to continue to do so in peace. She regretted what she'd told Hytham and Marcella – this *did* warrant a death sentence.

When she finished, the sun had set and the moon had risen to light her path back to the town of Cote and to the abandoned barn. Howling wolves in the distance kept her company as she walked, sticking to the shadows. All the while, she plotted the father's demise. How was she going to do it? How could she take his life? She knew that he had to be alone, but how best to get him there?

To figure that out, she would need to observe. She couldn't simply grab her sword and ram it through him. No… she needed to think like Hytham with his cat-footed gait. How would he assassinate Father Deoric?

The next morning, Niamh donned her kerchief and dress and settled in the churchyard, among the consecrated dead of the father's flock. By pretending that she wanted to pay her respects, she could sit for as long as she liked outside his walls and note his habits.

Father Deoric led a service every morning, afternoon, and night. He ignored requests from poor followers of his community, choosing only to allow those garbed in rich clothing to enter the cottage where he spent his time between his services. The altar servers and other people meant to help with the church life came to and fro, and Niamh noted it would be difficult to get near enough to Father Deoric to do anything at all without notice. She wasn't sure how to catch him out except when he left to sleep at night, alone in his quarters. But he did not go to bed until long after the village was asleep. She would have to hide until such a time to make her entrance.

Soon, the sun dropped below the horizon and the moon rose. The village put itself to bed after the evening prayer, and when Niamh observed the last man drinking his fill at the town tavern bundle off to his own bed, she realized it was time. Uncertainty struck her. The silence of the graveyard chilled her. She had killed before. But she had never killed deliberately in a planned manner. She had only killed during raids, when strangers with ill intent had come to her village to murder and destroy a way of life for their own gain.

Her eyes snapped closed as she forced herself to meditate on the choice before her, and she realized that this choice to take Father Deoric's life was similar to the choice to kill a Dane in self-defense. This man was doing harm to every follower of the old ways in his region. He was choosing to create an unsafe world. Killing him was the only way to keep them safe and stop the spread of misinformation that people should serve rather than live their own lives. She knew in her bones that he was not the kind of man who would change his behavior if she asked nicely.

When the moon reached the highest point in the sky, a young man exited Deoric's house, bearing what looked like the remains of the father's dinner feast. When the boy's back was turned away from her, she took the opportunity to clamber into the tree that hung over the father's house. Once settled in its branches, she continued to observe who came and went. She remembered Hytham's patience and his lesson to look around at alternative options rather than the straightforward path before her.

The boy disappeared into the church. Then, the fires went out inside, leaving the priest as the only one awake on the church's land.

Except for Niamh. Feet hitting the ground like a cat, she slid up to the house and through the door, taking the chance that the priest would be expecting another delivery.

"Boy, I told you to bring me another flagon of ale," the priest snarled from within the home, his back turned to the door and sitting at a desk bent over some sort of scribe work.

Niamh did not speak. She knew if she betrayed herself, she would be done for. He would fight back.

"Boy, I've told you a thousand times, you speak when spoken to," Father Deoric growled. "If you don't answer me, you'll be in more trouble than you've ever been in the past. I'm in no mood with those heathens breathing down my neck."

Heathens. Niamh clenched her teeth. She knew that he referenced her people with that word. She crept closer, staying in the shadows, moving from the front foray to the edge of the small room he resided in. Even so, the man didn't turn.

The priest took his time, grousing as he finished the sentence he wrote at his desk, and then finally looked over his shoulder at her. His eyes squinted in the darkness, and then they opened wide as he laughed in Niamh's face.

"You're not the idiot boy at all. You're one of them, aren't you? One of those witches that won't fall in line. Or, since you're sneaking in the shadows, maybe you're something more."

Hostility emanated off him in waves. But it wasn't merely that. His eyes were lit with cruel glee. She was a joke to him. She had never been treated before this way, and it stunned her.

"You think you and your little cult are going to survive?" he said, standing from his chair and taking a step toward her with his hands open wide. "You think that my people won't win? Our power is being established in every city in the world. We have hundreds at our disposal everywhere you look. We certainly aren't afraid of you, a little girl who plays with swords and herbs."

The emotions surging within Niamh were many and varied: rage at being talked down to, the fear of knowing that there were many more men like him than she could have imagined. She also found that she was ready to speak.

"You may think that you can overpower us, but you would be wrong. We are far more powerful than you could ever give us credit for." The thread was true; in her heart she knew that if his men came for Avalon, they would not win. People had tried and failed to keep the Women of the Mist down.

"You're going to be able to stop me? Your hands are shaking around your sword. You can't possibly kill me with that kind of fear. I wonder why they sent a child to do an assassin's work."

His mockery was getting to her, igniting her fury further to overtake her. She kicked out with her right foot, connecting it with his gut. His eyes went wide with shock as he made a surprised sound. When he fell backward, he hit his head on the table behind him, strewn with papers and books, quills and ink. His hand swept against an inkwell, and it flew backward, shattering against the wall and leaving a splash of dripping black against the wall, like the darkest blood she would ever see.

Niamh made her off hand into a fist and brought it down on his head, hitting him hard enough to rattle his skull. His hair was oily, slicked with sweat. His eyes shifted from full of mirth to a certain level of fear that gave Niamh a thrill.

"Not so sure you can beat me now, are you?" she snarled, bashing the side of his head again with her fist. "Why did you destroy the cairns?"

He gasped in pain at the second blow. "Because they were pagan relics. Is that what this is really about?" His voice remained clear even through the apparent pain on his face. He had no remorse.

"They're our burial mounds. We don't disturb your dead. How dare you disturb ours."

Deoric slipped from her grasp and tried to regain his feet, but his balance was wobbly. She had clearly done some damage. He struck out at her with an open palm, but she dodged it, moving around the table to grab the back of his neck. For a moment, she heard Hytham's voice in her mind, telling her that if she kept him alive a little longer, she could potentially get more information out of him.

But she had the advantage now. At any moment, the priest's servant would come in to check in on him, or to bring the wine that Deoric had asked for. She didn't have time to waste on asking further questions.

The dagger in her right hand would have to be enough, especially in this small space. She grabbed him from behind with her off hand and drew the dagger over his throat. Deoric choked and spasmed in her arms. She could feel the life drain out of him as his body sagged onto her. Niamh dumped his corpse on the floor, narrowly escaping being covered in his blood.

Niamh grabbed everything on the desk that looked important, skipping over personal notes and generalized speeches to his congregation. She also left the books filled with his religious beliefs, but she gathered the journals filled with notes about the people he took orders from. There were names and locations. She had hit a cache of information. She didn't have time to think about it or what it meant – only hoped it would be of some use to the Hidden Ones.

As she grabbed the last relevant piece of paper on the desk, she heard the sound of someone approaching the cottage. Her heart stilled in her chest as she glanced at the paper and saw familiar words there. A reference to Excalibur, out in the world, and in Father Deoric's own hand, bragging that it would be easy to steal back for his masters. She didn't have time to piece together what was happening, but a new sort of fear filled her.

The sound came closer. It was probably the boy responsible for bringing Deoric his every desire. There was no time to hide the body. No time to even consider it. Quick as she could, she ran through to the back of the house and scaled the wall, flinging herself out the window and hanging by her fingertips off the sill. Looking down, she discovered the drop was higher than she had anticipated. The papers felt loose where she'd stuffed them, and she feared they would float away from her and be lost. Especially the one dictating that the mighty sword of her people had fallen into unknown hands.

From somewhere inside, she heard the door open and the boy scream, though it felt as though she were very far away from what was happening. She leapt and scrambled up the wall to the roof, keeping her body low to the thatch.

She would have to escape quickly. Leaping down to the ground, she darted through the graveyard, and remembered what Hytham had told her once more. She scaled the church faster than she could think, dipping into the shadows of the tower, and waited while the guards swarmed the cottage, knowing that she would not be able to leave until well past dawn, well past when his body had been carried out of the cottage, well past when the town already knew of his death. An unknown woman to the village wandering during the daytime would be less suspicious than at night, when any good woman was in her own bed.

Ravens began to swarm the tower, crowding around so that no one could see inside her hiding place.

"Thank you, Morrigan," she chattered in a whisper, for the night was still cold, as she waited for the right time to leave. But she was unable to fall asleep on her perch and instead started to go through the papers stolen from Father Deoric's desk. What she learned was startling. Deoric really was part of an order, just like Hytham had said. She didn't know how it could be that Avalon had no notion of these men and their entwined networks on Avalon's own island, but if they did, they hadn't told Niamh about it. Perhaps this was why the Lady had sent her, to get as much information as she could about this order, too.

Once the sun finally rose, she clambered down the backside of the church, folding her headscarf over her head and blending in with the mourning crowd as she made her way back to the barn where she had stashed her breeches and her horse.

"Left in a pool of his own blood..." one woman murmured to another as she passed. "Throat slit like a sacrifice."

Dread filled Niamh, but she refused to stop moving, even as the whispers followed her.

"Was like some kind of pagan practice. Maybe a ritual killing?" another woman said.

Niamh swallowed the urge to correct the peasant woman, to tell her that wasn't their way, and then wondered what Avalon would think of her actions. Drawing attention to herself at this moment would not be wise. She could tell that the father's death was stirring anti-pagan sentiment in the village and she feared she had made life for Wisweth more dangerous.

It had only taken her two days to deal with the priest, and she had given herself a whole week to take care of the situation. Perhaps she could take Wisweth back to Avalon, to escort her to a place where she would be safe. After all, that was her other calling – to protect the pagan women and men of this island.

It would be the right thing to do, especially if these villagers were muttering about pagan sacrifices on the heels of the priest's murder.

Niamh picked up her pace and made it to the abandoned barn. If the villagers were truly that angry, she would wait to change her disguise until she was further away from the village. The father's funeral would distract the villagers. Even then, it was better not to waste any more time, but she needed to ensure her safety.

Mathan whinnied at her and tossed his head when he saw her.

"What's that, my love?" she asked, bringing the bridle down so that his nose just barely touched hers.

The horse whinnied again, breathing hot breath into her face, damp and musty like hay. His eyes rolled back in his head, a sign of fear, and she stepped back, hoping that he wouldn't rear up.

"Easy, love, nothing's going to hurt you," she said, and then she listened more carefully, wondering if the Goddess was speaking through Mathan. The horse was worried, but not about her. Without a question she knew what she had to do.

Jumping onto the horse's back, she kicked him into a gallop, racing out of Cote in the direction of the Wisweth's home. The whispers against pagans, and the knowledge that it had been Wisweth's husband's grave that was the site of the destruction almost certainly made for a decent theory that her ally was in trouble. If she wasn't now, she would be awfully soon.

I've been rash, Niamh thought as she rode past the farms and fields and entrances to forests. I didn't think through who would get hurt in the wake of his death. I only thought of preserving the culture.

As she crested the hill over the cottage, she could already see the smoke. The burning of a woman's home was a sight she had seen before, and it reminded her of other homes that had been torched in her presence – none of which should have been.

Niamh pressed Mathan faster and when close enough to the burning home, she tied her horse to a fencepost to keep him safe and unafraid of the flames. She approached the smoking building, crispy pieces of thatch falling at her feet. There were no signs of a struggle, except the broken crescent moon necklace somewhere near the entrance to the burning cottage.

Niamh felt a swell of rage, and sorrow, at herself, at the people who chose to murder an innocent woman, at the faith that led these people and this town to make such decisions as this. She was angry that she had allowed these Hidden Ones to convince her to kill a man and endanger a woman from her own community, and for a moment she feared she had lost her way. That in her attempt to follow Avalon's directions, she had inadvertently harmed those she was sworn to protect.

She knew that the next step was to speak to the Women of the Mist, to tell them what she knew, and to ask if she could go home. After all, this quest already had her in over her head. She was not a spy. Clearly, she had let her anger rule her decisions.

But first she would pray.

She knelt in the ashy dirt, the hot coals warming her skin even as she felt cold from the emotions of the morning's discovery and folded her hands into fists. She let the fury that came with the acknowledgment of this woman's death wash over her, Wisweth's name lost to the fear that she had of her neighbors, and she asked the Morrigan to take this woman's soul safely to the next world.

Once satisfied that the soul of the fallen woman had been taken care of, she turned around and silently got onto the back of her horse, fingers twining in his mane as she turned the stallion toward the shores of the lake that she called her spiritual home.

SEVEN

Glastonbury Tor rose high above the misty lake that shrouded Avalon in mystery. The very top of the Tor was covered in white mist, so Niamh knew that the high priestesses were there, making prayers and offerings to the God and Goddess.

She wished that she could go straight there, to offer herself up to them, to ask for guidance. But she knew there were proper ways to do that, and she had to adhere to protocols. She was not like the trainees who ran to the feet of the Lady begging for a blessing. She never had been. Around the curve of the lake, out of sight of the docks that were meant for visitors, hung a single indigo and white banner, a sigil of a hawk perched on the pommel of a sword, with one hand grasping the end. A feminine hand of power.

Niamh led her horse into the stable by the lake and walked, barefoot, over to the edge. Wading in up to her calves, she waited.

Her eyes lidded shut, trying to ignore the cold water, the

way that the chill worked its way towards her bones. She consoled herself, knowing that when the boat came, she would be warm on the other side of the ride. That when she stepped off that boat, dripping wet and full of the chill, she would be home. The thought brought her relief.

When she had almost given up on it, a wooden rowboat with no oars appeared in the mist. While the uninitiated may have been startled at the vision, she climbed aboard without a question, and was ferried through. This was all familiar.

The mist was all encompassing. The white fog wrapped the boat in its embrace and carried her through to the other side. When it finally cleared, she could see Avalon herself. Bright green moss and white stone buildings faced her.

Her first step was to change.

Niamh walked to the closest house by the shore, shedding her clothes and bundling them all up into the crook of her arm. As she stepped over the threshold of the stone cottage, she smelled the burning herbs of the baths not far away from her. Dropping her clothes into the basket by the door, she stripped off her boots and walked further inside. Her feet prickled with needles as she sank into the herbal bath. Once she was soaking up to her neck and her hands didn't feel full of iron, she pulled her hair out of its braids and let it snake into the bath with her.

This wasn't for her pleasure, though. It was done with respect. Bringing the dirt of the outside world onto Avalon's shores was considered disrespectful. Once she was clean, she re-braided her hair, carefully constructing a crown of them around her head. She slipped into the sage green kirtle and belt of a mid-tier priestess, put her sword back at her hip, and walked out of the bath house and dressing station into the main courtyard.

She wriggled her toes on the moss, smiling a little. She remembered how strange it had been when she trained here to have to go barefoot, but shoes were a mark of the "civilized" world, and they had no place here.

Groups of initiates in white robes clustered around smaller outbuildings, some with swords, some with nothing in their hands. Their hair was worn down if they did not wield a sword, but up if they were training not just to the religious life but to the life of the warrior. To protect those who needed protection.

She made her way past groups of women who were there to study – and only women, no men were invited to Avalon unless something truly special had happened. The men who served the gods and goddesses were further away, on the coast in their own sacred cave by the sea. She felt the eyes of the other women on her back as she walked.

She made her way past them and toward the sacred path up the Tor, laden with white stones. She followed it with memory, closing her eyes and putting one foot in front of the next, knowing that she would find her way because she had done this so many times as a student and a guardian.

When she finally reached the top, she dropped to her knees and waited. The dew soaked into her shift as her knees pressed into the earth, though not unpleasantly. She was safe here, and while she waited, she rested, thought, and asked for guidance. Soon, a hand touched her shoulder.

"Lady," Niamh began, keeping her voice steady, "I beg

pardon for my intrusion, and for the act of disobedience by leaving my quest unattended, but I am in desperate need of guidance. I made the kind of error that I don't think a woman meant for this quest would make."

"Walk with me," the Lady said, "and we will discuss what should be done." The Lady's voice was accented like a Pict and was clear as water. Now that she had been acknowledged, Niamh stood and studied the Lady. Ever since she had taken her vows and been fully initiated into the Women of the Mist, she was allowed to make eye contact with Avalon's leader. The Lady had red hair bound up in plaits, and she wore a shift of deepest blue, with a leather belt holding a sheath around her waist. That was an odd choice.

The Lady led Niamh further up to the sacred circle where they met to do their rituals. Niamh followed, curious as to why they were making this longer journey up the Tor.

What could the Lady have been doing up here? There was no holy day upcoming, no planned anointing of new high priestesses. They might have been planning a special ritual, but there would have been more present than just the two of them.

"I fear I've interrupted at a terrible time…" Niamh began, starting to think coming here had been a mistake. This seemed like a time of deep contemplation for the Lady, one that Niamh had clearly disturbed.

"No, in fact, I believe your instincts sent you here to receive more details of what has happened," the Lady said, taking them through a set of standing stones. Now, Niamh saw why they had come here, and why the Lady wore an empty sheath at her waist.

In the center of the standing stones was a table, laid with sacred objects. A cup, decorated to look as though the stem was the twined trunk of an ancient tree, with the branches holding the cup in place. It was encrusted with jewels. A plate, bare of any food, shone golden in the sparse light that came through the mist. The plate had a star inside a circle engraved in the center. A spear, taller than the Lady, twined with green vines and purple flowers. The sacred objects of Avalon. All save one.

Excalibur.

Niamh's stomach sank as she asked, "Lady... what... exactly are we doing here with the sacred objects?"

"I wanted to visually remind you of the stakes on your quest. That you are not merely investigating a new group, but you are out there to protect our most sacred artifacts. Have you heard anything from the Hidden Ones about such artifacts?" the Lady asked with a raised eyebrow, not answering Niamh's question.

"I have not seen the table set properly in my life," Niamh said, tearing her eyes from the artifacts and bowing her head. "No... no I haven't," she stammered, belatedly answering the Lady's final query. "The Hidden Ones do not trust me much, yet."

"It will take time." The Lady paused and let her gaze linger on the table. "No one has seen such a setting in a long time. Not in my lifetime, not even in the lifetime of the Lady before me. One piece is missing, though. As you might recall from your lessons, we gave Excalibur to Arthur when he pulled it from the stone. He was a true king."

Niamh did remember, but she knew better than to

interrupt when the Lady used that tone of voice when telling a story. It was a voice that could mesmerize.

"Arthur was a good soldier for Avalon until he obtained new advisors. At least, that was the story I was told. I've never known who they were, but they ultimately betrayed him. That betrayal led to his death. After that, Excalibur was lost, until we learned it had been buried beneath Stonehenge, but even the bravest of our witch-warriors were unable to recover it," the Lady said. Her voice and expression were a mixture of anger and sadness. "I have always wondered if the Christians got to him and told him he had to no longer wield a magical object from our lands, or if they wished to use that mighty sword for their own purposes. But regardless... it never returned and has remained lost to this day."

Niamh could see that the failure to return Excalibur weighed on the Lady. In turn, the stolen letter from the father's office weighed heavily on her, but she resisted interrupting the Lady out of respect.

"Or so we thought. Excalibur has been removed from its vault. From the reports from other witch-warriors, the vault was opened by a Norse."

Niamh failed to suppress a flash of anger. She knew that it wasn't appropriate to shout in the presence of the Lady, no matter how sure she was that the Lady would agree with her. The note she'd recovered began to make even more sense. Niamh took a deep breath to steady her nerves before she asked her next question.

"A Norse? They shouldn't be holding on to our sacred objects," she said, voice soft with shock.

"Your job has become more complex than to report on what you can find out about the Hidden Ones, Niamh. You are now also tasked with finding Excalibur and bringing it back to us. We believe that this Dane may have ties to the Hidden Ones, or that the Hidden Ones might be able to help you locate this Dane due to their own resources. But we must see if we can trust them first. Restore the Sacred Table and you will be able to ask for whatever role you want from Avalon."

This was certainly a gift. Avalon asked things of its people; it did not give people choices for their paths. Some were suited to monastic life, others to witch-warrior paths, and others to ritual practice. But the Lady, the Goddess, and the energy of the world steered those choices.

Niamh stared at the sacred table. The missing sword was painful, not just to the Lady, who took it personally, but to the whole of their practice. Every person who followed the old ways had the right to worship the sacred table, and one of their sacred artifacts being wielded by a Dane did harm to the faith of everyone in her community. It twisted their tales and lore, the building blocks of their beliefs.

"I'll find it," Niamh said, the promise heavy in her voice. "I already have a lead."

"I want to hear the full report of your adventures," the Lady said. "Let us have a moment of silence though until we are out of this sacred place and with our sisters."

After they studied the sacred table for a few more moments, the Lady led Niamh by a way she had never seen before, off the back of the Tor and down an unknown path. There were so many avenues on Avalon that came, went, and even seemed to disappear when their purpose had been used. The prickles on her skin told her this mossy path, guided by mushrooms and fireflies, was one of those. Eventually, they came to the edge of the lake, where a table and chairs sat out for the Lady and her attendant. No one was around, except the dancing insects who watched them while they settled into the wooden chairs.

Niamh felt strange. She had left Avalon almost as soon as she had finished taking her vows, sent back to Argyll to take her mother's place. Argyll had been without a witch-warrior for the whole of her four years of training, and it wasn't right to make them wait longer. If her quest was to continue for an extended period, her replacement would need to be identified, which was one reason for her feeling as she did. Not only that, but the way that the Lady treated Niamh now was different. Like an equal. She had never been allowed to sit with the Lady, always expected to stand or kneel.

She knew that the purpose of Avalon was to train witch-warriors who could protect the whole of Mercia, Caledonia, and Ireland. She had known that was her purpose, and now she was seeing how important it was for each initiate to study as hard as she could.

"How is your investigation of the Hidden Ones going, Niamh?" the Lady asked, pouring them each a glass of wine.

"It has been an interesting adventure."

"And have you infiltrated them yet? These hidden people who have come to our shores without invitation?"

"Yes, Lady. I have. They're in Lunden. Their names are Hytham and Marcella. I'm not precisely sure of their goals yet, but I do know that they are not for the church in the way that other invaders have been."

"Neither were the Northmen." The Lady's voice was crisp.

"True. I know that well enough." Niamh thought back to the last raid on her village. The dead bodies. The burning huts. The ruined crops and the terrified children. She knew the Northmen were just as bad as the Christians.

"So, why have you come back here instead of straight to your prey?" the Lady asked, sipping from her goblet and regarding Niamh with the look of a woman who expected more information than she had been given.

Niamh swallowed, hastily taking a deep drink of the wine in front of her. She had thought that the Lady might be unhappy with her return to the island, and she was right. She had left her quest too early, perhaps with too little information in hand.

"To tell the truth, this quest is more difficult than I had thought it would be," Niamh said, deciding that she needed to be as honest as possible. "I went to do as the Hidden Ones bid me to prove my loyalty – kill a priest that was causing trouble to them, but also causing trouble to our people... and while I was there, I met a woman – an older one who had been a part of our order before. The town blamed her for the priest's death. The death that I caused."

"Where did you hide his body?" the Lady asked.

"Hide? He was dead. His lifeblood had been spilled. There was nothing for me to do but leave his corpse because his servant boy was coming and I couldn't be spotted."

"You didn't think to hide the body to protect the witches

of the region? To keep the people who would be most thought of as the murderer safe?"

Niamh felt shame. She was used to fighting people out in the open, to the idea that the people who were going to die were expecting to die – and the people who found their bodies knew exactly why they were dead. She had been fighting invaders, not acting as the invader herself. She hadn't adjusted for her new reality, for her new role as a Hidden One. She looked down into her cup, the deep red wine like the blood she had let run out of the priest.

"I don't know if I can be good at this, Lady. I don't know that I have the wit for it."

"It was foretold that this would be your destiny, that you would be the one to follow this path. I cannot stop your destiny from finding you, Niamh of Argyll. I can only help you find the path and get back onto it when you fall astray."

"There's more," Niamh said, drawing the papers she had found out of her leather pouch at her hip. "These were strewn all over the priest's desk. They appear to be about the Order of the Ancients that the Hidden Ones oppose."

The Lady took the crumpled papers and began to leaf through them, her eyes taking in all the information that Niamh had brought to her.

"The Order of the Ancients is who fought with Arthur," the Lady explained, as she continued to read. "I knew they still existed somewhat, but I wonder… perhaps they are who we truly need to be worried about, not these Hidden Ones."

"The Hidden Ones do seem to have a reasonable pursuit of action against them."

"Nonetheless, we still don't know who has Excalibur or to who this Dane, who holds Excalibur, pledges their loyalty. It could be the Order of the Ancients, it could be the Hidden Ones, it could be neither. It could be the Dane is a mercenary working on behalf of the Descendants of the Round Table, those who are either by blood or by belief the progeny of those knights. Stealing it seems to be everyone's game, but whoever has it must be stripped of the sword. It belongs to us, not to anyone else."

"So, you want me to go back." It wasn't a question, not something that Niamh had wondered, simply stating a fact that she knew was true. "Even though I failed to protect the woman who was under our care?"

"Yes. You may have made a mistake, Niamh, but you are not worthless. Continue to learn from Hytham and Marcella. Tell the Hidden Ones that the priest is dead and find out more about their purpose. And no matter who has the sword, whether it be your new allies, or an old enemy, take Excalibur back."

"Do you think they have it?" she asked. "Or at least are behind its removal from Stonehenge?"

"I don't know. They might be. But so might be the Descendants of the Round Table. We won't know until you listen. No one has the ability to talk to us as we remain in secret, and I doubt anyone would admit to stealing it from its resting place. But if you listen carefully enough, you might be the one to find it. But Niamh, be wary. From this letter, it seems there are others than us after the sword. You may have far more enemies than you anticipate."

Niamh could tell without having to ask that her

audience with the Lady was coming to an end. She could feel the energy of her attention waning, as she turned to the business that the Goddess had her doing next. Niamh got out of her chair and knelt by the table in the grass, dew seeping through the kirtle that she wore.

"Your blessing before I leave?" Niamh asked, hoping that it would grant her some measure of peace when she went back to the Hidden Ones, to Hytham and Marcella whose eyes seemed too sharp to escape.

Without words, the Lady placed her hands on Niamh's head. Niamh closed her eyes, feeling whatever energy the Lady chose to give her. Then, the Lady handed her back the papers, stood without another word, and left Niamh in the grove by the water.

There, Niamh considered her options. She could, of course, ignore the Lady, ignore Avalon, ignore the Goddess, ignore her calling, and go back home. She could decide of her own free will that this was not the life for her. She could walk out into the mist and never return.

Or she could walk the path that had been set for her. She could choose to listen to what had been asked of her and follow. She could go back to Lunden to face the people she found frightening, who made her rethink the way that she did things, learn from her mistakes, and become a better fighter than she was now. She could make that choice. She would make that choice.

Niamh got up and followed the path – which somehow led back to the shore where her boots and breeches were waiting for her, freshly cleaned and ready for her to re-dress and enter the present world once again. She dressed and walked back to the boat that would take her to her horse for the ride back to Lunden.

Because Niamh knew that even though she was afraid for herself, she was more afraid for the people like her who could not defend themselves from men like Deoric, like the Northmen, like anyone who would come for her people. Because there was nothing she could do, except believe that she had been put on this earth to protect people like her.

EIGHT

Niamh returned to Lunden long after the sun had set when the whole city was sleeping. She assumed that Hytham and Marcella would be doing the same as the rest of the population, dreaming whatever dreams they could.

Thus, Niamh chose to enter the bureau by scaling the back wall off the alley and made her way in through the window to her sleeping space at the very top of the building. She settled into the bed of reeds in the dark and listened to the rain pattering on the roof over her head, grateful for the warmth of the blankets and furs over her.

Niamh was surprised that the rain was not the only sound echoing through the dark hours. Instead of silence in the main rooms of the bureau, she heard low voices. Marcella and Hytham weren't sleeping, as she'd anticipated, but instead were both awake and entertaining a third person whose voice was unfamiliar to Niamh, though the accent betrayed that she was a Dane. Niamh was not filled with excitement at the prospect of having to be friendly towards a Dane of any sort, let alone one who might be helping the Danes in their quest to settle on her islands. But perhaps this was an unforeseen opportunity – the person who took Excalibur was a Dane, after all.

Yet, she wanted to sleep. Between the long days of riding, the discussion with the Lady, and solving the issue with the priest... plus the grief around Wisweth's death... she yearned to rest in a bed, and not on the damp earth. Sleep, however, was not on the horizon. Even though she needed to recharge, she didn't know how long this stranger would be with Hytham and Marcella, and her presence was a mystery that needed to be solved. What if the visitor left? What if Niamh wasn't supposed to know she had ever been to visit? Perhaps the Goddess had guided her back to the bureau for this very reason.

She slid, belly down, on the rough wood floorboards to angle herself closer to the hole in the floor which led and looked down onto the main floor. From this vantage point, she strained to hear the voices as they drifted up the ladder to her sleeping place. Though she was a guest in this bureau, other visitors surely must have used the space in her absence. Glancing down through the hole, she spotted three people huddled around the fireplace. Marcella, in her furs, glanced uncomfortably at the other person, who wore feathers on her cloak and in her hair. Sacred bones rattled on her chest. Hytham sat on the other side of her, head tilted, listening intently.

The newcomer was unknown to Niamh, but she looked like one of the Northmen who came from far away. Curiously, not only did she look like one of those

Northmen, but she looked like one of their mystics who could see through the veil into the other worlds that everyone shared. Niamh smirked. Ah, yes, there were different belief systems, of course. Long-standing myths that others believed. They had their Thor and Freyja, and she had Ceridwen and Cernunnos.

"She is going to Ireland soon..." the Norsewoman said, answering a question that Niamh couldn't quite hear from Hytham. "She'll be heading to Caledonia beforehand... but I'm not sure when. There are some loose ends she has to tie up."

Who was *she?* The Norsewoman's leader, Niamh supposed.

"I'm curious, you said you had a visitor in your last letter..." the mystic continued.

"Oh, yes. Niamh. I'm withholding judgment. Hytham seems to be all ready to initiate her the instant she gets back – if she survives." Marcella this time, snide as ever. It was not surprising that Marcella wasn't cheering for Niamh to come back. If anything, Marcella probably hoped she was dead.

"Marcella is more suspicious than I am," Hytham said. He sounded tired.

"For someone who wants to work in the shadows you would think that you wanted to be more discreet," Marcella snapped back. "It's unlike you, Hytham. Before you landed on these shores, I heard you had a suspicious nature, always adhering to the rules and following protocol. Why the sudden leniency for this Niamh?"

Hytham took a deep breath. "I cannot imagine that your dislike of the woman would so overcome your desire for information." It was clear that he had been saying this over and over again. "We needed to find warriors who know this land better than us."

"So, you're using her for information?" the mystic woman asked.

"Not precisely. I genuinely believe her to be a good fighter, and knowledge of these islands and who the players are, such as the Women of the Mist, is invaluable. She has a good heart and instinct, along with a type of training that already places her above most. Marcella's dislike of Caledonians as a group aside, having someone like Niamh is useful. If she can trust us, she might open up to us, and we can understand the ancient workings of this place."

"They're all untrustworthy," Marcella said lazily. "You'll see."

It isn't me that Marcella dislikes, Niamh thought. It is the whole of my people.

"I've had experience with people like her. Deceitful. Only interested in looking out for themselves, or for people like them," Marcella continued.

Niamh couldn't change where she came from to please Marcella. She also couldn't change that Marcella's people had been part of an occupying force. Of course, they hadn't been *compliant* with the Romans. How foolish. Marcella would need to get over her dislike of Niamh and Caledonians in general. After all, Niamh could live in discomfort. She had before. Not everyone at Avalon got along, even in the service of the Goddess.

The conversation ebbed and flowed, but then changed tone, shifting away from Niamh as a topic. Niamh considered making her arrival known, but decided it wouldn't help if she scampered into view after they had been speaking of her – and especially with Marcella wishing for her death so plainly.

Once Hytham began telling an old story about an adventure in Constantinople, Niamh felt safe enough to climb down the ladder to enter the main room, making sure to snag her cloak so that it appeared as though she had returned only moments before, instead of the hour or more spent listening to their conversation.

"You're back," Marcella said, her voice filled with disappointment, confirming Niamh's suspicions that she would rather Niamh hadn't returned at all.

"Indeed," Niamh said and then turned to the unknown mystic. "I shall relate my travels to you at another time, as it seems you have company."

"It's all right, you can speak freely. Valka is one of ours," Hytham said. "She is the seer for the community I live in – Ravensthorpe."

Niamh was right on one count so far, and nodded her head at Valka. She wondered about the rest. She didn't like the implication of being lumped in with the Norsewoman as *ours* and restrained her instinct to bristle. She had to behave as though she could work with these people, after all, even if she didn't like the company they kept. Maybe she, like Marcella, needed to come to terms with her hatred of the Danes.

Marcella waved her hand at Hytham, attempting to silence him, but he plowed forward, pretending not to see her gestures.

"Valka is one of the advisors for us at the bureau. She also brings news of the other people associated with our organization when she can," Hytham said.

"I haven't met a seer from the Norse tradition before." It was the kindest thing Niamh could think to say. She had to behave. It was difficult for her to even look this woman in the eye, and harder knowing that if something terrible happened between them, Marcella was the last person on earth to consider protecting her.

Now that Niamh was closer, she inspected Valka with scrutiny. Valka was not dressed like a warrior, and there was something about her energy – her presence in a room – that told Niamh precisely what kind of advisor this woman was. She reminded Niamh of her fellow priestesses. Heavy with intention and a gaze that felt as though it could understand more about you than the human eye was meant to.

"You know me for what I am," Valka said, and it was not a question. Niamh couldn't tell if she was pleased to be spotted as a wisewoman or not. In her soul, Niamh knew she and Valka could be either fast friends, or bitter enemies. It was not clear which path they would take, but for now, her inherent distrust outweighed the possibility. The mere idea of being comfortable with a Dane was too much to contemplate.

"Valka has been instrumental as a healer and advisor to us," Hytham said, eyeing the two women and seeming not entirely comfortable with their connection. "Valka was interested in meeting you in order to understand more about the practices of your people."

"I'm not the only one. The leader of my community,

Eivor of the Raven Clan, is also interested in meeting you when she gets back from her travels," Valka said.

At that, both Marcella and Hytham gave Valka a silencing look. Valka responded with a look just as sharp and quick.

"You said I could speak freely in front of her," Valka said, giving the two Hidden Ones the same stern glance that Niamh saw mothers give their unruly children. It was a priestess move, through and through.

"Not quite that freely," Marcella snapped.

Valka turned to Niamh, placing the full weight of her gaze and mind on her. Niamh felt Valka's questions, the intent. She knew she would have to be careful with this woman, not just because she was a Norsewoman and therefore her enemy, but because she was a worker of energies in the same way as Niamh. It made Valka dangerous.

"It's nice to meet you," Niamh said. The lie lodged in her throat. She wondered what bloodshed Valka had seen on her travels from her homeland to Niamh's.

Valka kept her silence. Instead, her eyes roved over Niamh's face, taking in every pore and feature. It was uncomfortable. Niamh had been on the receiving end of such stares before, mostly from other witch-warriors trying to determine some secret thought or intention. The pit in Niamh's stomach grew with the silence, stretching far longer than she would have liked.

"How did your quest go?" Hytham asked, his voice friendly and cheerful in contrast to the silence.

Niamh thought about how to craft her answer and glanced away from Valka. "It could have gone better, but

the priest is dead and his followers no longer have a leader
to guide them into more trouble."

"What went wrong?" Marcella asked, picking up on
the issue with ease. She was smug, rejoicing in Niamh's
admitted difficulty.

"I…" Niamh considered crafting a lie, but it was difficult
to do so under Valka's piercing gaze. She didn't have time
to come up with a better story than the one that was true.
"I killed him when he was alone in a public place. The body
was found too easily and so the locals took out their rage
on an innocent woman who didn't commit the murder. I'm
sorry for her passage, and for the trouble she got into, and I
will do better next time."

"Hiding the body is just as important as hiding yourself,"
Hytham said, concern plain on his face. "Perhaps we need
to practice."

That sounded bloody and disrespectful, but Niamh
knew it was true, that the practice of hiding a body was a
part of the job she would have to do to survive with the
Hidden Ones. She nodded glumly.

Valka's gaze turned into one of curiosity, not concern.

"Yet, you did the thing you were asked, even if you
struggled with your stomach for it?" Marcella asked. "Even
if you didn't have all the skills on hand?"

Niamh couldn't bring herself to speak, and instead
just nodded her head, casting her eyes anywhere that she
could.

Marcella heaved a sigh. "Very well. She can become an
initiate, Hytham. If you still think she's worthy." Marcella's
voice carried skepticism, her eyes lidded with a mild

amount of disdain, almost as though she wished she hadn't spoken. But Valka seemed pleased.

"Why? I failed," Niamh said. She had anticipated that Marcella would get angry with her, and ultimately throw her out on her head, for her mistakes with the priest.

"You identified what went wrong," Marcella said. "Most people make mistakes in dangerous situations. Good agents are the ones who know how to learn to get better at their jobs, not the ones who defend what they did wrong."

Niamh considered this. On Avalon she had seen many young apprentices fail out in their first year because they were unable to learn from their mistakes, and so this thinking made sense to her. Honestly, she was surprised Marcella had somewhat overcome her animosity for Niamh.

"And because you didn't try to lie to us about what went wrong, we can trust you to report truth," Hytham continued for Marcella, standing up and walking to Niamh with intention. He placed one hand on her shoulder. "I welcome you into the order of the Hidden Ones. We will do well to have you in our ranks alongside us."

"As an apprentice," Marcella cut in, quickly. "To be trained as an assassin and not initiated. Not unless you want to have her go through the ceremony for the gauntlet." The last line was directed to Hytham.

"I told you, even if we raise someone to the level of assassin, we are not committing that act while I am in any position of power here."

Marcella waved her left hand at Hytham, and Niamh noticed the lack of a ring finger on that hand for the first time. Niamh was smart enough to know that some communities placed physical burdens on their followers as a way to show their faith. Avalon required a tattoo, which Niamh wore on her upper forearm. Not the loss of a digit as Marcella demonstrated that the Hidden Ones did. It made her stomach turn, and for a moment, she wondered what would have happened if they'd fully accepted her. Would she have gone so far as to bear that physical mark?

"Apprenticeship is fine…" Niamh said before Hytham could object, and she offered him a smile as thanks. This half-hearted initiation was clearly a fight that he had been having with Marcella for some time and she was glad to have earned some level of trust in the Hidden Ones.

Marcella withdrew her hand from view.

"Is there some sort of initiation for apprenticeship?" Niamh asked cautiously, wondering if she would have to make some other blood oath that would invalidate the oaths she had made to her people, to Avalon, to the Goddess that she served.

"No, you've already completed your first task and come home safely to us. But now we will continue to teach you the skills of our people more thoroughly, and give you the tools you need to practice the arts that we do."

From somewhere in the folds of his cloak, Hytham produced a metal gauntlet, which he slid onto her left hand. He waited for her to understand it, not using words, just watching with eyes and energy full of patience.

"This is the weapon that the Hidden Ones use. I want you to practice with it when you can. It is not yours – not yet – but it is the weapon that we prefer. But be careful. There is a reason Marcella is missing a finger."

She felt the weight of the metal draped over her hand and then up her forearm, and then she found it – a spot inside the gauntlet that, when she pressed it, shot out a single spike, a blade meant for death.

"Hytham," Marcella's voice was taut, "we don't give those to people who aren't fully–"

"She can learn to use it and we can revisit *full membership* another time," Hytham said with venom, and then turned to Niamh, focusing on her. "So that you can do what must be done with a swiftness. May the shadows always keep you safe."

Niamh felt the weight of his words like a mantle. This weapon was both a gift and a promise that the Hidden Ones were making to her. That they trusted her.

"Thank you for this gift," Niamh said, studying the metal gauntlet carefully and feeling a strange emotion overwhelm her. "I assume it is worn under the clothing so that it cannot be observed?"

Hytham smiled, almost sadly, and nodded. Niamh adjusted the placement of the gauntlet, making it almost invisible under the layers of fabric that she wore. She was grateful that it did not go further up her arm, so that she did not expose her initiation tattoo from the Mists.

"Like an adder," she whispered to herself, thinking about the energy and patience of snakes, the way that they waited until it was time to attack their prey. Only striking at those who came closest to them when it was absolutely necessary.

"With that, you are an apprentice of the Hidden Ones. We will share more with you once we have all gotten some rest." Hytham glanced at Marcella and Valka.

"It is very late or very early," Marcella said with a yawn, and with that she stood and left.

Hytham clapped Niamh on the shoulder one more time. "Do be careful with the gauntlet. I have always been a cautious man, but my experiences here have shown me that sometimes trusting in others first is necessary."

"You are following in Basim's footsteps," Valka said with ire. "Doing an act you once very much disagreed with."

"My past self would laugh," Hytham said. "Giving out such a gauntlet... who have I become?" His tone indicated soft self-mockery as he left the room.

Now, only Valka and Niamh remained.

Alone with the Norsewoman, Niamh wasn't sure what to do. Echo Marcella's earlier expression of tiredness, fake a yawn, and escape? She glanced around the room, studying the few adornments except for the furs and weapons. Such a lack of decoration struck her as strange. The cottages at home were so much more beautiful, with wall hangings crafted by the women, children filling the empty spaces, along with the clutter and sound of community. She remembered the small altars people built at their hearths. This bureau was not a home for the Hidden Ones, only a place where they came to fight and plan exclusively.

She thought back to Avalon and her conversation with the Lady on top of the Tor. She was here for a reason, and it was not because she wanted to be the kind of warrior that these people were, but because she had made an oath to the Goddess to protect people, and to learn everything she could about these new intruders.

"You should rest. Your mind is far from here. We'll talk in

the morning," Valka said, indicating that Niamh should go through the main room and back up the ladder.

While she would normally argue, Niamh realized that rest was precisely what she needed in order to do her best work. She nodded and touched the gauntlet around her forearm, feeling the hidden blade within it.

"Hytham has put a great deal of trust in you," Valka observed. "Have you earned it?"

The question made Niamh uneasy, and she did not answer, instead climbing the ladder wordlessly. Upstairs, she settled underneath the furs on her bed and closed her eyes, landing in a dreamless sleep quickly.

NINE

Niamh woke in the later hours of the morning. Valka was waiting in the entrance hall when she descended the ladder. The Norse seeress sat patiently in front of the fire, eyes half closed in meditation.

Niamh paused. She did not want to be the one to break the silence, even as old hatreds and suspicions rose within her. To say good morning would make her seem friendly to the Norsewoman, and even though she was meant to make allies and investigate the Hidden Ones, that did not mean she had to be *too* friendly. Instead, Niamh made her way over to the table where someone – Hytham, she presumed – had laid out bread and cheese for the morning meal. Taking some, she gazed out at the Tamesis, hoping that her silence would convince Valka that she was so dull that there was no reason to speak with her.

But after several minutes, it became clear that Valka was waiting for her. Niamh finished eating a slab of bread and cheese, and then, with great deliberation, settled down across from Valka and forced herself to be open to the conversation. It made her itch. It was not where she wanted to be. But, if she was to investigate the Hidden Ones, she needed to understand their allies as well.

"You came from Caledonia," Valka began, and her opening salvo was not a question. She wasn't inviting Niamh to speak. Her next sentence came after a lengthy silence, which Niamh felt could be deliberate either to keep Niamh off balance or justified her putting pieces of Niamh's backstory together. "Caledonia is far to the north, where some of my brethren landed with their ships."

This was not where Niamh had expected the woman to begin. She wished she had more cheese and bread.

"I'm sure you don't like people like me very much," Valka said. "You can barely look at me, can you?"

It felt like a splash of cold water to be confronted with her own dislike so brazenly. "No. My village was terrorized for two years with raids. We managed to stay standing, but it was hard won," Niamh said, and couldn't stop the animosity from seeping into her tone.

"Did you have something to do with that?" Valka asked, and the inquiry was not unkind. "Surviving the raids?"

"I did. I have always been good with a sword, and my home is important to me. I did what I could to protect us." She did not take full credit for how much she had done to protect her home, but she had to admit to Valka that it was a part of her overall experience that had first impressed the Hidden Ones. It wouldn't be believable to the mystic, that much was clear.

"You seem to be better trained than most of the women

I've met from your part of the world," Valka said, toying with the sacred bones along her neck.

That was a shock. Had Valka willingly gone as far north as Caledonia? Most of the settlers to Mercia had stayed where they landed, especially the ones who were important to their clans, like their seers.

"I suppose that's true," Niamh said slowly. "I got very lucky in the people who were around and had the time and wisdom to teach me. Unlike some of the other women here… Recently, I spoke with a nun who expressed concerns about the fate of a nunnery. It is something I mean to investigate when my duties with the Hidden Ones let me, but my instincts tell me that these women do not have the ability to defend themselves."

"Even though these nuns worship a different god? You would help them?" Valka looked suspicious.

"Of course," Niamh said. "It is… something I have struggled with, yes, but creating a safe haven for those in need has always been a priority for me. No matter the religion."

"That is an honorable sentiment. One I value." Valka sipped at the hot beverage she had in front of her and stared into its contents for a long moment before continuing.

"I have become fascinated by the practices of the witches in this part of the world. I have wanted to learn more about them since making my new home in Ravensthorpe. It seems important, even if I do not plan to worship your gods, to learn about them." Valka paused, licking her lips as if suddenly uncertain whether to continue. "I wonder if you might help me on this personal journey of mine.

Perhaps you might know something of the Women of the Mist?"

Niamh's spine straightened; her blood ran cold. She wondered how Valka could already know of the witches from Avalon, having only made her way to the shores of this island recently. But, if Hytham and Valka were close, he might have shared what little information he had on Niamh's true order. "I might. What have you heard about them so far?" Niamh asked, carefully turning the query back to the woman who had given it to her.

"I know they practice herb magic like I do, that they communicate with their gods – though I know not who their gods are. I know they train with the sword as well as the staff... though I don't understand why. Our seers are not fighters in the same way." Valka warmed to the subject, as if eager to have her knowledge confirmed or denied.

Niamh felt on guard. She wanted to open up to Valka, but her own misgivings held her back. The Women of the Mist didn't keep themselves entirely hidden, but since the arrival of Christianity, it had become a less open secret than it had been before.

"I don't know where they are, of course. The fact that they hide themselves in this façade of the mist seems untrustworthy, rather than standing out in the open and offering their services to all. I live on the outskirts of my village and am welcoming to anyone who would seek my counsel. Why hide?" Valka asked.

Niamh could only think back to Wisweth, who had died because Niamh had made the mistake of leaving the priest's body out where it could be found too quickly, the fact that the Christians seemed determined to remove paganism from her world, and they would take the Women of the Mist with them. She wondered how to connect with Valka, to explain without revealing too much the purpose of Avalon and how it functioned.

"You have problems with Christians in your home country too, do you not?" Niamh decided to start with that question first, as it was safest. The easiest one to explain away everything.

Valka's face darkened at the mention of Christians.

"They don't want us to keep our traditions at home either," Valka said. "They want us to accept their god and their leader and their practices and leave ours behind. But I will not leave Thor or Odin. They have guided me for a long time, and it is not their will that I follow this Jesus that the Christians speak of."

Niamh could agree with that, so she nodded cautiously. She hoped that if they could find common ground on things, the seer wouldn't look at her too closely. "Perhaps these Women of the Mist are the same as you – refusing to divulge their secrets even when it seems like their faith and beliefs are attacked on all sides."

Valka seemed to accept this explanation. "I see you have a raven stitched into your cloak," she said, nodding to Niamh's clothes and then taking a sip of her hot beverage.

"I do," Niamh said carefully.

"Is it for Odin?" Valka asked, almost hopefully. As though if they had someone in common then Niamh would be more comfortable, more trusting.

Unfortunately, Niamh could only tell the truth in this

instance. To lie would be a falsehood to her own Goddess, and she could not stomach that, even if telling that lie would protect her.

"No. I do not know your Odin, but I do treat with the Morrigan. She is a battle goddess, and her crows take the souls of the dead on to their next destination." Niamh found herself unsure if it was best to be honest about her faith, but she felt her icy exterior begin to thaw against her better judgment. If Valka wanted to know more… but Niamh drew back, knowing she was being pulled into a deception. She was too eager, and this was one reason she was not a good spy.

"Why are you asking so many questions about my gods and goddesses?" she suddenly demanded. "About my practices? Why do my beliefs matter to someone who seems to lay claim to land that doesn't belong to you? Why do you ask so many questions of my beliefs?"

The fire crackled in the hearth. Niamh's challenge was probably unwise, but she couldn't help herself.

"I wish to understand and question because I live here now. Even though I still believe in Odin and Freyja, I wish to understand what this land believes." Valka tapped the arm of the chair she sat in. "Your legends are different from ours, your afterlife is not a grand hall… I don't understand yet how your lands respond to you. I had hoped this would be seen as respect rather than not…"

It was an interesting idea to Niamh that the lands would respond to her. To her, it was less that the lands helped her, and more that she chose to cultivate a relationship with the energy of the land that she came from. She knew what it was like to feel the energy of the forest, or the shore. She knew what lived in those places, and what energies those animals could give her as well.

But she wasn't sure it was safe to tell Valka about it.

"I want to understand the organizations too," Valka said, sounding exasperated. "The Women of the Mist must be powerful if they have so many women at their disposal."

So it wasn't just an interest in understanding the place that Valka now lived. No, it was about understanding how to control or even manage or mitigate the people who lived here. Niamh felt her hackles rise again, but Valka continued, knowing she must have said something wrong.

"Eivor told me about a ritual that she witnessed a few months ago, where a man was burned to death inside a wicker statue of a man. Do your people usually commit ritual sacrifice like that?"

Niamh wanted to laugh, uncomfortable with the turn in conversation. "That's a rare practice. No one from my part of the islands does that." She felt as though Valka was asking questions about rituals not her own, practices she imagined were probably done out of desperation. She didn't know how she was going to get out of this conversation. The silence dragged on, and she knew that Valka was waiting on her to say something, to respond in any way.

"It's not as though we've left our homeland and settled on lands that don't belong to us, or taken artifacts that don't belong in our hands," Niamh finally retorted, unable to restrain herself from pointing out that there were unfavorable things coming from the other side. "And I think the communities that do that aren't in line with the Women of the Mist order, certainly."

Niamh knew that the Lady had warned communities against committing ritual sacrifice, knowing that it would only anger the Christians further. And yet, Niamh had perpetuated this violence unintentionally. Her heart filled with heaviness, remembering when she'd seen Wisweth's house burning.

"What else can you tell me about the Women of the Mist?" Valka asked. "Or perhaps about your own people and village?"

Niamh didn't care to speak much more, especially after being told that her people practiced ritual sacrifice. While Valka might be interested in learning about their customs, she also held the kind of beliefs about them that Niamh found reprehensible. In some ways, Valka's line of questioning was as bad as Christian queries, and she was a fellow pagan!

But she'd been silent on too many matters already. So, Niamh looked at the cackling fire and offered a small snippet, hoping it would close the conversation, "I know that they have a hidden home, where they train women up to be warriors and healers."

"Everyone knows that, it seems," Valka replied, pushing.

"Yes, everyone does," Niamh agreed. She hoped this curt reply would stop Valka from asking more questions. But Niamh should have known better than to think that a fellow priestess could be dissuaded.

"Did you train with them? You clearly have skill with the blade. Do you also understand herbs and energies?"

Niamh shook her head. She could not lie about her skills, but even less about the oaths that she had taken. The perceptible shake of her head, however, was not a verbal lie. It was not a verbal dismissal of the reality of who she followed.

"Interesting. So, you learned from the women of your village then?"

Niamh took a swig of the pale watery ale that was served with their morning breakfast, while nodding into her mug. Another silent lie. This woman was fishing for something. She would have to be careful she didn't unintentionally give something away.

"As I said, the women of my village were quite skilled." This was a truth.

She remembered the women of her village fondly, who would heal each other when one of the representatives of Avalon wasn't available. Boiling herbs for teas and poultices, tending to sick children when their burning foreheads felt like the hot coals in a fire pit. Some women took a season at Avalon to learn the basic skills of healing, or midwifery, returning home instead of pledging themselves to the Goddess and the full craft. She could have admitted to that kind of training, but it felt unsafe to admit any connection to the Women of the Mists in front of a Norsewoman. For all she knew, Valka was dead set on erasing them, just like the Christians were.

Valka didn't need to know any of this unless she had an alternative intent.

"I don't think that the women of my village, or any of the women working with the Mists, are incompatible with

your truths. Nor is our Morrigan incompatible with your
Odin. They're different paths, truly, different gods and
goddesses. But they don't seem to be completely against
one another, unlike the Christian god and ours," Niamh
said. She was trying to find a way out, unwilling to educate
this woman, but she hoped that by comparing their gods
and de-escalating from antagonism they would be able to
end this conversation.

Valka grunted, and Niamh could see it plain on her face
as the wrinkles around her eyes creased that she wasn't
convinced by Niamh's lies or her arguments. But it didn't
matter. As long as Valka didn't suspect her of being who she
was, it would be fine. She would be able to do her quest for
the Lady with some safety.

In the silence, interrupted only by the occasional
shout from the street and the crackling of the fire, Niamh
wondered what would come next. Would she be sent on
another task for the Hidden Ones by herself? Would Valka
try to extract more information from her? Would she be
sent back where she came from after her failure, asked only
to commit the murders that the Hidden Ones needed done
in Caledonia?

Despite the gauntlet on her forearm, she knew she hadn't
done well enough on her mission to Cote, that she hadn't
given the Hidden Ones precisely what they wanted. But she
hoped that perhaps she had done enough to get another
chance, and this time she would prove herself more than
worthy to earn their full trust. The papers of Father Deoric
were still hidden upstairs, the link to Excalibur safely
tucked away for her eyes only.

Without warning, Hytham slid in through the window, quiet as can be, and picked up his meal of the remaining cheese and bread and sat down with them.

"Niamh, I'm coming back to fetch you," he said eagerly as he ate his food neatly. "We have a mission to complete, and I would like to see you in action myself before we send you out on your own again."

Niamh's heart sped up. A mission with Hytham? On the one hand it was a chance to get him to trust her, to show him that she was worth investing in, but on the other, she would have to remember to cover for her own secrets and watch that she didn't reveal too much.

Niamh wrapped herself more tightly in her wool cloak. She knew this would be a more difficult test. After all, Hytham missed nothing with his keen eyes and his watchful mind.

"Of course I'll accompany you if you'd like my assistance," Niamh said, hiding the tremor in her voice. "Otherwise, I'm here to serve until asked to leave."

The commitment was a difficult one. Her heart yearned for home, for the isle of Avalon. She wanted to be anywhere but with these people who killed others because they felt it was their right. She especially wanted to get away from Valka, who did not seem to be on her side at all.

"What is the purpose of our trip?" she asked. The last mission had been bloody, and she knew this one would also result in another assassination and death.

"There is a pagan woman being held in a Roman camp some way outside Lunden. She is imprisoned there for committing acts of violence against the men in power near her village. Likely, she'll be put to death – but not if we rescue her and get her out of the area in time."

A pagan woman. A woman like her. Perhaps the Hidden Ones weren't all bad, and Niamh struggled to remember that Marcella's hatred of her people mirrored Niamh's similar hatred for the Danes. Perhaps she had been blinded. Perhaps they were trying to help those who were less fortunate, who had less power to stay safe. She couldn't tell, but maybe it wasn't all blood for power, after all. She wondered how it was they came to know about this situation.

"Of course, I'm happy to help one of my own," she said, "and help you as well."

"Yes, you've assessed it isn't entirely out of kindness – the man who is keeping her hostage is also holding information about the whereabouts of someone who is working against us here in Lunden."

"So we do both. Get the information that you need and assist someone that I would like to protect. How did you come to know about this woman's imprisonment?"

"News of her capture reached us because of the identity of our target," Marcella said, descending the stairs and smoothly entering the conversation.

"And who would that be?" Niamh asked boldly, resting her other hand on the gauntlet. She felt comfortable furthering her interrogation of their choices now that she was holding their weapon in her hand.

"His name is Cyrus. This is why I cannot go and Hytham must, because he will recognize me on sight. I won't be able to get close. He has known my face for a long while." Marcella looked frustrated, as if she'd been denied vengeance. "I am unable to walk freely around Mercia until he is dead and gone."

That wasn't necessarily a good thing for Niamh, though she would do her best to satisfy the mission to completion.

"I hate letting you take care of this issue, Hytham, and I'd rather let Niamh have the task of boiling bandages and night watch, but unfortunately the two of you will need to take care of this without me." Marcella stood in front of the fire, staring at it with a deep frown.

"You must miss going out on missions," Niamh said, risking Marcella's rage to detangle her history.

"Of course, I do. Do you think I like being trapped here, instead of being out there, fighting like I have learned to do? My skills are wasted in this building. All because of that Order of the Ancients scum," Marcella snarled back.

"Why is it that you can't just go and kill him?" Niamh asked, pressing a little harder. "Is his death part of our mission now?"

"Yes, of course. That should have been obvious. If he dies, I can go back to doing what I'm best at," Marcella demanded. "Kill him, but if you need motivation to do so, he's a man who believes that women are things. I should know. I came to this island with him and escaped on my own wits."

Marcella's eyes glittered, her rage something Niamh could almost taste. Niamh backed away from questioning the Roman further and turned her attention to Hytham. She opened her mouth to ask another question when Valka suddenly cut in.

"But are you ready to go on such a journey?" Valka asked Hytham. The woman rose and walked over to him and then seemed to inspect him. "Your health has never been the same since–"

"I'll be fine. Marcella said it herself, she can't go. It would destroy what little anonymity we have." Hytham brushed off Valka's concern. But Valka would not be deterred.

"Couldn't Niamh go alone?" Valka asked.

"Perhaps she should," Marcella declared suddenly, leaving Niamh confused as to her switch in tone. "She went by herself to Oxenfordscire and that was a longer ride with higher stakes than a simple prisoner capture."

"She cannot," Hytham said firmly. "The fortress is well defended, and Cyrus…" Here, Hytham looked Marcella straight in the eye, "… well, you know how well Cyrus fights. Would you send anyone in to fight him alone? Without protection or backup?"

Marcella looked profoundly uncomfortable. She wanted to say yes – it was plain as day on her face that she would prefer to send Niamh off to die at the hands of this warrior. Yet, to Niamh's relief, she couldn't quite bring herself to do so. Concern filled Marcella's face, as if she was unsure of Hytham's health being able to withstand carrying him through to see the mission's completion.

"Are you ready to fight at my side?" Hytham asked, directing the question to Niamh.

"If you let him go with you, and he gets re-injured, I will blame you," Valka said, looking at Niamh with conviction.

"If he goes and gets re-injured it will be his own decision, Valka. Not mine. I think it's clear to all of us that if he wishes to fight, he will find a reason for it." Niamh spoke with confidence. She could see that Hytham was spoiling for a fight. After all, she had been like him once, when an injury had taken her off the watch for her village for a little while and every day she had ached to return to the fight for her people. It spoke well of him, she thought, that the people he served with were so concerned about his wellbeing. It told her much about Hytham as a man, not just as a warrior.

From Valka's frustrated face, Niamh could tell the Norsewoman must have tended to Hytham after his injury, whatever it had been, and she was very clearly protective of his progress in this matter. Marcella didn't look happy either, but it appeared to be less personal for her.

"I have been resting for months. I have not gone on a longer journey than from here to the marketplace on foot, and when I have gone back to Ravensthorpe it has been on a boat rather than on horseback." As Hytham spoke, the pitch in his voice changed, and the annoyance was more than clear. "I have not been allowed to do my job, and I am getting tired of the restrictions on my actions. This is a fight that I can do. I can go with Niamh and I will be safe. She is a good fighter and will keep an eye out for me."

Niamh couldn't help but feel a swell of pride in her chest, knowing that Hytham trusted her. It mattered a great deal to her that the warriors she fought with felt that they could count on her on the battlefield – and Hytham was making it clear that this was very much the way in which he saw her.

Niamh glanced at Marcella's face, drawn shut with the frustration of not being able to solve her own problems, and at Hytham, who hopefully gazed at her, knowing that she had a decision to make. Without another thought, Niamh turned and together they walked down the steps to the stables.

She knew that she had to do this for the captured pagan women and for the oaths she swore to her gods, but also for the Hidden Ones, and she was grateful to be with someone who believed in her skill.

TEN

Hytham and Niamh rode north, alongside the Tamesis, as the river flowed from a harbor area which was littered with docks, Danes, and longships sailing out to sea with terrifying figureheads of dragons and wolves. Once they passed the busiest parts of the harbor and the main city area, they saw thick branches sweeping down to the river, and smaller cottages and farms placed further back from the road. It was a quiet ride. Hytham chose to keep his own counsel, and Niamh didn't know exactly what was safe to speak to him about – although she felt safer in his company than with Valka or Marcella. Valka could see too deeply into the energies of the people around her and Marcella was suspicious.

But Hytham seemed to genuinely believe that Niamh had come to the Hidden Ones with good intentions – which she didn't think was because Hytham was naïve. She recalled the conversation she'd overheard earlier, about how he'd once been cautious and how he realized he had to take the first chance at trust. Trust that he had put in her.

Her heart pounded louder, suddenly uneasy with the possibility that she'd have to betray him and ruin that optimism he had cultivated. She watched him as they rode, and noticed he kept his eyes and ears attuned to danger. If he had any suspicions, he would have alerted her at once. She could see that in the way his spine straightened at the sound of a fox bolting from a bush, and the distant thundering of hooves in the distance, his eyes tracked for the riders that never came – headed in a different direction.

She knew that they were here on this road together because of Hytham. If Valka and Marcella had their way, she would have been here alone, facing down a much bigger fight than anyone should have to tackle on their own. She was grateful for Hytham's stubbornness.

After all, it was easier to face a foe together, especially one as volatile and cruel as this Cyrus seemed to be. Avalon had its own share of enemies and hadn't always been popular with everyone on the isles. The Christians wanted to convert them, and the Danes wished to take their land, but the Descendants of the Round Table remained Avalon's greatest foes.

These supposed heirs to the famed knights hunted priestesses down for sport, trying to loosen Avalon's powerful hold on the isles. Their vendetta against Avalon ran deep, with lore indicating that it was the Women of the Mist who broke their sacred round table and attempted to destroy the revered bloodlines. She remembered hearing terrible stories of their cruelty and reminded herself that they could be out there now, searching for Excalibur to use the mighty sword to influence the islands.

As the farms and cottages thinned out and the wilderness took over, leading them further into the hills fit for wolves and the foxes, and less in the domain that humans tamed, Niamh found herself relaxing into her seat.

"So where precisely are we headed?" she finally asked, after several hours of riding with only the occasional whinny for respite from the silence.

"There is a settlement not far from here, run by Cyrus, a former Roman soldier. Marcella knew him from her march north, but, as she expressed, not with much fondness. She doesn't explain much, but she did say he had a streak of cruelty toward women that she found disturbing."

A shiver ran down her spine. She had known of men like that, men who saw women's bodies as currency, as something to be traded and borrowed rather than as people with opinions and claims and rights of their own. She had heard stories on Avalon, and she had experienced men like that when the Danes came to Caledonia. She did not believe that those exhibiting such cruelty should be allowed to live, even if Marcella's freedom in Mercia would cost her. If Marcella was allowed freedom to roam Lunden, Niamh worried she might end up on the end of Marcella's blade. Accidentally, of course.

The pit of fear grew in her stomach. In her village, men who found themselves possessed with a rage toward the mothers, wives, and daughters were not tolerated. They had sent a man packing not too long before she had left, for doing harm to the women in his family. He had been found torn apart by wolves a few days later. A just punishment.

Without speaking, Niamh kicked her horse, charging him forward with more urgency. Whatever was happening in that settlement or to the woman imprisoned there, she wanted to stop it before it got worse. She didn't need implications or suppositions, she just needed to make sure that the woman was spared from as much as she could be.

"And the woman – she has information that you need?" Niamh asked.

"She might. It's more likely that the information is hidden on the grounds of the settlement. We'll be doing a thorough search in addition to rescuing her. It's of course a bonus if Cyrus doesn't make it out alive. That would make Marcella happy, and making her happy certainly makes my life easier. But her dictation that his death be the point of our mission does not align with the greater goal."

It was not the first time that Niamh recalled Hytham being less than pleased with Marcella, who did seem more aggressive than he. For one as young as she, Marcella did seem hardened and overtly suspicious. But following the Roman army to wherever they chose to set up shop must have been difficult, and she knew that Roman women were not afforded the same freedom that she had to pursue study or interests. While she had been handed the mantle of witch-warrior by her mother, if she had not been suited to the role, she would have been able to defer to someone with more skills. Niamh had always had choices, but they had not been choices she had ever felt the need to exercise. Marcella, it seemed, had never even had that. Even Valka seemed limited in a way, without as many options or the agency that Niamh had taken for granted.

Even still, Marcella had managed to get out of whatever situation she had been placed in and was now running a small shop of assassins with a set of bruised knuckles and eyes that cut through even Niamh's resolve. Even though animosity ran deep between them, Niamh couldn't help but have some respect for the Roman.

In the distance, a keep rose up out of the fog and trees. A structure built mostly from wood, but some stonework kept the building secure from intruders.

"Hytham, we'd better stash the horses," she warned, pulling hers up short with a yank on the reins. "I think they'll be patrolling here."

Hytham stopped as well, glancing back at her with interest and surprise. "You think?"

Niamh pointed to the tower. "The towers aren't being manned, at least not well, and that means they don't trust their sightlines out on the plains. Too much wood and stone and fog. They'll have men on foot making sure that they don't have trouble coming their way. It's what we do in the north when we can't guarantee that our eyes are telling us the truth."

Giving away this bit of information felt wrong somehow, but she also knew that it was important for her to be truthful, and this *was* how she knew.

Hytham nodded and slid off his horse, tying his steed up to a tree well within the wooded area, petting its nose and reassuring it that it wouldn't be alone for long.

Niamh did the same, and then slid into the bushes along

the edge of the road, keeping a stealthy eye out for anyone marching up and down the road with a purpose. Hytham followed her, curiosity plain on his face.

"Do you think you're leading the charge?" he asked, voice so low that it might well have been mistaken for a distant wind rather than a man speaking.

"I think I know these kinds of woods better than you. I can get us inside that keep without being detected if you ask it of me," she shot back, remembering all the ways that she had gotten in and out of places she wasn't wanted when invaders had come to her homelands. "And I think you don't know what the mists can do for us here like I do."

Hytham chuckled low and slid closer to the ground, pulling the cloak of his hood up over his face, shrouding him further from view.

"On my signal," she said as they approached the tower, glancing out of the bushes into the waiting stretch of plains between them and the keep.

Niamh let out a deep breath and tried to resonate with the world that she knew. She was familiar with the personality of the mist – a cool and calm energy that had a mind of its own even if it was nothing more than wisps of weather. Once she had determined how the fog was developing thickly over the forest and plain, she could turn her attentions to the rest of their environment. She listened for the animals in the forest. There were no wolves baying in the distance, no foxes, no bears. She could not detect anything living that could cause a fuss in their area. The trees here were old and protected her and Hytham.

This was not an angry place. It was not a place that felt

as though it were against her, though it may be against the invaders who sat here in their keep. That would help her, because when the land is against you, there are fewer advantages to be had.

Her ears picked up the wind, and her eyes saw the sun being caught behind rain-filled clouds. She waited until the fog had truly come, and then she gestured for Hytham to follow her across the road.

Even though they were in broad sight of anyone coming down the road, the silvery fog shrouded their identities. No one would know if they were but a stray patrol, coming back from their duties because they were on foot. If they had ridden any further on horseback, they would have been spotted and immediately identified as invaders. Once they were across the road, she cultivated her next move. The fog made it difficult to see, but she felt her way to another grove of trees, leaning against their bark to blend in with tree after tree, becoming a part of the woodland.

Hytham followed along easily, observing her methods and combining them with his own cat-footed grace, staying in silence when he could have spoken to suggest an alternate method. It was as though he had decided she was enough… it was as though he was putting trust in her.

Niamh was filled with a sense of companionship she hadn't felt in a long time. Even if she was here to uncover the Hidden Ones' motivations and seek a link to Excalibur, this kind of mission was part of her witch-warrior work. If she helped the Hidden Ones –invaders in their own right – she would learn so much more.

Truth be told, in her deepest heart, she even liked Hytham

and *wanted* to help him. He was calm and collected, he was smart, and he wasn't cruel. She didn't sense that he was part of the Hidden Ones because he liked violence, but felt it was a part of a balancing act that was required to keep the world safe.

She watched him as he waited against his own tree, still except for the occasional stir of his head tracking some kind of movement in the woods.

Niamh moved forward, slowly and carefully placed her feet so that they made no sound. No leaves crunched, no tree branches snapped, no rocks tripped her. She lifted her right hand to indicate Hytham should follow as she located the next bit of snaking road.

Up ahead was a patrol. The men moved together seamlessly, their voices muffled by the distance and the fog, but she could hear them well enough to know what they were: Romans. They spoke in the language of Hadrian's Wall. Together, Hytham and Niamh paused to listen.

"Nothing for days, I don't know why we have to be out here at all," the patrolman at the front of their clutch of soldiers said. He wasn't dressed in any kind of uniform, which told her they weren't official, but simply the dregs of the army that had left long ago, men who had decided to stay, rather than go home in disgrace.

"It's cold and damp," another complained. "I want to go back to the fire rather than take this patrol one more time. There's nothing out here but rabbits."

Should have stayed in your homeland then, she thought, her anger sharpening as she watched them wander the road. She knew that they weren't paying attention.

There were only four of them.

This would be easy.

Niamh looked to Hytham, wordlessly nodding toward the easy prey in their path. Hytham flicked his wrist, indicating that she should advance, taking advantage while they had it. With that direction, Niamh smiled and moved into position.

Sliding an arrow into one hand, she brought her bow out and nocked the arrow, putting every ounce of strength that she could into her stance. The mist would make aim more difficult, but it didn't matter which of the patrolmen she hit. She didn't look to see where Hytham positioned himself, whether he had moved forward or opted to stay behind her. With a quick snap, the arrow flew free and went to its target.

The first man dropped. She had caught him square in the chest. The remaining three men looked confused, startled even. They barely had time to react, or to raise their voices when Hytham appeared behind one at the back and the man suddenly dropped to the ground like his strings had been cut. Niamh's smile became a grin. She nocked another arrow as Hytham faded back into the mist. She didn't want to let it loose until he was out of the way, but she simply couldn't see him.

The third man fell. Hytham darted away like a ghost as the fourth man started to scream for assistance.

But he never found his voice.

The second arrow found his throat first.

The four bodies in the middle of the road did not stir. Niamh strode forward to meet Hytham and together they studied the bodies at their feet. Niamh said a silent prayer to the battle goddess, hoping that their souls would be carried swiftly to whatever afterlife they cared to visit, not because she particularly liked them but because it would save her seeing their shades later.

Without speaking, they lifted the first body, then the second, then the third and fourth, heaving them along into a ditch near the side of the road. She now understood the importance of hiding her kills.

Her muscles ached in protest at the weight of each corpse. Dead men were heavier than live ones, refusing to distribute their weight in any sensible way, their limbs stiff and uncooperative. Their blood leaked from the wounds she and Hytham had made.

Once the last man had been stashed away in their makeshift graveyard, she glanced over their equipment, wondering if the men held anything of value in their pockets, but then she finally decided that her own weaponry was better than whatever they carried. She lifted her eyes to Hytham.

"Four less than they had before," she said. "I can't imagine they're going to be well guarded out here, not with the attitude they were throwing about."

"Little to do but drink and fight," Hytham agreed, picking up a pouch of coins from the belt loop of one of the men on the ground and tucking it away.

Together, they glanced towards the keep. It was time to figure out how they were going to break in. The entrance was empty of guards.

"Shall we?" Niamh asked, knowing there was little else to do but move forward.

"A perfect trap," Hytham said quietly, before shifting ahead of Niamh and drifting off to the left. "Never go through an unguarded entrance unless you want to die."

Niamh slid off to the right. It would be faster if they worked both sides of the battlements at the top of the keep. She didn't need to tell him the plan, and by now he knew she didn't need instructions either.

Scaling the wooden walls, her hands and feet struggled to keep purchase against the rain-washed wood. The ropes holding everything together were damp to the touch and prickled under her palms. Soon, she crouched just below the ledge, waiting until someone above her made a sound so she could pinpoint their location.

Sure enough, several minutes into the strain of holding on when her shoulders burned enough to wonder if she ought to drop off the wall and find an alternate route, she heard a sneeze directly above her head.

She scrambled upward, using her left hand to keep steady against the wall, while her right reached up and yanked the man down, flinging him behind her off the keep.

Even if he wasn't dead, he wouldn't be making a sound for a good long while. And that was an if. His life wasn't a surety after a fall like that one. Backbreaking landings weren't kind to the human body.

She lifted herself up further onto the battlements and peered into the keep. It was small with a courtyard, a few buildings for various purposes, and an armory, presumably. Somewhere for the commander to sleep, somewhere to keep hostages ... but she couldn't see anything particularly frightening or remarkable. The remaining guards seemed bored, and tired, and drunk. All of them studied the mist as if they expected nothing to emerge from it.

She knew Hytham would be dealing with whoever was to her left, so she turned to the right and started creeping forward, looking for whatever other sentries might be peering out over the railing for enemies that would never come.

Because their enemies were already inside the gates. After a few minutes of searching, it became clear that this operation was bare bones, using as few bodies as possible. She glanced down into the courtyard, the fog obscuring much of the view, and dropped down into a patch of bushes behind one of the buildings at the center of the keep. Here, she could hear men singing inside the building, a place for dining and celebrating. Looking around, she located a big enough box and pulled it across the door which made both an entrance and exit. They wouldn't be able to escape now, not with any speed.

And if she had to, she could burn it to the ground.

Moments later, Hytham found her, his hands covered in blood.

She didn't ask questions.

"Have you obtained any information on where they're keeping her?" he asked, voice low.

Niamh looked at him with concern, raising a finger to her lips to silence him.

"The men in the building behind you are making enough noise that we can talk," he countered, pulling her back against a wall into shadow.

"I haven't," she said, curt and to the point. "But I think we should take advantage of the keep seemingly unguarded." She glanced around and considered their options. She was unfamiliar with the lifestyle of such a place. In Avalon, the Lady's quarters were hidden, down a far enough track that they were not simple to find. But here all the buildings were clustered together, easily searched.

"But perhaps, if this is a trap like you'd indicated, we should be able to find the woman fairly easily," she whispered to Hytham. "Cyrus might be expecting someone to save her, and they have no idea we are here, yet."

Turning around, Niamh peered through a busted window of one of the smaller buildings to see what was inside.

Nothing. Just a stack of spears and shields, covered in rust and hay.

Behind her sat the kitchens and the dining quarters. There were only a few options left. Frowning, she gazed through the mist, wondering where a man like Cyrus would stash a woman where she would stay unbothered by the other guards. Niamh then sought out the furthest building, the smallest one. A single door, with no windows. She knew it would be locked, but if she was right, this is where the woman would have been stashed – secured, alone, and easy to defend. With her shoulder's full might behind it, she smashed the door off its hinges, and found herself face to face with a woman, covered in dirt and blood, tied to a chair. Behind, the soldiers in the bar seemed to quiet.

"That was too easy," she said aloud, lunging forward to untie her quickly. "We'll have to move fast."

The woman was barely conscious, but under the dirt and

blood covering her arms, Niamh could see the lunar tattoo of her people. She would get this woman her freedom as swiftly as she could.

In the background she could hear the shouts of a startled guard from the topmost part of the keep. Her noise must have alerted the others. Or Hytham must have found someone worth fighting.

She swung the woman into her arms, draping her lolling head over her shoulder and stumbling forward.

"I've got her!" she shouted to Hytham, who was engaged in fighting a man twice his size. The box holding back the bar's doors budged forward as yells became more prominent. Hytham's back leg was suffering under the weight of the man's blows. It wasn't clear if he'd been injured or if this was an old injury responding to the intensity of the fight, but she knew one fact: if Hytham died in this battle, the Hidden Ones would never trust her again.

Settling down the prisoner as gently as she could, she drew her sword and leapt forward, delivering a blow to the back of the man's head. She felt the wallop land through her bones, and the shattering impact on his shoulder made him drop his longsword as he turned to face the new attacker, leaving Hytham free to escape.

Niamh leaped to the side, dodging a fisted blow to where her head had been only moments before. She swung her own blade, connecting with the giant man's ribcage, and knocking him to the ground with the impact.

Recovering from the swing, she watched him, glancing ever so carefully to see if Hytham had moved out of the way or if he needed help.

It was a mistake.

She felt the impact of her opponent's fist in her gut a moment later, having left herself unprotected in the middle of a fight. The wind was fully knocked out of her, but Niamh used the energy of the blow to roll backwards, allowing herself to recover and regain her breath before charging forward, lunging her blade into the space where she anticipated his body would be a moment later.

The connection of her sword diving into muscle and sinew and bone made for an unpleasant sensation. It did not go smoothly into his body but fought and twisted with the body the blade was trying to control. The sword was a tool of hostility. She fought to drive the blade further into his belly, and she won – following him down as he gasped in pain and landed hard on the earth. His blood soaked his tunic and his other garments, and his eyes clouded with pain.

"Hytham, if you could get our guest, we need to move swiftly now," Niamh said, her voice tense as she tore the sword out of her victim's gut. He fell fully back in a bloody heap, and she sheathed her sword only after wiping it off on his cloak.

"Is this Cyrus?" Niamh asked, glancing at the corpse. Selfishly, she hoped it wasn't, because if it was, then Marcella was free to accompany Niamh on any quest she desired. But she also could see that Cyrus was a man that should not be allowed to live.

"I thought it was, but I'm not sure," Hytham said. "That was a tough fight, but he came down easily once you arrived."

"Two against one usually helps," Niamh said. "Now, if you need your information would you tell me where I might find it? Time is of the essence. Those soldiers inside the hall will notice they can't get out eventually when someone needs to vomit out the last of their ale. Then we'll have more trouble on our hands than we want." She grinned, even as the sounds from the bar seemed to get louder and full of concern.

The prisoner made a small, muffled moan as she tried to stand. Her injuries were more severe than Niamh could see or determined. Niamh put a hand out to indicate for her to rest a moment longer.

Hytham bent down and began to inspect the dead man's body on the ground. His hands moved carefully over tunic and armor, and he finally paused at the man's throat, on the clasp that held his cloak in place.

"This isn't Cyrus," he said definitively, fingers tracing over the clasp. "This isn't his sigil. He wears a bird clasp, and this is a bear."

Niamh allowed herself the tiniest amount of relief, knowing it to be short-lived. She would probably have to kill Cyrus in the long run – after all, such a man should not continue to live – but she did not want to give Marcella such freedom until Niamh was safe and back in her home village.

"The information, Hytham. Where should I look?" Niamh urged him to reply, and not focus on the dead man who was not their quarry.

"His quarters, if not on his body," Hytham said, dropping to the ground to search the corpse more thoroughly. "I won't be able to carry this fair lady far, my leg is…" He couldn't finish the sentence, merely nodded. "You'll need to search his quarters. Take anything of value – papers, journals, writings, and correspondence. You'll need to find Cyrus for Marcella and kill him, if he's in your way."

Niamh didn't waste her breath on another word. She simply ran for the next building, finding an empty barracks. She shut that door and glanced around. The only other buildings surrounding the courtyard were the armory, the dining hall, and the prison… but where would the soldier keep his belongings? Cyrus was clearly a commander. Thus, he wouldn't leave such things with his subordinates, certainly. Men like Cyrus always liked to keep to themselves.

Scaling the interior wall of the keep she made her way back up to the battlements and ran around until she found the entrance to the tower. Of course, Cyrus slept off the ground. He had to be the sort of man to let his followers die in their sleep if it meant he lived.

She found the ladder and scaled it up to the top and into a room, where a bed, boxes of treasure, and a desk lay waiting for her. No one to guard it because no one would dare come to his quarters without invitation. There were plush furs, curtains, and mead. Nothing like what was down below.

Suddenly, a scream of terror cut through the mist. Niamh knew she'd have to hurry. Either the soldiers in the bar had gotten out, or Hytham had to do something drastic to keep them safe. She regretted that Hytham had gotten injured, but for now she had to focus on the task at hand: finding

Cyrus, or at bare minimum, his belongings, and taking anything that might be of use.

It was clear that he had slept here recently. The chamber pot was full. The mead cup still had dregs in it, and the candles still burned. Cyrus must have been here while they fought. Maybe they had been meant to take the woman. Something felt fishy to her.

Niamh was aware that Cyrus might want some of his nicer items, but she wasn't willing to leave them for him. She grabbed a large fur and wrapped it around herself for warmth as her adrenaline from the fight slowly leached out of her, leaving her shaky. Then she began to look through the papers strewn about the room. Sorting through the table at the center of the room, she found a letter sodden with mead. It was addressed to Cyrus from "a brother of the table". Niamh felt a new kind of chill fill her.

This was what she'd needed. Proof that the Order of the Ancients and the Descendants of the Round Table were working together.

Were the Descendants those who might be working against the Hidden Ones in Lunden that Hytham had mentioned? Did the Hidden Ones and Avalon share a common enemy? This letter was obvious proof that Cyrus was working against Niamh just as much as he was Marcella. She continued to search, finding little else that was readable.

Seeing the name of the Descendants filled Niamh with the uncontrolled fear that she had been thinking about on the ride here. This was much bigger than just the Hidden Ones. This was much bigger than just trying to learn more about them. If the Descendants and the Order of the

Ancients had crafted an alliance and were trying to get Excalibur, things were even more complicated than she imagined. The letter from Father Deoric lingered in her mind. Obviously, the links between the orders was there.

Slipping the missive inside the folds of her clothes, she checked for any last items that might be of use and found a sharp dirk that she could slide into her left boot, a match to the one in her right.

Hopping back down the ladder she found herself facing a blaze of fire and smoke. The screaming had increased as the soldiers clawed their way out of the building and fought past the broken box that once held the door closed. The fire had spread across the keep. She didn't see Hytham, or their rescued prisoner, so she assumed they must have made their way out of the area.

Sliding down the way she came, taking the outer facing wall and making her way back to the copse, seemed like the most intelligent choice. Hytham had said he couldn't make it far with his leg as it was, and that was the closest and least obvious place for them to hide while she did her business up in the tower. Cyrus' death would have to wait for another day.

Yet she found no one in the copse. Bile sat at the back of her throat. Had she missed Hytham in the chaos of the keep? Had he been captured with the woman? She had looked, but perhaps not carefully enough. The chaos in the keep had been extraordinary.

So, she sat and listened, willing the forest to tell her if there was someone hiding where she couldn't see them, and tried to trust that Hytham would emerge.

She would not run back into the blaze until she knew for sure that they weren't hiding here, waiting for her to return. And she was rewarded for her patience.

An almost imperceptible whimper, a sound that could not have been made by an injured rabbit or a fox but by a person, reached her ears. A woman who had been frightened and hurt. A woman who had been tied up for too long. Niamh pushed through the bushes and saw the young woman with Hytham. Both of them looked worse for wear.

"Hytham, it is Niamh. I can get the horses." She spoke urgently, but Hytham only nodded, his face sweaty and his breathing coming out hard. Perhaps Hytham was in too much pain to speak. Instead of waiting for instructions, Niamh ran to fetch the horses. Time was of the essence for them to escape and get Hytham the help he clearly needed. Perhaps Valka was right… Hytham wasn't ready.

Yet, when she ran into the grove where they had left their mounts, she found that the horses were not alone. A small man wearing a Roman set of clothes stood with them, petting Hytham's horse gently.

"What have you taken besides my fur, lady?" he asked, turning to face her. His politeness was jarring. After all, she had not expected to be given a title by her enemy, or even treated with respect. "Did you take my prisoner? How about my letters?"

"I took everything that I needed," Niamh said, stepping forward with her hand on her sword. "Are you here to fight me, or just to gloat?"

At that, Cyrus laughed. She was tired of men laughing at

her. She drew her sword. Like Father Deoric, Cyrus seemed entirely too comfortable with the possibility of death at her hands.

"I will not be patient forever. Make a decision on what you want." She knew that it benefitted her to leave Cyrus alive, even if he was a dangerous man. If he was here to gloat, let him gloat. But she would waste no more time getting Hytham and the young woman to safety.

"I'm here because I don't need her any longer," Cyrus said, and Niamh knew he referred to the young woman they'd saved. "She gave me the information we needed. I suppose sending her back to her people will leave her in as much pain as dumping her body."

Niamh hated him. He knew that whatever he had done to her, she wouldn't go home a woman respected by her village. Further south, in the more Christian villages, there was greater attention paid to the purity and fidelity of women to their marriages. If Cyrus had violated her, there was little that Niamh could do to fix her path.

"But you seem like you could be a good replacement, especially since we'll need another body for the nunnery up north. Unless you'll be too much trouble for us." Cyrus' grin widened.

Recognition prickled in the back of Niamh's mind. The nunnery. The nun Niamh had met in Lunden had expressed concerns about such a place and had asked her to check on it. Perhaps it was more connected to the quest of the Hidden Ones than she had initially thought. She twirled her sword in her hand, biding her time.

"I would be. I don't like men who harm women. Even if

they're not one of mine," she agreed, goading him into the fight that she sorely wanted.

He struck out quickly, his short sword slicing through the air with speed she saw in only the most skilled of fighters. She deflected. He was a better fighter than the man at the keep, and still held all his stamina. Meanwhile, Niamh already felt the exhaustion from her exertions weigh on her. She would need to make this fight quick. Her arms protested as she cut through the air, arcing for the backs of his ankles, trying to immobilize him.

He saw what she was doing and nipped out of the way. The horses whinnied, and Mathan bucked. She cut again directly to his head, giving Cyrus no choice but to hop backwards, towards the horses. Mathan snorted, backing away from the body coming toward him swiftly.

Niamh struck again, not pausing, forcing Cyrus yet again to go backwards toward Mathan, who understood his duty. Mathan reared, bringing his hooves into contact with Cyrus' back. Her horse was the best ally that she could ask for, as Cyrus fell forward in the grass. Silent. Niamh then stood over him and flicked the hidden blade out of the gauntlet. It slid out with ease, almost nicking her finger. She paused, ready to kill him, and then hesitated. The image of killing Father Deoric flashed in her mind. The blood. The mistakes. The consequences.

She hoped he had come out here without alerting his guards or the other soldiers. She bent to see if he still breathed but could not be certain. Perhaps Mathan had been the one to kill him after all. But she did not need to land a final ensuring blow.

Niamh dragged his body further into the forest and took every weapon he had off his person. She couldn't carry his sword, so she chucked it as far as it would fly into the distance. Her next step was to stop him from getting too far, so she stripped him of his cloak, tearing pieces off it with her bare hands to create a little challenge for when he awoke... if he did. The blood from his skull seeped out slow and deep red. If he was alive, Niamh wasn't sure he would stay that way for long.

Carefully, she bound his hands and ankles, making sure that escape would be hard won. Her knots were not gentle. Finally, with the last strip of his cloak that she had made, she bound his mouth, so that he could not scream for help.

Her duty discharged, she gathered up the horses and brought them back to the glade where Hytham hid with their prisoner – though she was unsure whether the prisoner was friend or foe now. Something seemed wrong about the idea that Cyrus would run his keep so poorly. Niamh handed the reins of Hytham's horse to him, and he mounted with a grunt of pain, and then nodded, encouraging her to lead the way.

"Cyrus met me at the horses," Niamh said to him discreetly as she made sure he was secure and wouldn't topple from the saddle. "I think this woman is connected to the nunnery I found out about when I first came to you."

"How did you leave him?" Hytham asked, the question she had known would be his first.

The words suddenly dried up in her throat. She had to make a decision whether to tell Hytham that Cyrus was dead or alive. If she said that he was dead, it was *likely* truth, and Marcella would roam Mercia free – able to investigate Niamh and her origins as much as she liked. But if she lied... if she said he lived... which seemed less likely the longer that Cyrus lay on the cold earth with a head wound, then Marcella would still live in fear. And Niamh might be able to continue her quest for Avalon without the additional threat of Marcella swaying over her head.

"Alive. He was too fast. I wasn't able to catch him." The lie fell from her lips swiftly. It gave her time. She needed time. Marcella was canny enough to fish out the truth about her if she roamed without restraint.

Hytham nodded, but disappointment shone on his face. "Do not concern yourself with it. We will find another way to remove him at another time."

Niamh mounted and swung the listing young woman up along with her. They rode swiftly away from the burning keep, the information she had found kept close to her chest. The woman they had rescued passed out in front of her.

Niamh glanced backward, seeing the smoke as it mingled with the fog, indicating to anyone within miles that something bad had happened to the people who had come and taken over part of the land.

"You did well back there," Hytham said, after they had put enough distance between them and the fire.

"So did you," she said. "Starting that fire."

"In a way that would ensure many of the soldiers would not burn alive. After all, they had nearly broken the obstacle in front of the doors."

Niamh smiled. Despite her self-doubts, despite her

loyalties to Avalon, Niamh felt a bit of pride. She knew she had done her best to serve all her leaders, all her purposes at once. She had been who she needed to be for the Hidden Ones.

"Cyrus is someone who should not have power," Hytham murmured. "He abused the woman you're carrying, and he abused his power to harm others. He needed to be stopped. But, I don't... burn down the buildings of my enemies unless I have to. Do you understand? I only do this to those who deserve it. Marcella does not speak much of her experiences, but I know it was a terrible time in her life. Even then, knowing I could right a wrong for her, my honor is at stake. I do not take the lives of innocents and if I do, they are not taken lightly. I understand we have asked you to do things on our behalf when you aren't completely on board, but please know that our assassinations always have a purpose. This Cyrus? If I find him, I will kill him. In the future, if you have the opportunity to take his life, you should do so."

Niamh believed him. It sounded like the same code of ethics that the Women of the Mist operated from. To be in secret when necessary, but to do the things that needed doing for everyone's best interest. To maintain freedom for not just those of wealth and power, but for others who might have lived difficult lives.

She suddenly felt guilty for having lied about Cyrus. Most likely, she could have lived with his blood on her hands, but now she had ensured she would need to watch over her shoulder for his retaliation. Perhaps someday, she would be able to tell Hytham the truth.

The woman lying in front of her stirred with a moan. "I want to go home," she whispered, pain evident in her voice.

"Where is home for you?" Niamh asked, taking one hand off the reins to place it in comfort on the woman's back. She groaned again.

"We'll take you to our home first, dear lady," Niamh said. "We'll heal you and then take you home. You can't go to your family like this."

Hytham glanced at her, concern plain on his face.

Niamh stared back, determined. "We will not be leaving her anywhere, nor dropping her with anyone, until she has had a chance to rest. She knows things, Hytham. She is your information."

Hytham nodded and together they continued to ride into the countryside, leading them back to Lunden, where none of them belonged.

ELEVEN

The bureau was dark when they returned, barren of life or purpose. The absence of Marcella and Valka filled Niamh with relief and she wondered if the two were sleeping, or if Marcella had taken her fate into her hands and left to explore Lunden, confident that Cyrus' life had been taken.

Hytham limped into the bureau. The ride had been hard on him, as had the battle. Niamh knew that if Marcella saw him in this state, she would blame her. Imagining Valka's disappointed gaze even made Niamh squirm as if she had actually been responsible for Hytham's injuries. Again, she felt the urge to leave the Hidden Ones and find safety back in her homeland or with Avalon. Marcella was looking for reasons to get rid of her, even as Hytham worked hard to bring her into the fold.

But she wasn't safe on her own. The Descendants were active, and the Ancient Ones would no doubt know she was a new Hidden One. She had more enemies now than she ever had before.

She needed Hytham and Marcella and Valka, at least until Excalibur was returned. She needed them to keep her safe.

"Can I do anything to help you?" she asked Hytham as she deposited the unnamed woman, who was still sleeping, onto a pile of furs in the corner near the fire. Their charge slept on, unaware that she had been brought into a whole new place.

"I likely just need rest," Hytham replied, settling into one of the chairs by the fire.

"I do have some training in healing. Is there something I can do for you?" She repeated the question, ignoring that he had given her a no. She had seen patients like Hytham before, who didn't want to be treated as special. Who preferred to behave like cats who wandered off to die or to lick their own wounds in peace. "Before Valka comes in here and sees what we've done?"

Hytham sighed. "Perhaps you have a point. I did sustain a wound to my leg, but this weakness seems to affect my whole body. It feels like the problem lies within the muscles. They aren't always difficult, but after a blow they can spasm, flaring up the injury once more." Niamh lifted her hand to his leg, where she could feel the muscle trembling under her hands and saw the wound. Deep, yes, but nothing that would cause such weakness that she had witnessed on their ride back.

"How did they treat it?" she asked as she gently massaged the spasm, seeing if she could will it into stillness with her hands.

He groaned and then grimaced in pain. It seemed that the spasm hurt more than the actual wound. "Rest, medicine. Wrappings. The initial injury healed, but even now, it still continues to bother me," he said.

Ah. Wrappings. That was something she could work with. She'd tended many a warrior after a fight, and this was familiar ground. It was also ground that made her look useful to the Hidden Ones.

"Where do you keep your medicines and herbs?" she asked. "I'll see what I can do."

Hytham gestured toward the kitchen and a specific cabinet. She found it full of bandages, herbs, and ready-made poultices easily at hand. Of course, people who fought for their daily practice would have such things in plain sight. It was true in Avalon also.

She grabbed a variety of herbs, as well as bandages that were about the width of her fist, and she went back to the common area where Hytham waited, eyes slightly drooping from the pain.

Without speaking, she mixed the herbs into some water and set it to boil at the fireplace. While she waited, she began to clean the wound and then patiently wrapped Hytham's muscle spasm. Her hands remembered the rhythm of wrapping bandages easily. When the poultice was ready, she spread it over the wound. Looking at it, she didn't worry. It would heal cleanly.

"You're talented at this," Hytham said as he watched her. "You must have been well trained."

"The women of my village were talented, yes." Niamh fought back the instinct that he was fishing for information, but after having fought by his side, she found her fondness for him growing.

After the bandages were tightly and safely wrapped, she moved back to the fire to remove the boiled water and made a tea for him. "Drink this. Go settle into your sleeping place, and I will bring a wine flask filled with hot water in a little while. You'll sleep with it on your leg to help the muscles relax."

Hytham regarded the tea with some distaste. "How long will that make me sleep?" he asked grouchily.

"As long as you need to. Now, off you go. It works quickly."

"But what about..." his eyes drifted to the sleeping woman they had saved.

"I don't think she's going to be of much use right now," Niamh said softly.

Hytham nodded and rose from his chair and carefully walked to his bed. But he paused at the doorway to look at her.

"I don't think Marcella and Valka fully appreciate that you are a good woman," he said. "But I do. I hope that no matter what happens next, you've found value in our mission and that you'll stay."

Niamh smiled softly. "Thank you. That means a lot."

Hytham nodded and left the room, and Niamh turned towards the sleeping woman she had freed. She gnawed her lip. If this woman was part of the Women of the Mist, she could not risk her speaking with Hytham and revealing more than she should. It left her in a quandary regarding what to do.

She boiled another round of water, this batch much

bigger than the last. Then, after she found a pail and poured the boiling water in, she left it to cool down to a reasonable temperature to the touch. She took the promised wine skin full of water to Hytham's chambers and then puttered about the bureau, gathering up clean shifts and rags, and bringing her comb from the room that had become her own.

The third round of boiling water became a tea, which she set in front of the woman they had rescued. The young woman blinked sleepily, until she became fully awake. Her eyes darted around the room, unfocused in their fear.

Niamh moved slowly over to sit beside the woman, bringing the pail of hot water with her. She had a stack of clean rags in her hands. In many ways, this was the calmest Niamh had felt in weeks. Being a healer was something she enjoyed, and caring for both Hytham and their charge gave her a chance to focus her mind on something positive and clear. There was no misinformation, no misdirection, no amount of calculation necessary. It was just about healing both body and mind.

"With your permission, I'm going to undress you and wash your wounds," Niamh said, using a calm and firm voice that gave no space for argument. The woman nodded and propped up on an elbow, undressing quickly. Taking the bloodstained and dirt caked garments, Niamh tossed them in a corner. They were torn and unwearable, best suited to rags.

She dipped the clean fabric scraps she'd gathered into the hot water, and began to wipe the woman down, gently cleansing each limb and wiping her face with a deliberate care.

"Are you one of us?" the woman finally asked in a cracked voice. Niamh glanced around and saw that the door to Hytham's chambers remained closed, and that no one else was present. She chose not to answer verbally, knowing the danger. She lifted her right-hand sleeve, showing the woman her own lunar tattoo.

The woman sagged with relief, all resistance to treatment fading from her body at once. "My name is Ebba, and I would like to go home once you're finished tending to me."

"I think I can arrange that," Niamh said, as she cleaned a gash across her back. Ebba flinched at the touch, but she did not ask Niamh to stop. "Is there anything you haven't told us yet that we ought to know?

"Cyrus is kidnapping women and committing them to a nunnery. I was one of the witnesses, but I escaped to try and spread the word of what had been done there. I think it's why he took me to his keep." Her eyes filled with fear, but also determination. "Something is happening at that nunnery. It's not just a place for women who choose to become brides of Christ. There is something sinister happening there. I saw a woman who wasn't a nun being hauled inside. They interrogated her."

Niamh could feel the threads coming together. The nunnery that the young initiate had told her about, referenced again by another woman full of fear. Something was wrong there, and Niamh became determined to do something about it. Something like this fell within the Hidden Ones' jurisdiction and they could help her.

"They were taking this woman because she had been transporting letters with the seal of the Women of the

Mist on them. They demanded to know everything about Avalon's sacred artifacts, but especially demanded to know more about the location of Excalibur." The woman looked up at Niamh in despair. "Did you know that they are looking for Excalibur?"

Niamh's blood ran cold hearing the name of the sword spoken so freely in the place where she was doing her best to pretend that she knew so little. But regardless of how carefully she had constructed her cover, she was going to have to go to this nunnery and find out exactly what was happening.

Cyrus had been part of the Order of the Ancients, communicating with an unknown Descendant of the Round Table. Father Deoric had correspondence with another, indicating that they would take the sword back. Clearly, both parties were aligned and assumed that the Women of the Mist or the Hidden Ones knew where Excalibur was after its removal from Stonehenge.

The only problem was the Women of the Mist didn't know. That left the Hidden Ones.

And she couldn't let Hytham speak with this young woman. All would be revealed, and even though she was starting to have a soft spot for the Hidden Ones, she did not quite understand their motivation for taking Excalibur... or where they might have hidden it.

"Where can I take you to get you home?" Niamh asked. "Are you a witch-warrior for a specific place?"

Ebba shook her head. "Only a healer. If you can get me to the river bend of the Tamesis to the north, I should be able to walk home from there. My family will make assumptions if I am delivered by a stranger, and they aren't assumptions I wish to draw."

"You mean to say they won't believe that you were stolen away?"

Ebba looked down. Niamh didn't need to ask further. She knew that Ebba would be safest if she was to go home on her own power and volition, and to weave a tale that would be bought by those who would need it.

"I'll take you once you're dressed," Niamh said, not wanting to waste time. Hytham would rest, but when he was up, he would want to speak with Ebba. And since Ebba knew enough about who she was to be a liability, she would have to go soon. While Ebba dressed herself in borrowed garments, Niamh climbed up to the nest she had been assigned as her room to change into clothes not soaked in blood, and found a letter waiting for her from Valka.

Her hand trembled seeing the unfamiliar scrawl. Valka's handwriting was deliberate. Clearly, she had crafted the letter in Niamh's language, rather than her own. It was an invitation.

I was intrigued by all that you had to share when it came to your own practices.

Niamh smirked. Not that she had shared much in their conversation.

We seem both far apart, and also close together in the ways that we walk and observe this world. I would like to get to know you further and understand the ways of your people better. Should you be open to this invitation, please come find me at your convenience. Distrust lies between us, but I know we can put such hesitations to rest.

The note left Niamh torn. On one side, she did not want to know Valka further. She did not want to have to guard her energies, or her knowledge. If anyone could discover her secrets, it would be Valka. She did not want to be discovered.

But she also realized that Valka could be precisely the ally she needed when it came to the nunnery. Women of the old ways and the new were being harmed by those who wanted power. While Marcella and Hytham were both against the increase of power for the Order of the Ancients, they did not seem likely to meddle in the affairs of commoners. But Valka… Niamh had to imagine that Valka had defensive abilities, even if it wasn't with a sword and a bow. Perhaps this was an opportunity. After all, she could not trust Marcella, and Hytham's reoccurring injuries would not allow him to embark on such a journey so soon.

Yes, perhaps such hesitations could be put to rest.

After changing into a long kirtle, she flung her cloak over her shoulders and went back down the ladder. Ebba was ready. With so many enemies whose faces Niamh did not know, she knew just as well that Ebba would not be safe on the road by herself. Nonetheless, she took Mathan and the two of them rode to where Ebba announced she would continue alone. No other words passed between them. Niamh watched her leave in silence for a moment longer than necessary, before returning to the bureau.

When she entered the bureau, Hytham and Marcella waited for her by the fire. Niamh had dreaded this moment, but it was one that she knew she would have to face.

"Did she leave by her own power, or did you assist her?"

Marcella asked, the edge of accusation plain in her voice.

"She asked to leave. I questioned her about Cyrus and his activities and found that there was little to be gained from keeping her here when she was desperate for the safety of her own family and home." Niamh removed her cloak and hung it on a hook. She did not sit down, but stood in front of the Hidden Ones, as if on trial.

Hytham turned to look at Niamh, questions clear in his eyes. "Did you think that was your role?" he asked, obviously unhappy with her.

Niamh wanted to shrink like a flower in frost. Her decision had cost some of the trust Hytham had in her, and she knew her reassurances and gentle care meant nothing in the face of this. Trust could be undercut so quickly, and Niamh's small lies had finally come to light. "I thought you had left me in charge of her," Niamh replied.

"You said she had information for us," Hytham pointed out.

"Which I can relay to you now."

The heavy silence that followed told Niamh three things:

That Hytham had left her in charge, and he agreed with her.

That Marcella was unhappy with his decision, and Hytham was going to pay for that choice in one way or another.

And that Niamh had a chance to direct the flow of this conversation by revealing what they needed to know while keeping parts of it secret.

Without a beat, she pulled out the letter she had acquired in Cyrus' chambers before Hytham had set the whole keep ablaze and dropped it into the hands of Marcella. She had read the letter and its contents, though it had not made much sense to her at the time.

"I found this when I made sure that we hadn't left anything behind in Cyrus' chambers. It includes information about identities of three of his collaborators, including people who are searching for an artifact of great power," Niamh said. "I hope one of these names identifies your enemy here in Lunden."

"We'll need to discuss this," Marcella said after reading the missive. She then stared meaningfully at Niamh, dismissing her with a glance.

"You can't send me away now," Niamh said, looking at Marcella directly. "You accepted me as an initiate. And furthermore, I'm not done. Ebba, the woman we rescued, was connected to the nunnery that we heard about a few weeks ago. Something is happening there, and it's connected to the Order of the Ancients. It was why Ebba was taken by Cyrus."

Marcella shook her head, but not out of denial. She knew Niamh was right. Whether or not Marcella wanted to allow Niamh to join the Brotherhood, the choice was done. Niamh might only be a potential member who needed to prove her skillset, but she was still working with the Hidden Ones. She went on their assignments and did it to their satisfaction. She had a right to be here. So Niamh sat down, daring Marcella to order her to leave again.

Marcella didn't.

"That woman you brought had information, and if you hadn't needed to lie down for a nap you would have been able to get it," Marcella said, voice taut, eyes boring into Hytham's like daggers. She was obviously looking for a way to place blame.

"I trust Niamh. So far, she has made excellent decisions to both keep us safe and maintain the integrity of our missions. If the prisoner was cooperative on the condition of her release, she might have given us information. If she was too traumatized, she would not. But the true information is what's inside that letter. Cyrus won't be looking for any artifact. He must be searching for Excalibur."

They spoke of Excalibur. Niamh was shocked that the information had come out so easily. Her heart pounded in her chest so loudly she was afraid that Marcella and Hytham would notice, but they were too focused on their own disputes.

"Along with his associates," Marcella snarled and tapped the paper dismissively. "These round table children. I've been sending agents to scour what I can of Lunden for weeks trying to learn more about them... sometimes risking going myself. Sticking to back alleys and bars. Unable to go anywhere of real importance because of Cyrus."

"Tell Niamh what you know," Hytham pleaded. "We can also let Eivor know what to be on the lookout for now. That these enemies might be coming for her."

Marcella scowled. "These Descendants of the Round Table have been surveilling pagans for weeks, enlisting them when the Order of the Ancients needs locals to do their dirty work. Their alliance is deadly and could transform the workings of both politics and religions across these islands. Rumor has it that they had some kind of plan or capability to jumpstart their hold over the development of the islands and their peoples, and this just confirms that using the mythos of Excalibur will simply push those of a pagan mindset over to the all-encompassing iron fist of the Order of the Ancients. Whoever wields the sword would be the true king of the islands, eh? A king that no one would question. Well, they are determined to ensure that king is one they can puppeteer. But all of this is information *we* already know."

"The information in the letter isn't nothing, Marcella," Hytham argued.

"It isn't as much as I wanted."

"It never is for you," Hytham snapped back. "Niamh did an excellent job of keeping me safe, and of making decisions on the fly. We don't want to lose her, which we will if you keep pushing her away and behaving as though she has neither skills nor our trust."

"But she doesn't have our trust," Marcella said. "She may well have captured yours, but mine is significantly less easy to steal, and a little Caledonian brat who happens to be good with a sword isn't going to steal it so easily."

Niamh felt like she'd been slapped. Even though she knew how much Marcella disliked her, having it confirmed so blatantly right before her eyes was a shock.

But it was of little consequence. Marcella could hate her to the ends of time, and it wouldn't matter because Niamh had confirmation that the Hidden Ones knew about Excalibur and that this Eivor was a link to its location. She didn't know if she could hold her façade any longer.

After all, it was the Hidden Ones who had taken

the sacred artifact from underneath Stonehenge. And, surprisingly, this revelation made Niamh burn with resentment. Excalibur was part of the Sacred Table, the holy regalia that belonged to Avalon. It didn't belong to the Hidden Ones, or their leader, and certainly not to any Danes who didn't believe in their ways. And it shouldn't be used by the dreaded Descendants of the Round Table to further power through lies and deception on the isles.

But how could she go charging off into the night in search of this Eivor, when women at the nunnery were in such trouble? She couldn't think in the room. She needed air.

Niamh rose from her seat. "I think I need a brief walk. When I return, I want to discuss going with Valka to investigate this nunnery that Ebba had mentioned. I think it may be connected to all that we are investigating as well. Perhaps there are more leads to the Descendants of the Round Table than we know."

Without waiting for a dismissal, Niamh fetched her cloak and headed out into the Lunden streets, where she planned to bury herself in the crowds to think and parse through the emotions that seemed to overwhelm her.

But before she'd cleared the steps, she overheard what Marcella almost certainly hadn't meant for her ears:

"I may need to go to Ravensthorpe to speak with Valka again, to see what she thinks about this Niamh. She spent some time with her, and we did not have time to form an opinion before she was required back home. And you are going to recover well before the long ride north. Eivor will need to be warned of the dangers to her new sword as well requiring our help. I do not trust sending any messages or any messengers."

"Niamh will have to come with me," Hytham said.

"Of course, she can't be left in the bureau by herself. She must be watched. Now that she knows the full extent of our mission, it is your job to make sure she doesn't do anything that could cost us," Marcella ordered. "You decided to trust her, so on your head be it. If she betrays us, it will be your fault. And if she brings us glory, that will be yours as well."

Niamh pulled her hood up and stepped purposefully into the street. Part of her wished she hadn't heard that, the churn of guilt strong in her gut. If Hytham was to get in trouble for Niamh's decisions, it would cost him. Even the thrill of finally homing in on her target – of completing her mission for the Lady so she could go home – soured within her. This Eivor held Excalibur and Niamh was determined to get it back. Yet, could she jump on her horse now and leave the bureau behind to acquire it? Or should she stay, maintaining her façade for a little while longer to accompany Hytham to the north? It was inevitable that she would have to betray him and ruin all the fondness they had built for each other with either choice.

But her commitment to the Women of the Mist was strong. It was the most important thing in her world, and if she had to betray a man she had only just met for the people who had raised her, she would do it.

After all, Excalibur wasn't just some sword that a king had held once. It wasn't just a gift to Arthur. It was an object of great power. No one, except those who had held it, knew its true power, knew what it was capable of. But Niamh knew that it was important enough that the Lady of Avalon had sent her to go and retrieve it at all costs. The worry on the Lady's face had not been a trick. It was the true fear of not knowing where the most powerful artifact of their people had gone, and not knowing who had the ability to use its power for ill or good.

The Lady would have gone herself to find it, it being hers to care for, but Niamh knew as well as anyone that it was not in the Lady's power to leave Avalon. The green shores and the lake protected her, and she was as much a head of state and a ruler as any king or queen or emperor. She was at risk if she left, and so instead the Lady had sent one of her warriors to find it.

Niamh knew the task at hand. She hardened her heart to it.

This was why she was here. Not for Hytham, not for small errands, not for intelligence. She was here because there were people not from these shores who had their hands on one of the most precious artifacts belonging to her people. They had Excalibur, and they shouldn't.

But here she was stuck: she didn't know who Eivor was, or where they were, or what their plans were for Excalibur.

How had this person managed to get it out from underneath Stonehenge? Who had given them the tools to uncover it when many before had not been able to?

Most importantly, Niamh knew that her quest had become more complex. Niamh gazed at the clouds above her head. She knew that it was going to be important to get Marcella on her side, to trust her just as much as Hytham. Because she was never going to get anywhere close to the sword of her people until she had the trust of everyone in *this* bureau, and the people they worked with beyond.

Niamh had only one choice. She had to get to Avalon to tell the Lady where Excalibur was, no matter the cost of her time. Once she had reported in, she could investigate this nunnery, and then do whatever Hytham and Marcella asked of her next until Hytham was recovered and they could travel north together. Niamh knew that she could not be rash and go straight to whoever this Eivor person was. She would have to bide her time, and that meant going back to the bureau, going back to this woman who hated her, and finding ways to make her way to Eivor's side, so that she could take the sword back for Avalon once and for all.

TWELVE

When Niamh returned to the bureau, only Hytham remained in the common area. He looked agitated. Niamh couldn't blame him. After all, Marcella had been clear that it wasn't only Niamh that she distrusted – Hytham's own instincts had been questioned.

Niamh lingered next to him before speaking. "Hytham... I understand that warning your friend Eivor is of great importance, but we need to find out what's happening at that nunnery." She paused, knowing that her next statement would annoy him, but was the truth, so she forged ahead. "And we know that you can't go with me. With everything Marcella revealed, I think it might make sense for me to take Valka."

At that, Hytham glanced up in surprise. "Valka?"

"Yes. Two women traveling to a nunnery won't be seen as strange, especially if we disguise ourselves. However, a man and a woman, heavily armed, one with an obvious limp, will be."

Hytham turned back to the fire. "That is true. Valka might be hesitant to leave Ravensthorpe, but you make a good argument for why it might be necessary." Hytham was thoughtful. "We will need to ride north to warn Eivor about the combined forces of the Order of the Ancients and the Descendants of the Round Table. Anyone allied with the Order of the Ancients should be someone we are wary of. Will you be back in time to ride with me?"

"Of course. This will help me... patch things up with the seeress. Last time we spoke, I was uncertain of her intentions. Valka sent me a letter asking me to spend some time with her, and I think this might be an ideal time to do so. Away from Marcella. Away from this building." *Away from you too,* Niamh thought regretfully.

Hytham nodded, even though he looked uncomfortable, as though he was about to do something that he might regret later. Niamh hoped against hope that he would choose to help her, instead of restricting her further.

"You'll need to go now, then," he said. "Marcella wants us to focus our efforts on Excalibur, and on the Order of the Ancients. I think you're right that the nunnery situation is involved, though not perhaps as central as it might be. But this could very well tell us more about the Descendants of the Round Table."

"It is important to me to try and make those women safer than they are right now," Niamh said, wanting to emphasize the fate of those in danger, rather than the machinations of such powerful orders. It was the truest thing that she had said to Hytham thus far, something that had come straight from her heart. "And if the Descendants are involved, even more reason to undertake the mission."

"I understand," Hytham said. "You've never been to Ravensthorpe, have you?"

"Might I ask for directions?" Niamh asked with a small smile.

"Ride northwest from Lunden and look for signs of Danish settlements. It's not far from Grantebridge. Valka's hut is near a waterfall. People are familiar with it, thus you shouldn't get too turned around, and if you do, ask for help. If anyone does ask, tell them you're bringing a message for Valka of the Raven Clan."

Niamh tried not to shudder. She had never ridden into a Dane settlement by choice, and never under the guise of being their friend. It was not something she had ever planned to do voluntarily, but now, for Avalon, she would have to.

She would need a good cover for why she went to Avalon, too.

"What if I get lost?" she asked.

"Then come back this way and by the time you return my leg should be well enough to take you. But I trust in your ability to travel. When you get back, Marcella will be angry," he warned. "She too planned to go to Ravensthorpe and consult Valka, but I will tell her of your intentions."

"She will be angry no matter what I do," Niamh said. "Marcella has set her mind against me, and the best way to convince her otherwise is to move forward."

"Travel safe, my friend," Hytham said, and reached out, clasping her hand briefly.

Niamh took in a deep breath and bowed her head in

farewell. Then she strode out of the bureau without a second glance, hoping that she would not encounter Marcella on her way to the stables to get Mathan. Luck was with her, as she hopped onto his back and rode out of Lunden without anyone to stop her.

She directed her horse towards Avalon.

Arriving once more on the shores of the lake, she swiftly made her passage, not bothering to stop and change her clothes when she arrived on the other side. This was not a ritual call, or one where she was expected to perform the duties of a priestess – this was Niamh coming to report as a warrior on patrol. Even so, her actions would be frowned upon, but she had not a moment to lose.

The Lady was kneeling in the chapel of the trees. Head bowed, knees planted in the earth, the arches of trees enveloping her in a green glow as the sunlight trickled through the leaves into the space. It was a spectacular place, and even in her state of speed, Niamh took a moment to glance up, take a breath, and give thanks for the world that she lived in, for the gifts she had been given by the gods and goddesses, and for the safety that she had in this very moment from harm.

"Lady, I come with news of Excalibur," she finally said, after waiting for a few minutes to breathe in the presence of the trees.

"What news of our sword?" the Lady asked, not turning around to face her, but lifting her head so that she could hear better. The Lady's long black hair fell in a cascade about her shoulders.

"I know who has it," Niamh said, steeling herself even

as she betrayed the people who had given her training and trust. "Eivor of the Raven Clan of Ravensthorpe. I'm not sure if she is part of the Hidden Ones, but I do know they trust her and she works with them. She has it. I'm certain. Her people are planning to travel to her location, and they mentioned the sword. A letter I found on a mission with them indicated that others were looking for it."

At that, the Lady stood, turning around and looking at Niamh directly. "You know who has the sword? And you haven't taken it yet?"

Niamh had expected this response. After all, it was the same reply she would have given if she were in the Lady's shoes. It was the action she almost leapt into when she first learned of the sword from Hytham. She remembered that she had reason for her decision to wait and thus she didn't allow the sharpness in the Lady's voice to unsettle her, but ploughed forward with the report.

"Yes, Lady. I know who has it, but I don't know where it is. Or rather, where the bearer of the sword is. It sounds like she's recently been across the sea, but… she might be on the move. The only people who do seem to know where she is are the Hidden Ones."

The Lady looked somewhat mollified, but not for long. She began to pace, her gown dragging in the grass and the damp, the color of her gown growing darker in the train as she fussed.

"Who could be working against us? Is it Mordred's Descendants of the Round Table? Or is it someone else?"

"It seems to be all of them, Lady. The Descendants, plus a new powerful order called the Order of the Ancients that

I spoke about before... and the Hidden Ones may not be working fully against us, but they do support a stranger holding Excalibur instead of us. Yet, my Lady, Avalon have not quite made themselves known to the Hidden Ones, so we cannot be sure if their intentions are directly against us."

"A whole web of enemies, and you're the one taking the web apart with your hands," the Lady muttered, staring at her. "Are you staying as safe as you can? The Descendants know your face, don't they?"

"Most likely," Niamh said. "Some of the Descendants would be able to identify me. They hunted me along with the other priestesses when they tried to invade Avalon a few years back. They have been trying to eradicate our presence on the isles for a long time, but they have never been strong enough or had the influence to do so. I have no doubt they have close record of new witch-warriors emerging from Avalon to protect their homes."

Even though Niamh suspected the Descendants had aligned with the church to discover more of the witch-warriors on the isles, the Lady – and Avalon as a whole – remained secretive about why the Descendants despised the Women of the Mist so.

Niamh shook the unpleasant memory off. "My intentions are to deceive the Hidden Ones longer until they reveal the location of the sword or take me to it. In the meantime, I am going to befriend a Norse seer. She... well, she might understand our beliefs better than I anticipated, and is greatly trusted by the Hidden Ones. I think she might be someone who I can use as an ally to understand the role of the Hidden Ones better and whether they mean Avalon harm by using Excalibur. She might be someone I can trust if I need help asking for the sword back."

"*Ask?*" The Lady's voice was taut, imperious, and most of all, enraged. "We do not ask for what is rightfully ours. You will demand it. Or take it back by force if necessity requires. We do not ask politely for our own artifacts and sacred sigils; they are ours by right."

Niamh was surprised by the Lady's emotional state and felt abashed. She had hoped that this would give her leeway to halt an ultimate betrayal and maintain Hytham as a friend, but clearly that was not what the Lady commanded of her. She understood that they wanted Excalibur back, but the strength behind the Lady's emotions was quite something to behold. Niamh may have known that intellectually the return of the sword was important, but to the Lady it was an emotional matter.

"Why would Mordred's people even try to ally with the Order of the Ancients?" Niamh asked, changing the subject. "While they're deeply pagan and don't align with Christians often... or would agree with what I know of the Order of the Ancients, they don't have any claim over Avalon or even the sword. Our leadership has always been women. I would anticipate that using the sword to regain power would only result in them having to acknowledge that the sword came from Avalon.... and they simply seemed determined to wipe us out. Why such a hatred of us?"

A shadow of concern passed over the Lady's face. Deep lines ran around her mouth and eyes. She sighed and clasped her hands, saying, "Mordred's people are aware of the Women of the Mist, as you know. What you don't know – what we have tried to keep secret – is that some of them are not just descendants of Arthur's knights but also our sons. Avalon's sons. Sons who chose to follow the paths of power rather than the paths of energetic will."

Niamh's mouth went dry.

The Lady continued. "Mordred was the son of the Lady who ran Avalon during Arthur's reign. The leaders of the Descendants now are from the bloodline of priestesses who have been cast from Avalon forever. I know it's hard to believe that the events of three hundred years ago have bearing today, but their leader has claimed his ancestor's name and thus, Mordred seems to have returned and now believes that Excalibur belongs in his hands. He would want to be seen as the rightful king, with the true king's blood running in his veins. Fulfilling a prophecy, as it were, of the true king's return."

The puzzle pieces began to click. The Descendants of the Round Table wanted their king on the throne, cemented in place with Excalibur as proof to the masses. And with the Order of the Ancients backing them, the Descendants would push through any agenda the Order of the Ancients had. Even if that meant destroying the Women of the Mist… and quite possibly the Hidden Ones.

"What will this mean for us?" Niamh asked, not sure what the answer would be.

"At this moment, I cannot say. But they know who we are and would do anything to keep us from maintaining control of Excalibur."

"But why not seek out Excalibur to begin with and take it from its resting place under Stonehenge?" Niamh asked, knowing it was an impertinent question.

"The sword was protected. When the Descendants first decided they wanted to reclaim the sword, we sent out witch-warriors to kill those who got too close to the truth, which ignited their furious response upon us. We knew *where* the sword had been sealed away, but not how to re-open the vault. I have since learned that certain artifacts were needed to release the sword and believe that the Descendants simply could not obtain all of them. I am uncertain who originally took the sword and hid it, but I am certain Arthur died believing that no one should have the power of Excalibur. I have always assumed it was someone who wanted to honor his wishes."

The implications of the sword seemed even larger and more world-encompassing than Niamh had ever imagined. With so many factions now working to have it under their control, and the sword loose in the world...

"Lady, what does it mean if Mordred's people, or the Ancient Ones, or even the Hidden Ones, were to keep Excalibur out of our hands? Isn't it just a piece of the Sacred Table? Couldn't we simply forge another?"

"No. Excalibur was made... We don't know by whom, but we know that it can do things no other sword can. We wouldn't know how to replicate the magic that it performs, and that magic is part of what makes it sacred to us." The Lady smiled. "Would you have us give up our history so easily, Niamh?"

Niamh disregarded the pointed question, even as her

cheeks burned. "But we always have said that it was forged at Avalon. Is that not true?"

The Lady looked uncomfortable. "We found it in the lake. It washed ashore, and when the Lady long before me picked it up, it glowed. Later, it was sealed in a stone until a rightful holder could come along to claim it."

"And that was Arthur," Niamh said breathlessly.

"It was. We believe it picks leaders for Mercia. That is why we need it, Niamh. We need its guidance to find the next Lady. And the one after that. We need it to find kings and queens. The sword knows who it can trust with its power, and it speaks that trust with the cues that we have been trained to look for."

"So now our enemies wait for the sword to be in a position where they can take it," Niamh summed up, "and hand it off to those who believe it will place them in power."

The Lady looked somber. "Yes. This has become a more dangerous quest for you. No longer are you simply embedded with an enemy, but the whole future of the islands rests on you recovering the sword."

Niamh wanted to disagree, to say that the Hidden Ones weren't their enemy. That they were friends and if only Avalon wasn't so secretive and distrustful, they could have the Hidden Ones on their side. She wanted to say all this, but something about the Lady's face kept her silent. Niamh was meant to believe the same doctrine that the Lady believed when it came to the Hidden Ones. She was not sure that the Lady was incorrect when it came to Marcella... but Hytham? He was a different sort.

However, Niamh knew her place. She knew that it was

not hers to question, and she did believe that no one, not even Hytham, should have the sword of Avalon. It belonged with the Lady, and likely under stronger protections than the ones that Eivor had been able to remove it from.

She nodded and bowed before the Lady. "I will do as you say," she said. "I will bring the sword back to where it belongs."

"So may it be," the Lady replied, before turning her back to Niamh and kneeling in the grass, facing the center of the grove of trees.

With a heavy heart, Niamh made her way back to her horse, and rode swiftly in the direction of Ravensthorpe. She kept her attention sharp for those who might mean her harm, but no bandits came, no wolves darted out of the woods, no adders slid in her path.

Her next stop was Ravensthorpe.

THIRTEEN

Hytham was correct that Ravensthorpe was easy to find. She followed his instructions and made her way past Grantebridge and could see the little hamlet across the river from her. She hesitated to ride straight into town – even though she'd begun to see that not all Danes were going to attack her on sight, the old knowledge that many had and might do again grounded her.

Instead, she skirted the river and stashed Mathan somewhere safe, as the horse was in desperate need of a rest, a fair distance from the center of town. She followed the river until she could find a bridge and crossed.

From here, she could see that there were several roads leading into the settlement, each one undefended. The Raven Clan must have been comfortable here. Able to easily activate their safety precautions should the need arise. Niamh assumed they would not attack a pedestrian on the road towards their village and remembered Hytham's guidance to call on Valka's name if anyone did question her.

Valka's letter had become crumpled in her pocket as she pulled it out and looked it over once more. She made her way to the seer's hut and heard the sounds of a waterfall nearby. She climbed down the rocks to the side, and strolled up to the front door, which was open to let in the day.

"Valka?" she called into the small home, which dripped with hanging herbs and deer skulls. It reminded her of her mother's cottage in an odd sort of way and she couldn't help a soft smile of remembrance. It was becoming more difficult to hold on to her old beliefs, as hard won and strong as they were. Valka was not the men who had stormed her own village time and time again. She was a herb worker like Niamh. She took care of her people.

"Can I help you?" Valka's voice drifted out from the very back of the cottage, accompanied by clanking sounds. It was obvious the seeress was busy at some kind of work.

Niamh was surprised that Valka was not coming out, weapon in hand, to investigate the stranger at her door. Perhaps things were truly that peaceful here. Valka sincerely felt that safe in her new home – something that Niamh, in her whole life – had never felt.

Niamh eased her way carefully through the front door and made her way through the cottage, making note of all the tools and herbs that Valka had at her disposal. She also noted the lack of weapons by the door and shook her head in disbelief.

A strange sort of jealousy filled her. She had never felt that she could fill her home with only herbs whilst leaving herself unguarded. It was a privilege she ached for. While

Niamh loved her sword and the power it gave her, her true calling lay with herb craft and healing.

"Valka, I'm sorry to come upon you like this, but it's urgent," Niamh said as she crossed through the back of the house into Valka's kitchen area.

If she had thought the first rooms had an impressive quantity of tools, this one took her breath away. A giant hearth with a cauldron twice the size of any Niamh had seen in a village, with hooks for smaller ones, was the main focal point of the room. Jars of dried herbs and spices, some of which seemed unknown to Niamh, were displayed with care. Valka stood at a table in the center of the room, a heavy stone bowl in front of her, hands busy with the work of grinding herbs into a paste.

"Niamh, I'm surprised to see you here, but pleased that you decided to visit instead of simply returning my letter." Valka's voice was inviting, but her eyes were full of that curiosity that made Niamh anxious.

"I have come because I need your help," Niamh replied, stomach churning with anxiety. She didn't know if Valka would say yes. If she didn't, Niamh would have to head into a dangerous situation at the nunnery alone. More than that, and despite the Lady's warnings, Niamh also nursed the hope that if she made friends with Valka, then Valka might be able to help her smooth any conversation revealing Niamh as an agent for the Women of the Mist to Hytham. She needed Valka to come with her.

"My help? Do you need healing?"

Niamh chuckled, shaking her head. "I do not, although I think you would prefer that after I tell you what I do need. I need you to come with me on a journey. Do you remember the nunnery I spoke of when you visited us in Lunden?"

"I do… but why…"

"Marcella is still unable to leave the bureau safely." The lie passed her lips with ease, but the next would be more difficult. "Hytham is choosing to rest after our journey to the Roman keep – do not fear, he is simply recovering from the excursion – and since my Hidden Ones' tasks are at a standstill, Hytham has given me leave to investigate the nunnery. He knows it is important, but his absence leaves me without backup. It was confirmed that women are being taken to the nunnery for some nefarious purpose. I mean to understand what that purpose is."

Valka's eyes lit with understanding. "You need me to be a second pair of eyes, in case something befalls you while you are investigating?"

And I need you to tell me everything you can about your leader, Eivor, while you do, Niamh thought to herself privately.

"I worry going alone, but also believe I will require your healing abilities. If these women are unsafe, they might require such aid. I wouldn't ask, except that I think you understand. And I think, even though these women are of a different faith from you, you hate seeing women treated badly."

"When do we need to leave?" Valka asked, beginning to put the paste she was making into a jar for safekeeping and giving Niamh a warm smile.

"As soon as you can," Niamh replied, relieved. She had

her. She could make this plan work. And, it seemed, the Dane wanted to work with her.

"Then I'll get a horse. I can meet you on the road outside of town before first light."

Niamh went back to get Mathan, and when she returned to the agreed-upon meeting place, she was surprised to find Valka came alone. Somewhere in the back of her mind, Niamh had supposed that Valka would come bearing guards, weapons, and a disposition meant to inspire fear. Niamh shook her head at her preconceptions. She still had a lot to learn.

They rode out towards the nunnery – a half day ride at best – and to the east. The closer they got to the town where the nunnery was located, the fewer pagan symbols were found alongside the route.

"There are fewer signs of the goddess here. More of Christ," Niamh explained quietly to Valka, realizing how nervous she'd become.

"Nothing from our practices either," Valka confirmed, answering the unasked question. They were both thinking the same thing: the Church was strong here, and anyone who opposed it must have been given ultimatums. Leave or convert.

"I don't like it," Niamh said. It made her queasy, seeing how little the old ways were tolerated in this part of Mercia. She could feel it in the land, and in her own heart.

"Remember what you told me," Valka said. "This is about those in need, not the religion they worship."

Niamh and Valka found a small stable that had been built for visitors, and tied their horses up to posts, leaving them to eat hay and drink water while they continued on foot.

"It will be easier to blend in," Niamh said, gesturing for Valka to walk beside her.

As they approached the center of town, Niamh noted the large church and crosses, along with those attending a midday service. Hordes of attendees swarmed out of the main doors, alight with how good the service had been.

"I'd like to speak with some of the women in town first," Niamh said, watching the crowd thin out. "Someone who will give us more information on the nunnery before we go there directly. I just don't know who..."

Valka scanned the streets, and then frowned. "I sense we have not gone unnoticed," she said, just before they were attacked from behind.

Their attacker was small, about a foot shorter than both of them. Niamh struck out and found the back of her attacker's neck, grasping hold of it like a kitten. What she found was something like a kitten, a child of no more than twelve, squirming viciously in her grasp.

"Let me go!" the child shouted, punching at the air.

"Behold. Someone to talk to," Valka said, almost laughing. "Odin provides. I don't think you're going to be able to harm us, child."

The urchin punched at the air again, hoping to make contact with either Niamh or Valka, but failed. Once they finally stopped fighting the empty air, Niamh set the child down.

"Now. Why are you attacking two strange women in broad daylight?" Valka asked, kneeling to make eye contact with the fierce little girl.

"Because! Strangers don't belong around here. I hoped I could get the bounty for catching anyone who looks like they aren't supposed to be here." The girl bared her teeth at Niamh and Niamh had to hold back a smile to take the child seriously.

Yet her words were odd. Odder still that a child would be hunting a bounty, but orphans were common in these parts.

"You mean the local government rewards people for turning in strangers? Even if they're just passing through?" Niamh asked.

"You're not just passing through, lady," the girl replied, eyes narrowing. "And it's not the local sheriff or nothing, it's the priest. He doesn't like strangers coming in. Says the pagans will try to drag us all back to the old ways. He says there are punishments if that happens. Bad ones, too."

If the Church was trying to get strangers to stay away, that added a lot more credence to the theory that they were up to no good here.

"If we can give you enough coin to keep you fed and housed for..." Niamh glanced in her less than ample coin purse, "... a few days..."

Valka coughed into her hand and Niamh could swear that she heard the word "weeks".

Niamh amended her statement. "A few weeks. Do you think you could tell us a little more?"

"If you can get me out of here, I'll tell you everything you want to know."

"I'm part of a settlement, a half day's ride from here, that would be happy to take you in," Valka volunteered without hesitation.

The little girl eyed them suspiciously, but the gleaming coin and the chance of freedom seemed to outweigh her hesitations. Niamh knew the child would be well taken care of in Ravensthorpe. And with that, the child started to talk.

"The new priest here – well, he's not new, he's been here about a year – started to get rid of all the pagans. If you didn't convert and you were a woman, he tossed you into the nunnery. If you were a man, he ran you out of town. He wants us to be a Christian village. He says his friends want a place where it's safe to meet and that anyone who is sneaking into town is dangerous and must be brought to his attention at once."

Niamh could guess who the friends were. It didn't take much to assume it was the Order of the Ancients. While Mordred's Descendants wanted the sword more than anyone else, they were unabashedly pagan. They would not be getting rid of pagan women and men – unless they were pledged to Avalon.

"And what is happening at the nunnery? We've heard rumors," Valka said.

"Oh. Well. We don't really know. It's on the outskirts of town. Women just disappear in there. Sometimes they come out, but they don't usually. Sometimes, they're even brought here. I assume it's because they need to be converted."

The child didn't seem too concerned about it. As though the notion of disappearing women was common, but for this village that did seem to be the case. What it must be like to live in such an unsafe place!

Niamh knew she couldn't fix the village as a whole, but

she could figure out what was happening in that nunnery. And the best way to do it was to go in with how she'd been taught from Hytham: to let the shadows protect her.

"Will you stay with the girl?" Niamh asked. "I think a stealth mission might be more suitable to breach the nunnery and rescue anyone. I'll need you on the outside to help in case any are injured. And, if I'm taken, you can get the girl out and spread the word to Hytham."

Valka looked uncertain, as if she could object, but Niamh clasped her on the arm. "I do not want the child left alone to tell of our presence," she said in a low voice. "Other coins might speak more loudly to her than what we can offer."

Valka nodded in agreement, and together they headed off down the alley and out into the streets to retrieve their steeds and find the nunnery.

Niamh felt the trembling pull of the Goddess. So far, her journey had led her here, and in this moment it seemed just as important as finding Excalibur. This was one of the things the Goddess was asking her to fix, and she would not disappoint.

FOURTEEN

Niamh spotted the large, well-guarded nunnery in the distance. Well-armed soldiers surrounded the building. The tall stone walls were covered in spikes, with few doors and windows to allow for entry. Many of the windows had bars over them.

Whoever had constructed this place did not want anyone getting in or out. Niamh would have a hard time getting in by herself, but she knew that if she brought Valka and the child they would end up with a whole new set of problems. They dismounted and hid their horses before approaching the nunnery further.

As Niamh crept along the edges of the wall, looking for an eventual crack to creep through, Valka and the child kept back and out of sight of the guards. Niamh wished Valka would remain further back, but at this point she couldn't very well argue with her. Inspecting a crack in the wall, Niamh grimaced with frustration that she was too large to fit.

"How are you going to get in?" the child asked.

"Looks like you might need to act more like Hytham than you're used to," Valka said with a smile, holding the girl's arm.

"I could go instead," the child whispered, but Valka shushed her.

"I admire your willingness," Niamh said under her breath. "But trust is harder to come by." She then clambered up into a tree, gesturing for Valka to watch out for her. Leaping from the branches and onto the top of the solid rock wall covered in spikes was terrifying, but soon enough, Niamh found her way inside. Bells rang for the next round of religious services. The guards were plentiful inside the walls too, all of them watching the nuns carefully for any sign of misbehavior. The women – because after observation and despite their garb, Niamh realized they weren't just nuns – were tending gardens, making repairs to armor, and boiling bandages out in the courtyards.

This isn't a place of religious worship, it's a jail, Niamh thought, disgusted by whoever had brought these women here. She could see it on their faces it hadn't been through choice. Two guards were hassling a woman who wasn't working quickly enough for their liking. Niamh scaled down the wall and lay in wait among the bushes.

She hadn't brought a veil or anything to blend in as one of the women, so she would have to do this in speed and shadow. She waited until one of the guards came up close to the bush she hid behind, and for the first time since receiving it, she truly used the blade on her left wrist. She reached up and grabbed him, flicking her wrist and letting his weight sink onto the hidden blade. He barely made a sound as she dumped his corpse in the bush. Now, she understood why the gauntlet was such a powerful tool – and why Marcella had been reluctant to give it to her. Faster and quicker than a sword, Niamh marveled at how the blade slipped back into its hidden sheath.

She made quick work of his clothes, swapped her armor and cloak for his, and most importantly, donned his helmet. Now she looked more like a man here for the purpose of keeping the women in line than what she really was: a woman ready to make trouble.

At least this way they won't notice me for a good long while, she thought. Although the women I am here to talk to probably will take some convincing if I look like one of their captors.

She strode out of the bush and navigated through the main courtyard in plain sight. No one gave her a second glance. Not even the nuns.

She made her way to the interior of the building. Each step took her further away from possible escape routes. Niamh had never felt so alone, or unsafe. She was here in a Christian house of worship, being used to keep women like her hidden away so that they could cause no trouble to the men who were in power.

Niamh took a left and found her rage was growing. She was glad that Valka waited for her outside the walls and that she and the young girl wouldn't have to see this. The cells… that was the only word for them… were locked. She peered through the barred windows and saw women inside. They were not at prayer, but many of them stared out the meagre windows at their disposal, gazing onto inner courtyards. With each cell – she counted ten – she imagined there were more in other hallways. Her rage increased. This had to be the work of the Order of the Ancients, trapping those who would stand against them. She wondered if this place was a secret kept from the Descendants – that, if the Order of the Ancients was slowly whittling away at those who might support or believe in the true king agenda, then they could usurp power from the Descendants and betray them just when the Descendants thought they had everything they needed to control the isles.

Niamh felt powerless. She was just one woman. She couldn't possibly take on all of the guards here and rescue every single woman who was kept captive. How could she even begin to undo the evils of this place? She wasn't going to get an opportunity to get inside again.

But she could use her work with the Hidden Ones to take the whole organization down. She could help them undo the work of the Order of the Ancients. In this, they were unambiguously on the same side. She couldn't do everything on her own, but she could do something. And she would have to try.

Niamh started by going back out to the courtyards. A few women were tending to some small garden patches in the center of the inner gardens.

"Come with me," Niamh said, her voice low, making eye contact with the woman who seemed to be the most in charge, while standing over her in a menacing way, as if inspecting her work.

The women scowled at her. "I haven't done anything wrong. I told you everything I could!" The other woman beside her looked confused, almost as if ready to shout.

"Listen to me," Niamh said, "I can help you get out."

The woman's scowl turned into one of surprised hope. Niamh shook her head. She couldn't allow the woman to show joy in this moment.

"All of you, follow me just like you would follow any of the guards. Pretend I'm taking you away to be interrogated."

Niamh led the three of them back to the crack in the wall, sneaking each of them through between glances to be sure that they weren't being watched. Luckily, without heavy armor, the first two were able to push through, but the third remained unable to fit. Niamh shared an agonized glance with her until the woman said, "Don't worry. I'll spread the word and help you get as many as I can out."

Niamh nodded. She couldn't do this for all of them. It made her feel sick.

The woman continued, pointing across the courtyard to a building. "The keys to the cells are either hanging in the guard house, or the lead guard has them. If you get those, you can get enough of us out that the guards can't catch us all. Thank you for coming to get us. We thought no one cared or remembered."

"Another nun in Lunden told me about you," Niamh said fiercely. "You had not been forgotten."

Valka gestured through the hole in the wall, indicating that Niamh should follow – but Niamh shook her head, ignoring her. Instead, she turned around, intending to hunt for the keys. She couldn't stop those in charge of this place from kidnapping more women, but she could at least rescue as many captives as she could.

Valka clearly disagreed with her decision, but without the benefit of speech, all that Valka could do was stare into Niamh's eyes before she ran back into the nunnery. She hoped no one would find the corpse near the bushes, but she could not move him without being spotted.

The keys were not hanging on the wall. She would have to find the leader of the guards to make that plan work. Could she do it in time? Could she do it without drawing too much attention to herself?

Niamh had to believe that the Goddess had given her the skills to do so. She had to believe that the sparse lessons from Hytham would guide her. This was what she had been asked to do for her people. Niamh continued to operate in plain view, pretending to be a guard.

As she came around to the chapel, however, she found that there was an even bigger problem.

Cyrus. He stood at the entrance to the chapel, a bandage covering his head, slowly moving with the assistance of others. He must have survived and had been brought here to heal. He could recognize her, especially since they had fought so recently. She would not be safe if he did so. He would be the one to bring all the guards down on her head, and there would be no escape.

Niamh backed down the hallway and thought. If she couldn't set all the women free, what could she do to make sure they were safer?

But it was too late. She had been spotted. Cyrus paused

and squinted, and Niamh knew that the sword she carried would be recognized and be her undoing.

"Stop that woman!" Cyrus shouted.

Niamh turned to run and found herself instantly surrounded and outnumbered. If she didn't fight with every scrap of ability that she had, she would find herself imprisoned in the very place that she desired to destroy.

She could not afford that. More than her own skin, the women who were being kept against their will could not afford her to fail. Niamh approached the group of men blocking her way to the exit and removed her sword from its sheath.

The fight was brutal. She couldn't keep track of her opponents, or for that matter, their weapons. She was certain that this fight would be her end ...

Until she heard the scream of other women joining into the fray. They fought back with tools from the garden, branches, and swords stolen from the fallen soldiers. Yet, they were still no match for those trained in combat, and many fell. Niamh screamed in rage as she fought on but knew she could not sacrifice herself. In the chaos, she ran for the wall, hoping the women who survived would follow.

Some women did, but not as many as Niamh had hoped. She led them to the wall and scaled it to reach the tree, while others tried to fit through the crack in the wall or follow her. Soldiers scrambled after them. When Niamh dropped from the branches on the other side, exhausted, Valka grabbed Niamh by the shoulder and hauled her toward the horses.

"Where are the other women?" Niamh asked as she

flung herself on Mathan and reached for one of the women who had escaped. Some of the others, she counted three, sprinted in opposite directions, heading for the safety of the woods, outpacing any soldiers in pursuit. She thought she had at least saved five and sent a prayer up for their safety.

"They ran, much like those others," Valka said, mounting her own steed and hauling the young girl in front of her. "They did not want to wait, especially since we still had the element of secrecy. What happened in the nunnery?"

Niamh hated what she had done. She had to get back to Hytham and report what she had found. They would need to come back here at some point, and save those women trapped in the cells. One thing she knew for certain: the Order of the Ancients had to be stopped. "I met Cyrus," she said. "We fought, but the women tried to fight by my side." The rest of the story went untold, but Valka seemed to understand, nonetheless.

"You did what you could. Something like this sounded like terrible luck. Perhaps I should have armed you like I would one of our warriors. We use mushrooms and herbs to assist in battle. Have you ever fought with such assistance?"

"I have not had the pleasure, no." Niamh chuckled despite herself, but she had seen such fierceness from the Danes in battle. They were relentless and seemed like the fear had been sapped out of them. "Do you use these medicines to see through the veil?"

"The veil? I'm not familiar with that concept, but I do use mushrooms and some herbs to help people commune with Asgard," Valka smiled.

Niamh felt as though they were making progress – a bridge across their cultures. Even though she still carried distrust for the Northmen, she was willing to work with *this* Dane to create a better world. After all, Valka had come on this quest and shared with its failure. They were not on opposite sides any longer.

FIFTEEN

Once Valka and the two new Ravensthorpe residents had been safely deposited, Niamh rode back to Lunden. It was a long hard ride. Niamh was still furious at herself for being spotted by Cyrus and for not ensuring he had been killed at the keep, for having not been careful enough to make a bigger difference with the women in the nunnery, for leaving many of them there and making things worse for them. It had been a mistake to go there, to try and rescue more women. She shouldn't have fought and should have allowed herself to be arrested instead.

Those women in that nunnery weren't safe, and so long as she had the connections with the Hidden Ones, she might be able to make more of a stand to protect them than she could on her own. Hytham would help her.

At this point, she struggled to see how the matter of Excalibur was more important than these women in captivity, but she knew her orders and she was working to obey them even as she struggled with her emotions.

Upon her arrival, she saw Marcella standing in the doorway, and it was Niamh's first signal that she was going to have a harder time convincing the Roman woman of her trustworthiness.

Marcella's face was hard as stone, and her hand rested confidently on the sword pommel at her hip. "I see you've returned to us once more, Caledonian." The hostility in her voice was deeply vicious.

Niamh knew that in Marcella's mind there were no good excuses for why Niamh had journeyed with Valka and had obtained Hytham's blessing to do so.

Would Hytham continue to support Niamh, or would he feed her to Marcella's rage? Niamh may have trusted Hytham, but she understood he had a certain amount of loyalty to Marcella, who was a full indoctrinated member of the Hidden Ones.

"I went to Ravensthorpe to speak with Valka, only to hear that she had left with a Caledonian," Marcella snapped, unsheathing her short sword and jabbing the blade at Niamh as if in emphasis.

"I–" Niamh started to speak, to explain, but Marcella stopped her.

"No, Caledonian, this is where I talk and you listen. Carefully. If you step out of line again, if you don't check your actions with me beforehand, I will kill you. I will not hesitate. As for Hytham…"

Niamh needed a good lie and quickly. One that would spare Hytham whatever punishment Marcella may be planning for him. She clearly hadn't spoken to Hytham yet, as Niamh deduced from Marcella's dusty riding clothes.

They must have arrived at nearly the same time, which gave her an advantage.

"I had wanted to pray, Marcella. I asked Hytham for permission to go and seek out the guidance of my gods. The city is too loud and full of people. I had to go to the forest. And what of your safety? Should you be out so blatantly when Cyrus still seeks you out?"

"Do not speak to me of Cyrus." Marcella's eyes flashed. "What kind of gods do you have that require such a sacrifice of your time?" she asked, her tone sliding from accusatory to snide.

Here, Niamh could weave in the truth. The lies she would have to tell Marcella would be many and varied, but they did not need to be all encompassing. She had simply wanted to spare Hytham another argument with Marcella.

"While I was praying, I had an idea. Valka had said she was interested in spending more time with me, and so I rode out to meet her. The nunnery that we had discovered on our last mission wasn't far, and rather than coming back to fetch you, I simply asked her to come along and assist me to investigate."

"Damn the nunnery," Marcella spat. "There are bigger things at stake that require attention."

Hytham joined them then, drawn by their arguing voices, and he walked down the steps easily. Niamh could see even at a distance that his limp was better. She hoped her medicines had worked for him.

"And now we can see to them," Niamh said, moving forward to enter the bureau. Marcella blocked here with her forearm. She paused, then stepped backwards.

"Are you really going to stop an initiate of your own order from entering the shared sanctuary that we have?" Niamh asked. She did not want to come to blows with Marcella, but she was almost certain they were close to it.

"But why would you leave so suddenly after what we'd learned? In the dead of night as though you had reason to escape us?" Marcella asked, refusing to let Niamh move further. "Speak truth. Are you part of the Order of the Ancients?"

"No!" Niamh cried. "I found I was being called by my goddess. I did not want to wait to heed her, and so I left. I believed you would trust me to return. You can speak with Hytham or Valka to see I am not lying. I gave you my word. Why is that not enough for you, Marcella?"

Niamh knew it was a dangerous question to ask, to open the door to a blunt conversation about Marcella's mistrust, but if Marcella believed she was part of the Order of the Ancients, she couldn't let that stand.

"Will this help?" She tore the gauntlet from her arm, and handed it reverently to Hytham. "I am no longer in possession of something that you believe should not be used by me. I never counted it as my own, only something to learn by."

Niamh felt the danger in the knife's edge of the energy between them. One imbalance and there would be nothing but death and pain. Marcella seemed disinclined to allow her past without a fight. One wrong word from her and Marcella would take advantage and send her on her way.

Behind her, a merchant and his cart rolled past, rattling

away through the mud, completely unaware of the incident that was about to unfold between the two of them.

Hytham still kept his silence. Niamh realized, after looking at him, that he too was waiting to hear Marcella's final answer.

Yet, whatever that answer may be, Niamh was unsure whether Hytham could do anything to fix the problem. If Marcella hated her this much – suspected her of being a member of the Order of the Ancients – Hytham wouldn't be able to stop her from putting an end to Niamh's life.

"Marcella, why have you not invited her back inside our walls? You do this every time she returns, refusing to allow her sanctuary. At this point, I have to believe it is because you feel something personal, rather than a direct threat to our organization. She has done our business for us. What more must she do to satisfy you?"

Marcella turned to look at Hytham with distaste. She clearly didn't have a good answer, as she kept her silence for a long time.

"If you really don't trust me, why don't you just fight me? If I can beat you and I don't kill you, don't you think that's enough proof that I'm here because I want to be?" Niamh spoke before she could stop to be rational. Trial by combat was normal where she came from, many people solved their disputes in this manner. Niamh was no different. She knew that if they fought, some of the tension would bleed out of both of them. She just had to hope Marcella took her up on it.

"Because I don't understand why she had to leave without a word to us, stealing out in the night like a thief or an escaped prisoner. Might as well have been taking our secrets to our enemies. Might as well be trying to undermine us from within." The snarl at the end of her words was perceptible. Then, without another word, Marcella stripped her cloak off, tossing it onto the ground in front of Hytham. She stepped forward, forcing Niamh out into the middle of the street.

"You want to fight me? Fine. Let's fight. If I don't kill you, you can stay." Marcella's acceptance of such combat surprised Niamh, but she didn't hesitate to confirm. She too dropped her cloak, throwing her saddle bag to the ground. Niamh didn't dare to close her eyes, concerned that Marcella would strike without warning, and instead called the energy of the wild boar to her to keep her safe during this fight.

"She's not yet sworn to us, Marcella," Hytham called out. "We gave her an honorary position so that she could do what we asked, but she hasn't gone through a formal ceremony. If you kill her now, we lose a valuable asset."

Marcella did not hesitate, moving forward toward Niamh with her blade drawn and her eyes full of hatred. "I don't particularly care, Hytham."

With that, Marcella charged. Niamh had not seen Romans fight before – Danes, Picts and other Caledonians to be sure – but Romans had never come as far as her village in her lifetime. This was a new fighting style to her, dictated by Marcella's blade, which was short and stubby and suited to the kind of combat that kept fighters close together.

Niamh took the distance to step aside and avoid being stabbed, but now they were close together and Niamh could see how angry Marcella was. The creases next to her eyes were visible, and even when focused on the fight, Marcella shook with rage.

Niamh did not intend to kill Marcella. She didn't particularly want to. But now it was possible she would have to just to survive.

"Marcella, stop this!" Hytham shouted again, trying to get the two women to disengage their blades.

Niamh's sword clanged against Marcella's and she locked against the pommel, matching gazes with her opponent.

"I have done nothing to you, Marcella. I have listened to your advice and asked you to trust me, but your unwillingness to give me even a sliver of trust has undermined the Hidden Ones." With those words, Niamh shoved back against the sword with all her might, putting her weight on her back foot when Marcella gave way.

They were, by this point, gathering a bit of a crowd. Merchants slogging their carts through the street were now a rapt audience, and more were coming. This was not the kind of attention that the Hidden Ones needed. Niamh could feel anxiety building in her stomach. Marcella wanted to get rid of her at any cost, but the cost of their hideaway was too great. If Marcella was worried about Cyrus, she certainly had broadcast her image to the townspeople at this point.

Instead of letting the fight continue, Niamh jumped forward, bringing her longer sword down within a hairsbreadth of Marcella. Marcella lunged to the side, and then stared.

"She pulled that, Marcella. She didn't have to. She could

have cleaved you in half if she'd chosen it. Swallow your pride and let her report on what she's found. Based on what I suspect, we want to hear it," Hytham said, sounding tired.

Niamh felt sick looking at Marcella. She would have to work with this woman who would gladly kill her after her mission was accomplished. But unlike Marcella, she had the ability to hide her distaste.

"You're right, Hytham. I do have something interesting to report." But Niamh did not sheathe her blade. She waited for Marcella to call an end to their squabble.

"Put your blade away, Marcella, be done with it," Hytham said.

The air between them was tense, and watching Marcella make the decision not to kill her was the hardest thing that Niamh had ever done. She knew that she could not sleep at the bureau again. With the stealth Hytham had exhibited, she knew Marcella was just as dangerous.

Finally, Marcella sheathed her sword, and stalked back into the bureau, shoving past Hytham. She didn't speak another word to either of them.

"I don't think we should follow her," Niamh said to Hytham after sheathing her own sword. She glanced around at the audience watching their dispute and tried to remember their faces. Knowing who was present would be important if word got back to Cyrus.

"No… I don't think that would be wise," Hytham agreed, "but we can't stay here in the street, either. Let's walk. You can tell me what you know and we can make a decision together."

"Your leg?" Niamh asked.

"Well, thanks to your ministrations."

Niamh offered him a small smile and followed him, walking through the gathered crowd and out into the streets beyond. Instead of heading toward the docks or to the river, Hytham directed them out into the city, searching until they found an abandoned house, and then climbing to the top to sit on the flat roof which gave them a view of the city at large.

"Tell me, what did you find when you met with Valka?" Hytham offered.

"You don't want to discuss what to do about Marcella?"

At that, Hytham laughed. A true laugh that echoed off the buildings that surrounded them.

"No. Marcella is not a problem that you or I can solve. She is going to have to sort things out by herself. I don't know if it's that Marcella has a strong dislike of other women, born of her time with Cyrus who would pit every woman against the other, or if it's just that she was born with such fury... but we cannot help her. We cannot fix her. All we can do is hope that you standing up to her makes her rethink her choices."

Niamh wasn't sure that was true, but Hytham knew Marcella better than she did. She shook off the adrenaline of the fight, and turned her thoughts to her recent adventures.

"Hytham, the nunnery is a prison. Valka had to help me escape when we ran into Cyrus. He's alive. And he knows my face well... and the Order of the Ancients is very clearly doing more to undo the pagan way of life in these lands than I thought."

Niamh swallowed, because she knew that she was

treading a dangerous path, one that she could not retreat from.

"I think that if they get their hands on Excalibur, the sword they are searching for, they will be able to do real harm to the pagan ways and people. That cannot be allowed. I want to fight against the Order of the Ancients as best I can. To help you. Working with Valka has shown me that there is more to people than I realized. I did not... understand my hate and dislike of others until now. In a way, I am as poisoned by hatred as Marcella. But I am doing my best to fight it."

Hytham's eyes warmed as he listened to her. A smile played across his face, as though he had been expecting these revelations all along. And though Niamh knew that she would never actually be a part of his order, as she would be a witch-warrior of Avalon for the rest of her days, she also knew that this allyship meant the world to her.

"I want to make you a proper member of the order, Niamh. I believe that you would be a true asset to us, and we could be so to you. If you have no one in this world, let us be the ones that are there for you. We choose our family, bound by the oath of brotherhood."

Niamh felt uncomfortable. She knew that she would be making a false oath and to do so in the face of his kindness was something she could not do.

"Let us set aside the matter of my oaths today, Hytham. It has been a difficult day. Instead, let me tell you what I've learned. The Ancient Ones are involved in the nunnery up north. They are keeping pagan women there against their will. I was only able to free a handful before I was discovered, which led to many deaths. I fear for the women who have been left behind. At least we now know where they are. We know that the Order of the Ancients is operating against women in this land with the assistance of the Church." She paused, knowing she was making a leap, but her instincts told her she was right. "Hytham, I think the Order of the Ancients is trying to stamp out paganism because they know that with groups like the Women of the Mist they are less capable of maintaining power."

It was a risk to bring up her own order, but it felt right to tell him what she believed to be true. She knew she had to filter some of the Lady's knowledge to him.

Hytham looked surprised.

"The Descendants of the Round Table are pagan, Hytham. This I have known and have not told you. Their alliance with the Order of the Ancients – people who seem committed to the Christian Church, makes little sense to me… unless they've promised the Descendants power. Excalibur is that power. It holds visions of sacred myths of the true king, as Marcella described. Yet, the Descendants believe they are truly of Arthurian bloodline – specifically of Mordred – and also the Women of the Mist. If a Descendant wields the sword, they could have a strong claim to the pagan population to promote conversion to Christianity, and, all the while, the Order of the Ancients would be puppeteering them from the inside. But, I believe the Order of the Ancients' purpose is twofold. They will betray the Descendants and fully replace any Descendant king with one of their own. Then, they will lay claim to all peoples – pagan or Christian alike – along with a legitimate claim to the isles as a whole. Wherever Excalibur is, it is in danger. There is both a pagan organization and your own Ancients trying to get it."

Hytham looked thoughtful as the pieces started to come together. But Niamh had to press forward. She knew that the Hidden Ones still thought of the Women of the Mist as potential enemies… and such an outlook needed to change, especially if they were going to protect the people Hytham believed deserved protection. They would have to work together.

"If they are operating in that way, and I strongly suspect they are, then the Women of the Mist are likely your allies. They would not support the Descendants using such a sword to perpetuate such tales. They would be able to help you in the fight against the Order of the Ancients," she finished.

It felt too vulnerable to offer more.

"Are you certain that the Order of the Ancients and the Descendants of the Round Table are working together to get control of Excalibur, and that the Women of the Mist would oppose them both?"

Niamh nodded in agreement. Here was the part where she would have to be careful. "Hytham, if you know where that sword is, it matters to the people of this island. It matters, and we cannot let it fall into the hands of either order. They would do things with it that are not wise."

Hytham gazed outward to the horizon, calculating all the information that he had at his disposal into a conclusion.

Niamh saw the choices coming: on one end, she could tell him of her true nature and position with the Women of the Mist. Or she could swear a false oath and ask for forgiveness from the gods and the goddesses when she returned to Avalon.

It had been the right choice to go and visit the Lady. It had been the right choice to tell Hytham some of Avalon's secrets.

But if Hytham asked her to take an oath that would negate those she had made to Avalon, it would be soul-rending for her. She couldn't do it. Making oaths was important to her, her word was the only thing she had in this world. No children, no family, just the promises she made to the people who looked to her for service and guidance.

"And Valka, what did she say?"

Hytham's words startled her out of her thoughts.

"Valka didn't say much about Eivor, but she does think we need to rescue the women at that prison of a nunnery," Niamh said. Valka had been just as horrified as she when they discovered what the nunnery was truly for and had wanted to burn it down.

"Well, you're going to meet Eivor," Hytham said, wearily standing from his position. "We'll leave at first light. We will discuss your future with the Hidden Ones when we return. By that time, Marcella will have had a chance to look at the realities of your actions – not the perceptions of what she believes."

"I'm going with you?" Niamh asked barely believing she had gotten away with it. "After what Marcella said about me?"

"I will need someone to watch my back on the long journey. You know it well. We're going to Caledonia."

And Eivor has the sword, Niamh thought, realizing that the end to her quest was close at hand. Soon, she would be able to get the sword back and take it to Avalon. She smiled at Hytham and knew in her heart that she would never take that oath, because when Hytham returned, it would be without her at his side.

SIXTEEN

Niamh had not seen Hadrian's Wall since she left her home. She had assumed she would not live to see it again. But here she was, riding behind Hytham toward it. Unlike her last time at this place, she did not need to sneak around the wall, trying to remain unseen. No, such stealth would be needed when they crossed the border, ironically. Now, she rode up to the wall with bravery, not afraid of the guardians who awaited her.

There were many who chose to guard the wall: Picts who wanted to keep the Mercians and Northmen out, Romans who still thought it was their business to attend to the wall. It was a Roman soldier that Niamh and Hytham came upon. She felt anxiety, wondering what kind of trouble they might get into, but the Roman man was haggard. His gray hair and crow's feet around his eyes told her that they were not in for a fight. They left their exhausted horses there and continued over the border on foot.

The heather was in full bloom, but Hytham's limp

had become worse on the long journey north as much as he pretended it did not hinder him. It was closer to midsummer than it had been to Beltane, and the passage of time had made the animals come out in full force. The rabbits frolicked through the highlands and the cows munched happily on every flower they could get their mouths around.

She ached to get to a midsummer observation, to light the bonfires and to sing the songs of her people. But she was here on business, and they were going somewhere with a purpose. She was far from that lone Caledonian and her assistant leaving their homeland.

It was a somewhat peaceful way to return home. Niamh found herself wistful for a return to the shores of her homeland, a return to a calmer life than the one that the Goddess had chosen her for. Hytham had been a fine riding companion to the wall, teaching her the ways of the Hidden Ones, giving her lessons in the craft of the blade beside their fires as they rested on the way north. He also told her of Ravensthorpe, of the community that this Eivor had created with her brother. Of the place where he planned to return once the bureau had been established.

They were a day into their walk through the highlands when Niamh felt she had to force Hytham to take a rest.

His wounds were more severe than he had admitted to Marcella, or to Niamh when she first treated him. His body did not want to stay in joint when it met force. They watched the sun set, and Hytham began to talk.

"It was in a fight that Eivor herself witnessed, that this happened," he acknowledged, watching as she re-wrapped his leg to treat the muscle spasms which had overwhelmed him once again. The pain radiated everywhere for him, keeping him in a weakened state. Niamh felt shame for not prioritizing his health.

"I took a blow that damaged me severely. I've been told that this is my life now. That I will never recover." Hytham didn't sound angry about his injury, more disappointed.

"Aren't you unhappy with the changes to your body?" she asked, as she tightened the bandages once more.

"When you are a fighter, your body is always in danger of change. I accepted that when I took on this role in my life. I have to accept this every day, as hard as it is."

It was odd to be caring for a man who she was about to betray, but she knew in her heart that she could do no less. Niamh turned to the cook fire and boiled water, going back to the same trick of filling a wine skin to keep his muscles warm and relaxed in the night.

"You should sleep and take the shift. I am used to long days without rest." Niamh handed the skin off to him. She knew that she needed the sleep, but she also knew she had done battle after birthing a babe whose mother had been two days in labor. She could fight if she needed to on little sleep.

As they continued their journey into the highlands, Niamh let Hytham make the mistakes that she never would have made in coming through these hills. Of course, she saved him from ridiculous fumbles, like walking into a bog, but otherwise, she knew she had to make her presence known. She followed roads she would have avoided, she went through valleys that she knew were watched by the local communities of Picts, and she carefully flashed the ravens on her shoulders when she knew they were being observed, so that they would know she was one of them.

Eventually, they came across a skirmish. It was as though Hytham had been looking for it, drawn to the clash of battle. Niamh could see groups of Danes and Picts fighting in the distance. They were fierce. The Picts – not a group of them that she knew personally – were throwing fire, and the Danes dodged them expertly as if they'd seen these tactics before. Leading the charge was a tall woman with blonde hair and tattoos, dressed in armor and furs.

She wielded Excalibur. She fought effortlessly, bashing the long blade into her enemies without fear and lifting it above her head for an even greater stroke. Niamh felt breathless seeing such a sight, and for a moment she wondered if the Lady had been wrong – perhaps Excalibur did belong with Eivor. She banished the thought.

There weren't enough Danes to fight off the Picts, and before Niamh could stop him, Hytham ran forward to join the fight. Niamh shouted his name, but drew her own sword and jumped into the fray. She did not want to kill any of the Picts – especially after flashing her raven sigil of Avalon on their travels north – and she dealt incapacitating, but not deadly, blows.

Even so, she could not help but be distracted by Excalibur. Her eyes weren't constantly focused on her opponents, but rather on the excellent warrior. Eivor fought with determination and immense strength, cutting swaths of Picts down with a bright grin on her face. A deep scar marred her face and throat, something that made

Niamh realize the warrior had been marked by a great animal.

"Hytham!" the Dane finally shouted, joy in her voice, when a moment of reprieve occurred during battle. "I see you've come to join the fight!"

Hytham crushed an opponent with his own sword and stood back, matching Eivor's energy with a smile of his own. He responded, but Niamh couldn't hear him as another round of Picts set to overwhelm her.

One parry, one thrust, one parry, one thrust. Almost mechanical, Niamh worked her way up to the front of the fight, so that she could stand in the presence of Excalibur's power. She could feel its energy, calling to her. She *had* to get that sword, no matter the personal cost.

Yet, fighting next to Eivor was invigorating. She was a talented warrior, and Niamh did not want to be on the wrong side of her blade if she could help it. Niamh almost felt that Norse energy seeping into her, fueled by some kind of ability that shielded her from fear and terror and made her certain death would not find her this day.

As soon as the last of the Picts had retreated, Niamh bent over to catch her breath as Eivor approached Hytham and began to speak to him after pulling him into a hug.

"It is so good to see you outside of Ravensthorpe, Hytham. But where are your horses? You shouldn't be walking such a great distance!" Eivor pulled back and looked Hytham up and down. Her concern seemed genuine and she turned and gestured to one of the other Danes who immediately responded by returning with a horse.

"The others can walk," Eivor said. "It is only a short way

back to our camp. After you saved us from the Picts, it's the least I can do." Eivor winked at Hytham.

"No one saves the great Wolf-Kissed," Hytham said and Eivor threw her head back and laughed.

Eivor was right – the walk back to camp was short and it was full of Danes who wore many furs along with braids and beads in their hair. Hytham dismounted, and now Niamh could get a better look at the woman who had taken Excalibur. She had blue tattoos on her face that contrasted nicely with the scars, and hair that was braided into one long tail. Now that she was not in the heat of battle, Niamh ached to take the sword from her, but Eivor sheathed it on her hip, where everyone could see it.

Niamh felt the energetic pull of the sword, calling to her like it knew that she was there to rescue it. She felt it asking to be taken home. And she knew, sure as anything, that she would not be able to take it off Eivor without a fight... a fight that Niamh was uncertain she would win. She needed to take the sword of Avalon carefully, quietly, and without a fuss.

"Eivor, I cannot tell you how good it is to see you again," Hytham said, as some of the Dane warriors surrounded their leader. Niamh found herself trailing behind him and wading through the small crowd, not wanting to get too close in case the energy of the sword became too much for her, in case she could not resist taking it.

"Hytham, tell me how Lunden fares? What of Marcella? Have your fights gotten worse?" Eivor's eyes twinkled. "Although I see you did not bring her, you did not come alone."

Eivor's eyes locked on Niamh's face. Niamh looked away, hoping Eivor did not see the clear conflict there. In the distance high above them on a cliff, over the green and heather valley, a single white stag stared down at them. Niamh's heart raced. She made eye contact with the stag, and thanked Cernunnos for bearing witness both to her action and to her patience.

"What is your name?" Eivor said asked, bringing Niamh back to the present.

"Niamh. Of Argyll," Niamh said, strengthened by the sign.

"And what brings you to the side of Hytham of the Hidden Ones today?" Eivor's tone of voice was almost jovial. A wisecrack at Hytham's expense. As though the idea of being part of their order was funny. Niamh wasn't entirely sure how to respond, pausing to look at Hytham for direction. At this, Hytham stepped in, saving Niamh from having to speak for herself.

"I sent out a letter, asking for people with the kinds of skills that the Hidden Ones seek out to come and visit me in Lunden. We are in need of more people who can do what you and I do, Eivor. We need people to help us against the Order of the Ancients."

Hytham was speaking so freely in front of her now that it was a bit of a shock. This was one of the reasons that Marcella had fought so hard to keep her out of the inner circle, Niamh thought. Because once you were inside, all their secrets flowed like a rushing river of information. There was nothing that Niamh could not ask in this moment that would not be answered. But perhaps, this was a reason why they had flourished when Avalon was struggling. Too much secrecy and you faded into myth.

"The rush of battle has made you careless, Hytham. You are much more open than you used to be. Is it wise to speak so freely?" Eivor said.

Hytham sighed. "Marcella had the same question, but Niamh has proven herself. She saved me from sinking into a bog on our journey here."

"Ah, then the woman has my thanks. Who am I to doubt you when you have questioned me many times and still accepted my choices?" Eivor said. Eivor seemed as fond of Hytham as Niamh had come to be, and considerably warm-hearted for a Dane.

"I admit I don't know this land as well as the people here do, and I am doubly grateful that we have found those who would understand it to help us."

At that, Eivor laughed. "It's true. The locals of this land have been quite helpful when they learned we are not here to destroy them or take their land or burn their fields. We just want to live in peace alongside them." At this, Eivor looked directly at Niamh. "I assume you've seen violence at the hands of some of my brethren. I promise you, my settlement has been built on land gifted, not stolen by my own hands."

Niamh was surprised to be spoken to so directly. "Ravensthorpe is a lovely place," she agreed.

"You've been?" Eivor looked surprised.

"Yes, she and Valka have been developing a bond," Hytham said.

Eivor appraised Niamh once more with a long look, and

then turned back to Hytham. "We have much to discuss together. Will you walk with me a ways? Niamh, feel free to make yourself at home. Help yourself to ale and any food cooked on the fire. You've earned it after today."

"Thank you," Niamh said and bit back her next words that Hytham should sit and rest. At this point, if Hytham was tired, it was to her benefit. She ached knowing that her betrayal was coming all too soon.

Eivor and Hytham walked off, already in deep conversation, leaving Niamh alone in a camp full of Danes, all of whom eyed her, distrustful of the new Celt in their midst. Or perhaps Hytham was less well liked than she had expected, as well.

Niamh found herself anxious about what to do next. Marcella was suspicious, and grudging, but these Northmen were outright hostile, looking at her as though she had to prove her worth in a way that would satisfy them. And what would satisfy the Danes? What would satisfy anyone? How could she convince them that she was a safe stranger, rather than one who needed to be watched? It appeared simply helping in one battle did not mean she was part of the group.

A burly man carrying a large sword came trudging toward her. She could not imagine what he was going to do, but she didn't want to find out. She had one card in her pocket to play: an ally's name.

"Is Valka here on this trip?" Niamh asked him. She hoped they understood her language, or at least that they understood the name. Niamh didn't speak their language, as she hadn't had the opportunity to learn.

"No, Valka didn't come this far north with us. She stayed in Ravensthorpe to tend to our people," the burly man said. He lowered his sword. "But you know Valka?"

The eyes of the assembled warriors turned on her, less fueled with suspicion than with curiosity now.

"Yes. Valka and I met when she visited Lunden a few weeks ago. We talked of many things that interested her. I would call her friend." Niamh swallowed hard.

The Northmen all looked at her in curiosity. Niamh reminded herself that perhaps she had let old fears get the better of her. Even if she saw these people as a threat, it could be because of her past... and what she planned to do that would not endear her to them in the future.

"Valka tends to keep to herself," one man said grudgingly, nodding to her. "If you speak true, then no doubt Valka had purpose in her discussions with you. She is a seeress. Come. Eat. Drink."

Niamh smiled and stepped forward, taking a cup of ale and tasting the bitterness. The valley seemed to be full of Danes. Clearly, Eivor had brought great warriors to the highlands of Niamh's homeland with her. They were dressed in armor and carried all sorts of weapons, and Niamh sized up what she was up against. She could not challenge Eivor in combat, as she had done Marcella. She would have to use every trick she had learned to get the sword and steal away into the night undetected.

She knew that the Lady would want her to do whatever it took to help Avalon, and that by getting Excalibur back into the hands of those it belonged to, she would be helping her own people in their quest for survival and autonomy.

She walked through the encampment, looking for signs of Hytham and Eivor. At least, if she was going to be here, she could wander freely and find out more about what the Hidden Ones and the Raven Clan were up to.

But it was more difficult to find her targets than she had imagined. Each tent looked the same, filled with identical survival items, the same furs and hay beds. They had not decorated their traveling arrangements, nor made it easy to see which tent belonged to which leader.

Her mind roved in circles, torn between her duties to the Women of the Mist and her fondness of Hytham and the Hidden Ones. Even here, Hytham chose to trust her, chose to listen to his own instinct over that of Marcella. Hytham was not watching Niamh, preferring to let her take care of herself. Which left Niamh with a purpose, and one that would shatter his confidence in her, instead.

Niamh paused and stared up at the tall crags, searching for more wildlife to ask guidance from, but nothing revealed itself. She took a breath, steeling her resolve, and knew if she were to take the sword and flee back to Avalon, she would need to make sure she had the supplies to do so. She would have to steal more than Excalibur. She darted in and out of the tents, carefully making sure that no one was inside before she entered.

In each tent she found things that would help her to survive, from flint to hard rolls of bread. She found furs from creatures she had never seen, altars to gods she had never heard of, and then finally she entered what felt like a strategy tent. She had never seen a map before, after all, Avalon didn't bother with such things. It took her breath away. Here, hanging on the wall, she could see how far she had traveled from her home, all the way to Lunden and beyond. It made her feel so small. On the map there were notes in a language she could not understand, but she could glean that they were tracking something. Members of the Order of the Ancients? Locations? She didn't know, but she ached to understand more of the world from this perspective.

In that tent she found letters about the Order of the Ancients too. Niamh stopped breathing as she read.

The Descendants of the Round Table seek claim of the sword known as Excalibur. We will pledge ourselves to the Order of the Ancients if you can bring us what is rightfully ours.

Niamh wondered if Eivor was collecting this as evidence, or if this was intercepted information passed from the Lunden Bureau to Eivor. It certainly confirmed that the enemies of Avalon were using their sacred sword as a bargaining chip. She re-centered her focus. She needed to find the sword and somehow get Eivor away from it.

Leaving the tent full of clues and information behind but taking the letter indicating the allyship of the two orders to give to the Lady, Niamh began to search for Eivor's tent in earnest. The other warriors and those filling the encampment paid her no mind. No one seemed to bother her. After all, she was Hytham and Valka's friend.

She finally came upon one tent that carried a trunk big enough for swords and shields and a variety of kinds of armor. It also seemed to carry Eivor's personal journal, letters and writings that she had done during her travels, some in Hytham's own hand, and Niamh knew that if she were found here, she would not be able to explain why.

The sound of Northmen speaking in the distance kept her heart pounding in her chest, until she heard the distinct sound of Hytham's laugh just outside the tent. A voice that she would recognize anywhere, and she threw herself under the furs on Eivor's bed, hiding safely in the many layers that kept Eivor warm at night. She could not risk going outside and being seen spying by one of the other warriors, and yet the room remained sparse enough there wasn't anywhere else to hide.

She couldn't see when they entered the tent, but she kept her breathing low. Outside the tent she could hear the crows coming and wondered if this would be the time that they would carry her soul to the next life.

"So, she says she's from north of here," Eivor said, as she entered the tent, her footfalls stopping at the edge of the place where Niamh hid. They were talking about her, it was clear.

"Yes. I don't have contacts this far north, and the fact that she came willingly tells me that she needed to escape. This part of the world seems harsh." Hytham stood closer to the flap of the tent, based on the echo of his voice.

"Interesting," Eivor mused. "Hytham, you've changed. Putting your trust in someone so new? It seems different from how you used to be."

"If you recall, I put much trust in you. I trained you in our ways and you never promised to be part of the Hidden

Ones. Working with Marcella has made it more challenging to be the man I want to be," Hytham admitted. "Her rage is troubling. It clouds her leadership and makes it difficult to be honest with her, or to behave in a way that feels honorable. She is far too reckless, and yet sees my choices as reckless."

Niamh held her breath as Eivor leaned over the sleeping space, taking one of the smaller furs off the cot. She didn't hear it hit the floor, which meant that Eivor must have draped it over herself for warmth.

"Tell me more about this evidence you've found about the Order of the Ancients concentrating their power with these Descendants of the Round Table," Eivor said. "I've also intercepted some correspondence indicating this as well, but you've been enmeshed in this far more than me." She paused. "I would stay and help, you know I would, but I'm needed across the sea in Ireland. My cousin calls."

A thud echoed in the tent.

"Do not concern yourself with that," Hytham replied. "The Hidden Ones are prepared. But I do come bearing a warning. We should find Niamh. She can explain more."

"Let's go get a drink," Eivor said. "I want to know everything, but the day is long and you need to put your feet up."

Hytham's voice trailed off, and with a sound of heavy fabric slapping shut, Eivor and Hytham appeared to have left the tent. Niamh waited, counting her breaths, until she was sure that Eivor wasn't coming back.

Then she slipped out from under the furs. And what she saw was utterly baffling.

SEVENTEEN

In front of her, lying on the table where Eivor kept all her papers, journals, and several knives, was Excalibur. It lay there in a plain brown leather sheath, waiting for someone to pick it up. It lay there knowing, even though it did not have a mind, that it was meant to be held by someone like Niamh.

She approached it slowly, with reverence. This was it: the final piece of the sacred table. The holy sword that she had been sent to retrieve to protect her land and serve her people. She willed her hands to stop shaking as she lifted the sword into her hands.

The pommel was metal and silver that sometimes looked bronze and was decorated with a series of circles intercepted by gold crisscrosses. When she reached out and unsheathed it, the blade itself appeared melded from all kinds of other swords, forged into one strong being that glowed when held by the right bearer. Niamh felt a small pang of sadness when the blade did not glow for her. But she had known that she was only the messenger, a temporary hand that would take the sword back to its rightful place, not the actual person meant to hold its power.

Even so, the power rumbling through the weapon was extraordinary. Lifting it felt like holding a heavy snake in her hands. Excalibur pulsed with strength, and it felt amazing to behold. The energy had to be from its makers, those who wanted this to be an important piece fit for a king or queen to protect their people. But it was also a gift from the gods of this land, a promise to keep everyone who followed them safe and protected.

Niamh removed her own sword and slid Excalibur into her own sheath. It didn't fit well, with about an inch of the blade sticking out from the top. Tearing at a cloth that Eivor had left on the floor, she used it to wrap the visible pieces of the blade and the pommel, disguising it as much as she could as any old sword. She glanced at the sword that she had brought with her. It was unidentifiable. Not a remarkable blade, or even one that meant something to her. She had carried it for the purpose it had been intended, to get her to this moment. Some nameless blacksmith in the Northlands had made it, forged in the heat of their fires. But now it would serve a different purpose. She laid it down in the same spot that Eivor had so unceremoniously dropped Excalibur, and with her eyes closed she prayed over the old sword, that it would remain disguised as Excalibur until such time as was safe for its true nature to be revealed.

Then she quietly and carefully exited Eivor's tent.

The trouble was, she wasn't certain what to do next. She

had Excalibur. She could leave. But if she left without saying goodbye to Hytham, was that a betrayal of their bond? She knew that Hytham trusted her, but if she allowed Eivor or Hytham to see her with Excalibur on her hip – as poorly disguised as it was – she knew she would be sunk. The best thing to do, no, the right thing to do, was leave. To escape while she could, while no one knew what she had done, and hide in the hills until she could make her way back to Avalon and to the Tor.

Niamh turned with regret from the center of the camp. She felt in her heart that it was the wrong thing to do without some parting goodbye to Hytham. But what could she say? She knew this was simply her heart and personal wants speaking, not the priestess that honored the Women of the Mist.

For a moment, she basked in the present, listening to the sound of fires being lit and tended to as the sun continued to fade. The sky was bright orange and pink and purple, glowing with the colors of the setting sun. Drinking songs from another land echoed in the valley, and she knew without a doubt that even though she was in her homeland, this was far from her home.

The darkness settled quickly, and Niamh took a deep breath, letting the priestess overtake any personal desires she had, and she set out into the camp. She crept behind tents, hoping to avoid the bonfires to get to her horse, but it seemed that such stealth was known to others beyond herself.

Eivor and Hytham strolled through the shadows, both of them deep in conversation and seeming to avoid the boisterous celebration of the others when they came upon her.

It was one of those strange moments, where time felt sticky and lengthy. Everything slowed, and Niamh felt like she was walking through sap. She turned to leave upon spotting them, but Hytham called her back. Cold sweat dripped down her spine.

"Niamh, we were just discussing something you might be able to help us understand – the nunnery you investigated. Can you attest that it is truly a prison, or are some of the women devoted nuns? If there is some connection to the Church, we may be able to utilize one of Eivor's Christian contacts who is not in league with the Order of the Ancients or the Hidden Ones to help us after our time here."

A small shred of relief wormed its way into the anxious terror Niamh felt. She was glad Hytham had kept the nunnery in the forefront of his thoughts and seemed to be considering how to help these women when they were in peril. She just hoped that neither of them would notice the sword at her hip – and momentarily wished the sacred sword didn't have to be quite so large.

"It's a good thought. From what I recall, there weren't any devoted nuns, but I was originally told about the nunnery from a nun in Lunden. Perhaps we need to speak with her to make a connection first. Of course, I can't be the one to interact with the Christians. They won't do well with someone like me," Niamh said, shifting so that the hip bearing Excalibur was more fully in the darkness.

"However do you mean?" asked Eivor.

"Niamh is a devout follower of the Goddess," Hytham

answered. "Many of the women who are imprisoned at the nunnery are pagans, and while Niamh has excellent self-control, she did happen to be spotted by those running the institution…"

Niamh desperately tried to think of ways to get out of the conversation but found herself picking up on Hytham's trailing thoughts. "I would not be a good fit to make inroads with the Christians, no." Her eyes darted around them. Was there a way out? Did she have the strength to attempt to knock both of them out cold without a fight? She didn't want to attack Hytham, but it might be her only choice. Except that a fight would draw the attention of the many soldiers just waiting for one. She couldn't afford that. She tried to calm her wild thoughts and think things through logically. Around them, the bonfires blazed as new fuel was added.

Hytham continued to speak, but Eivor suddenly silenced him with a single raised hand. Her eyes narrowed as she peered at Niamh's hip. "Niamh, whose sword is that?" Eivor asked, her voice turning deadly.

Niamh didn't answer. She couldn't find the words to speak.

Eivor didn't wait for an answer. She turned to Hytham, and smoothly drew the sword from his hip. "If you're planning to take that to the Order of the Ancients, you'll be disappointed by their company," she snarled. "I think you'll find that you're disposable to them." She leaped toward Niamh without hesitation.

Niamh scrambled back, drawing the almost too large Excalibur out of her sheath and holding it in a defensive stance with two hands. Behind Eivor, Niamh watched in despair as Hytham's expression transformed from shock to confusion to dawning understanding.

In front of her, Eivor raised her blade.

Niamh did not want to fight this woman. She had seen her decimate a Pict not more than a few hours before. Niamh was an excellent fighter but armed with a new weapon and in a defensive stance... she knew she could not finish this fight.

Eivor struck out, and Niamh had no choice but to engage. Instead of withdrawing, Niamh slid Excalibur down, locking hilts with Eivor. She knew that the sword Eivor had taken off Hytham was less weighty than Excalibur. She could break the blade and get away – except that Excalibur trembled in her hands and she knew the sword was not fit for her stance.

"If you give the sword to me now, I won't kill you. I'll just send you back to whatever hole you crawled out of," Eivor said, her voice calm with a growling edge or rage to it. A grit that Niamh could not ignore.

"I can't give it to you," Niamh said, feeling herself weaken against the Dane's strength. The pressure between them was building. Niamh would have to be fast. "It isn't yours. You stole it. The people it belongs to need it more than you do."

With that, Niamh threw all her weight into the hilt of Excalibur and shoved. Eivor stumbled back, and Hytham's sword wavered as she did. It didn't break, but Niamh realized she had provoked something feral within Eivor, and it was like a wolf had been released.

Eivor roared, shouting something in her own language. Then the Norse warrior charged, and Niamh knew she could not afford to get locked into combat as the entire camp was roused into action.

Eivor lunged for her, and Niamh took the advantage to roll out of the way. Scrambling to her feet, she turned and ran, hoping foolishly that Eivor would not pursue her.

"If you took that for the Order of the Ancients, they won't help you!" Eivor yelled as time sped back up again and adrenaline brought clarity to Niamh's world. Footsteps sounded behind her, but if Eivor was a battering ram in battle, Niamh was smaller and faster, outpacing the Dane as she disappeared into the surrounding area.

"Niamh! Come back! Explain yourself! Why do you have the sword?" Hytham's voice now, calling her back, pleading. But she couldn't. She had to move forward.

She ran through bushes and brambles, not bothering to disguise her movements. There was no time to do anything but put as much space between her and the Danish camp as possible. She kept going until she saw the meadow where the horses were being kept. The men milling about saw her, but she was on the far end of the field. Before they could react, Niamh took action.

She mounted the first horse and slammed into the saddle burdened with her stolen tools of war and her reclaimed sword. She knew that the duties of a sworn priestess would be more difficult than just the fighting, but she had no idea it would have such personal costs like the friendship of Hytham.

Her breathing came fast and hard, and she ended up

having to trust the horse to see for her, because her eyes blurred with tears. She could not cry now. She could not weep or mourn. She tried to shove the feelings down, to force them to go away. But the loss was too great, and she laid herself on the back of the horse, who galloped into the hills, and sobbed.

After the tears had dried, and the chaotic fearsome shouts behind her became dim and faded, she forced herself to focus on her escape. Traveling along the lonesome road was too obvious. One woman with weapons and a horse practically begged for bandits, or for Eivor's own horde to easily track her movements. She turned her knee into her horse's flank and headed up to where she had seen the stag, facing up the crags.

She knew that she could hide from these Northmen better than anyone. These were her hills and her valleys, her fjords and her lochs. This was her home.

The cold wind bore down on her as she reached the top of the first crag, where she could watch down into the valley for Eivor or her people. While she couldn't expressly make out Hytham or Eivor, she could only determine that there were people down below – and many of them would be coming after her.

She knew the best decision was the same one a fox would make when it stole a village chicken. A fox doesn't stop to see if the villagers notice, and the wolf doesn't check to be sure that the owners see the lamb is dead. Learning the lessons of those hunters, she turned her way north, and headed into the lands of the Picts. They would see her raven clad shoulders, and determine she was one of their siblings. With any luck, they would help her, especially if they noted that the Northmen were striking out with their flaming swords and their arrows in her pursuit, because the Danes were not welcome in these lands, and Niamh would use that to her advantage.

It was not long before the terrain became more treacherous. The rocky crags were steep, and her horse balked at the notion of trying to climb the slopes in the dark. He bucked and whinnied, and rather than fighting, Niamh hopped off and tied him to a tree, slinking into some bushes to keep her protected from any observing eyes. She would have to wait until first light to urge the horse on any further.

The stars twinkled overhead, her only company besides the wildlife in these parts. A murder of crows flew by. She could feel the danger in the air – the unnerving sensation of being hunted. The skin on the back of Niamh's neck was cold, and goosepimples rose on her forearms. She huddled in her furs when she heard her name being called.

It was Hytham, calling her to come back. Pain threaded his voice, the betrayal of someone who he had fought so hard for in the name of trust. She could hear the frustration in himself, for having trusted someone he should not have. And she could also hear anger. Rage. Niamh had to fight her own instincts to return to him, to tell him that she would come back, that she would fight by his side once again. After all, she could not promise that. She could not give him what he wanted.

She had to follow the orders of the Lady, and that meant hiding from him.

As Hytham grew closer, she moved away from her horse, finding a hiding spot in the grasses even further above this ledge. The stones slid under her feet, sending gravel flying, the gentle breaking sound of rocks destroying the silence of the night.

Hytham followed the sound and she watched as he made it up to the horse. Here, she would have to be the quietest that she had ever been, watching as he adjusted his leg back into place as if in pain, and regarding her horse with frustration.

"You can't tell me where she is," he said, accusation in his voice.

The horse snorted at him.

"You can't give her a message for me, either. If she even comes back for you." He reached out and undid the careful knot she'd placed on her horse's reins, smacking the horse's rear once, as hard as he could. The horse kicked, bolted, and fled down the hill, whinnying.

"You'll have a harder time getting away with that sword now," Hytham said bitterly, speaking as though he knew she was there, even though she had left little trace.

He stalked back down the hill, the disappointment seemingly weighing down his shoulders like a stone. Niamh felt his cold rage of having been betrayed, and she knew that if she met Hytham of the Hidden Ones again, it would be at the other end of his blade.

Once Hytham had disappeared, Niamh began a slow trudge across the dangerous terrain, knowing that every step away from the camp took her farther from Hytham's wrath. It would be a pain to get to Avalon on foot, but it would be too dangerous to search for her horse and even less safe to steal one from Eivor's camp. She had already taken one precious item from them. It would not be wise to take another.

Making her way through the Pictish countryside, she wondered how many days it would take to get where she was headed with this precious sword on her hip.

Too long, especially now that she'd been outed, someone would send information out describing her face, her clothing, down to the last detail. It wouldn't be an easy trek without some kind of transport. She would have to find a horse.

Glancing across the horizon outlined in the rising sun, she looked for settlements, marked by the smoke that came up out of their morning fires, meant to roast meat and boil water. Far down, several valleys over, she could see another settlement – likely Pictish – keeping their own fires lit.

That's where she could find assistance, even if they weren't her family or her usual allies. They would help her against Danes. Everyone would help her against them. Even the Christians, though she wouldn't seek them out without dire need.

She climbed down the far slope, much steeper yet than she had come up. Her feet struggled for purchase and her hands bled on the rocks, torn by the rough edges and the steepness that pulled her down ledge after ledge. She knew that she could not keep up this kind of descent without costs, but the knowledge that a horse might be available kept her going.

Her knees ached from the strain, and it felt like hours,

but eventually she made it to the bottom, to a brackish fen.

Across the fen was a small village, built a little less cannily than her own, mostly out of stone with little wood to be seen except around the firepit. Men wearing nothing but fur and blue paint walked through the village in the early morning light, armed to the teeth with weapons and their own fierceness.

Niamh had both been allied with the Picts and been against them. But in her current state, wearing a kirtle and a raven shouldered cloak that made her look like one of the Women of the Mist, she was not sure that they would take kindly to her presence in the middle of their home without invitation.

So she crept along the edge of the fen, sticking to the bushes and carefully moving around the snakes that nested with their eggs close to the water's edge. She could hear the women of the village in the distance, singing the cleaning songs that were known in Niamh's village too. Perhaps she could speak to the women, and they would help her, even if the men might be hesitant.

Light of foot, she got through to where the women were doing the laundry, stepping out of the bushes next to a woman who appeared close in age to her. The woman stopped beating the cloth and stared at her until all the others noticed her presence.

"Give me one good reason why I shouldn't scream," the woman to her direct left said, eyes full of determination.

Niamh questioned herself. So far, she had failed in her promises to protect. Wisweth had died because she had killed Deoric too quickly. The women at the nunnery were all still imprisoned. She had let down these women in a terrible way... but they were also her best allies.

"Because I'm from the northlands, like you, and I'm in terrible danger," she said, speaking truth for what felt like the first time in weeks. It was a relief to her, to be able to be honest. The lies were building in her chest like a poison.

"How far to the north?" the suspicious woman asked. "D'you have any herbs from the shore? I've got a babe with colic. If you've got what I need, I will help you."

This was a transaction that Niamh could help with. She could save herself using her knowledge. From inside of one of the pouches on her belt, she withdrew a small jar.

"This is seaweed, from the islands. It will clear up the colic if you make it into a broth. Don't feed it to them straight, you understand, but slow and steady and warm. Like a tea."

Niamh looked past the woman out to the far distance, the sounds of anger reaching her ears. "In fact, if you would be so kind, I need somewhere to hide. The Danes who are looking for me... I think they're here."

There was a commotion up at the mouth of the entrance to the village. Niamh could see Northmen on horseback. She cursed her slow getaway, and supposed it made sense to look for her here, in one of the few populated places nearby. One of the women grabbed her by the arm, and at first Niamh moved to object, but then she realized that she was being taken to safety.

The woman was older, and the lines on her face told Niamh that she had seen many winters and borne many children. She had probably lost many people, too. She brought Niamh into a small hut and shoved a batch of clothing at her without a word. Niamh changed quickly out of her warrior clothing and into the clothes of a washerwoman, binding her hair back in the way that these women did.

But what was she going to do about Excalibur? She couldn't leave it in this hut, not without it being guarded. Yet its large size necessitated that she hide it. There was no possibility of blending in with the Picts while wielding such a weapon. Excalibur was meant to awe, without subtlety.

The woman glared at her, trying to emphasize the necessity of speed. But Niamh cast around, noting the worn leather harnesses and sagging old saddlebags along the wall, and finally wrapped the sword in her own clothes and shoved it inside an empty barrel. If the Danes burned the village to the ground, it would be lost, but if they left... the sword would be fine, and she would still be alive to take it to Avalon.

The older woman gestured for Niamh to follow her, and she regretfully left the hut with one backwards glance. It didn't feel wise to leave the sacred sword in an old rotting barrel, but she wasn't sure what other options existed.

Outside, she joined the circle of women beating the dirt out of furs and other fabrics worn by the rest of the village. It smelled awful, but she was used to it. She had done such tasks with women in her own village – even the local witch-warrior had to help with the laundry. It was not above her to help with the children, either. She laughed, watching a young boy dash through the circle of women, naked as the day he was born, chased by a passel of other children who were coming to catch him.

Niamh plunged her hands into the mess of fabric and pulled out something that she imagined had been drenched in blood. In these parts of the world there was no red dye, and yet it was stained so. She took the cloth to the cold water of a stream, freezing her hands as she plunged it into the water. The icy touch matched the blood in her veins. In the background, she could hear the Danes questioning the men at the front of the village. They were looking for her. Describing her clothing and her face, and asking if they had seen the sword.

The Pictish men did not budge, instead showing hostility to these Northmen. For one thing, the men didn't know she was there. She kept her head down, listening to the women singing their washing song and letting the beat keep her heart steady and her hands from shaking. If she were caught now, she would have no way to defend herself, and the sword would be lost to her.

"I want to search the village. She's probably hiding here," one harsh Norse voice said, clearly heard across the distance. "Hytham said she might be hiding among the women."

Niamh ducked her head down, taking the stream-cold cloth and flinging it over a line. She grabbed a stick and beat the cloth to get rid of all the dirt, blood, and grass. She used the cloth to hide herself as she listened to the discussion about her whereabouts.

"We told you, we haven't seen her. She's not here and if you lay one more toe into our village, we'll make you regret it. I have archers waiting for my order," the leader of the village spoke in halting Norse.

If the Picts gave her up it would go badly for her. The Northmen would not spare her if they thought she was one of the Order of the Ancients. And Eivor seemed to believe that if she was not one of them, she was at least cooperating with them.

She wondered if Hytham agreed. But that was too painful to contemplate, so she went back to eavesdropping as she beat the cloth in time with her unsteady heartbeat.

The Danes paused. If the Pict leader truly had archers at the ready, they would be dead in an instant, having brought few reinforcements.

The leader of the Northmen finally stepped back, no longer directly physically in the space of the Pictish leader.

"We'll come back," he said darkly, turning his horse and leading his men away.

Niamh let out a deep sigh and knew she could not be here when they returned.

As soon as the hoofbeats had cleared the air, she turned around and fled back to her clothes and her sword. She bundled her own clothes into a saddlebag, ignoring the protests of her own mind. The Picts may have shared a homeland with her, and some beliefs and traditions, but they would not protect her like one of their own.

She left through the front door of the hut and listened for horses. Turning to her left, she headed back toward the fen, and found a pen full of steeds, none with saddles. It didn't matter. She grabbed the first one with dangling reins and slung the saddlebag over its midpoint, then hiked herself up, skirts and all, with Excalibur at her side, onto the horse. Riding in skirts wasn't her favorite, but it would make her less obvious than her own clothes did, shaping her appearance as a woman riding to birth babies rather than a warrior fleeing.

The woman who had helped her earlier stopped her just as she was leading the horse out of the pen.

"You cannot take our horse," she snarled. "Get off him and walk."

"Do you want me to be anywhere near here when they come back? You can tell your leaders and the Danes I stole a horse for all I care… they know I didn't have one. But if you let me go now, I'll be far away and you won't have to deal with a pack of Danes hunting for me on your lands."

"Why shouldn't I just hand you to them?" she said, glaring at Niamh. "After all we've done for you, you expect more?"

"I am a daughter of the Mist and I carry the Lady's sword back to her. The Danes took our sacred artifact and let it be wielded by one of their own against Excalibur's own people. It is my duty to bring it home."

Her truth was a gamble. If she was a Pict that stood with the Pictish gods and not with Avalon, she would stop her, but… if Niamh was lucky… if the women of this village had been trained like her… if she chose to follow Cernunnos…

The woman dipped her head. At first, she thought, out of fury, but then she stepped back, leaving the way forward open to her.

"Lady, you may pass," she said, speaking the language that they shared.

"I will return the horse when I am done," Niamh said, a promise she knew she would keep. And if not this horse, then another to resupply their herd. She was not unkind, but merely desperate.

And so she rode south, desperate to reach Avalon as quickly as possible.

EIGHTEEN

Riding past Hadrian's Wall, past the northern forests and deep into the midlands, Niamh realized she neared collapse. She had been alert for days, barely resting or eating as she fled Eivor's wrath and Hytham's rage, and both she and her horse were exhausted. But every time they had stopped, she sensed danger wasn't far behind. The forests had been loud, insisting there was always some predator not far away, spurring her to mount again quickly and continue on her way. As she rode, she realized that she was not merely running from Hytham and the Hidden Ones, but from The Descendants of The Round Table and the Order of the Ancients. Niamh had made more enemies in one moment than she ever could have imagined.

She had known this quest would be dangerous, but now she was aware it was deadly. All her new enemies would kill her for Excalibur if they had the chance. Hytham might hesitate, but Marcella wouldn't. Marcella would do whatever it took to keep Niamh from completing her own mission.

As dusk descended, Niamh stopped and risked her location to build a small fire in the middle of a glade, then slipped her small ankle knife out and began to hunt, leaving her trembling horse to graze in the meadow while tied to a tree.

It brought her no joy to hunt rabbits – they were gentle creatures who deserved to be left for their natural foes like the fox, the wolf, and the snake – but she was out of the stores she'd carried with her, and her weakened state demanded that she eat. It had been so long since her last warm meal.

She hunched far from the fire, folding her legs underneath her, and waited for the forest to gift her what it would allow her to kill. She was still dressed in the clothing from the Pictish village that had given her the horse – a long tunic style dress draped with a shawl, and a headkerchief that kept her hair out of her face. To be honest, she was just as comfortable hunting in these clothes as she was in the trousers she favored for long riding journeys.

As she waited in the ever-darkening forest, she realized this was the first time she hadn't been alert since leaving Hytham behind. Her heart ached at the thought. She had become comfortable with him – she had even been fondly contemplating that while Valka had been somewhat over curious about her practices, the Dane seeress had been genuine. The Hidden Ones had not been hostile, not to her or her people – excepting Marcella – and they had not wanted to change her ways. They had wanted to learn from her, to teach her new skills, and to become allies.

"I wonder if I had come to them as who I am, if they would have worked with me?" she said out loud, her lone voice carrying into the wind and to the guardians of the forest. She dismissed the thought quickly, knowing that even if she had arrived at the Lunden Bureau and said that the Women of the Mist wanted to work with the Hidden Ones, the Hidden Ones had been in possession of Excalibur to begin with. Putting her cards on the table from the start might have guaranteed that the Hidden Ones kept the location of Excalibur to themselves, and since they did not understand its true nature, it would have been vulnerable to the likes of the Order of the Ancients or the Descendants of the Round Table.

As much as her decisions weighed on her, she had been right all along not to fully trust them. If she had told the Hidden Ones that Avalon needed Excalibur back, that her people deserved it, she would have been told it was nothing more than a sword.

She could let her own personal doubts hound her, but her heart knew she had been right to complete her missions. She would mourn the relationships lost, nevertheless.

Excalibur hummed with power at her hip, reminding her that it was much more than a mighty blade. It was everything to her people. It was an honor to be able to bear it home.

At the edge of her vision, something rustled in the forest. It was quick, a blur amongst the foliage, nipping from bush to bush. The forest had provided. It was a rabbit.

Niamh slowly crouched, limbering up by bouncing ever so gently on the front pads of her feet. Her body sprung to life as she came out of her meditative space, and her hands and blade became one. She darted to the next bush, where the rabbit had fled, and quickly slit its throat. The rabbit didn't have time to react, and her heart was glad of that.

"I'm sorry, little friend," she said quietly, carrying the rabbit's warm body over to her fire. She skinned the beast quickly, mind wandering back to her predicament like a dog with a bone, while she completed a task that she had done over and over a thousand times in her life and put the rabbit on a stick to roast over the flames.

A quick glance towards her horse told her he had eaten his fill and was now sleeping. With that reassurance, Niamh unbuckled the huge sword from her waist and laid it nearby the glade, covering it with fronds and foliage in the event she fell into a deep sleep and was taken upon unawares. Only then, did she feel able to close her own eyes for a few moments while her meal cooked, under the assumption she would be better focused after some rest for the long journey ahead.

Or at least, that's what she hoped.

A set of howls emanated from the north, the snarls and barks indications of an angry pack of wolves. They were common enough in these parts that Niamh knew she might have to deal with them, but these wolves didn't seem to be hunting her. They sounded as though they were reacting to someone moving through the trees. Wolves did not attack people with malice unless hungry, or if they had good reason. These wolves lived in a forest full of meals to catch and good caves to rest in, so the wolves were reacting to whoever was in the trees.

Niamh did not want to know who it was. Her mind

flashed a dozen possibilities. Faceless assassins. Betrayed friends full of rage. Without another thought, she pulled her meal off the spit, and threw it into her saddlebag. She would eat it later, regretfully cold, but it would be better to be eaten cold than to be left charred and inedible for her corpse. She had risked a fire, and her luck had not held out.

She knew if she rode out of here, she wouldn't get far without detection, so instead she took the borrowed horse and led him by the reins away from the fire, wishing for all the world that she could have rested a while longer. Her vision swam from hunger and exhaustion. She checked for her bow and arrow, ready to take these men out one by one if she had to.

Sure enough, the thunder of hoofbeats arrived not much longer after, and she strained to hear the voices as those hunting her crowded around her fire.

"She's gone," an unfamiliar voice said. The accent did not sound like a Northman. It was a Briton.

"You should have ridden faster," a second unfamiliar voice snarled. "We need that sword. He'll be angry that we weren't able to get it."

Who was he? Who did these people represent? It wasn't the Hidden Ones, or scouts from Eivor's Raven Clan. Niamh chewed her lip and eased further back into the forest, her stomach twisting at a new thought. It could be someone from the Descendants of the Round Table, or from the Order of the Ancients themselves. But how did they know that she had Excalibur? Would Hytham have partnered with them for the mere purpose of catching her? The thought seemed so absurd she banished it.

"If anything, at least we have confirmed it's loose in the world and she is the likely source for it. She's only one woman. She can't stay away from us for all that much longer," the second voice said, the leader, she thought. She was too afraid to look, to stand up away from the bush that she had hidden alongside. She hoped they didn't look too closely at the trees, either, where her horse stood, looking for all the world as if he were bored.

"She's been trained by those damned Dogs of the Mist, so we may be up against more than we bargained for," the first voice spat.

Niamh could tell this man hated her people. He must be one of Mordred's, to refer to Avalon as such and with such hatred. From her reconnaissance, the Order of the Ancients merely planned to use Excalibur and any reference to Avalon as pawns in their ultimate scheme, while the disdain in this man's voice spoke of something much different.

How was she going to get out of this forest alive and back on the road? They knew she was here. They would listen for her horse's hoofbeats, they would stalk her, and then they would kill her and take Excalibur. She reached to her hip and realized that in her rush to get out of their way, she had left Excalibur in the glade.

Swearing to herself, loathing her carelessness, she looped the reins around the nearest tree, and began a slow but deliberate crawl closer to where the men stood, raging about the Women of the Mist who kept them from the power they craved.

"If you ask me, we should attempt to invade their Avalon again and burn it to the ground."

Niamh recalled Hytham's teachings even as her heart thundered in her chest, and she crept closer. She could see her new opponent's face as he spoke reflected in the firelight. He was a Briton, dressed similarly to the other men she had seen in Lunden. He had bright blue eyes that were lit with fury and a scar across his face. Neither of the men, who were dirty and ill equipped, had their weapons in their hands. If they had been hunting her, if they had even thought for a second that they would catch her, they would have had their swords in hand. But no, they were the kind of men who assumed that their prey would not stalk them back.

She couldn't help but smile as she got to her feet and nocked an arrow. They had given her enough information to identify them, but now it was time she ended their quest. She shot the man with his back to her in the neck. It went through, spurting blood into the other man's open mouth as he continued his screed about her people. The survivor gaped, clearly in shock.

Niamh leaped forward, knocking him to the ground and pinning his hands. Nose to nose, they stared at each other. She kneed him in the gut and shrieked, coming up against hard armor instead of soft belly.

He smiled and resisted her strength, lifted up his hands, then grabbed her wrists and threw her off him. Niamh landed hard, feeling every one of her ribs crunch with the impact.

"We did find you," he said with a smile, standing and bringing his foot down hard in her side. "Now, where is the sword?"

Niamh was suddenly glad she had left Excalibur hidden

in the glade where she had been sleeping, dug in the dirt and covered with fronds so that she could rest without fear of it being taken.

"What sword?" she asked, gasping for breath as she reached forward and grabbed at his ankles. He stomped, crunching her left hand. Niamh knew her scream could be heard for miles.

When the pain receded, she rose, taking a leaf out of Marcella's book, and charged him like a boar. It worked. He was too startled to react as she knocked him down again, crushing him into the ground.

"Who do you work for?" she snarled. "How did you know I was here?"

Her opponent started to reach for his sword, but she got there first, drawing the sword in reverse and bringing the blade up to his neck in one swift motion. She nicked his throat, leaving a thin line of blood.

"I will do it. I will kill you. It will not be pleasant for me, but it will be necessary," Niamh hissed, and then repeated her questions. "Who sent you and how did you know I was here?"

The man stared at her. She swiped at his neck again, drawing another thin line of blood.

"The Order of the Ancients has eyes everywhere. We saw you take the holy sword of Excalibur from Eivor of the Raven Clan. You may not serve us, Avalon scum, but we have those who do in her midst. We know what you are as we have seen you all over this isle this last month, causing us trouble." With that, he kneed her in the gut, but this time she was ready for it.

She rolled away, but the stolen sword made it difficult, and after a short scuffle, it was flung just out of her reach. She scrambled for her dagger in her boot, but he also had more than one weapon on his person. He pulled a blade out. It was the length of his arm and it dripped with black ichor.

Poison.

She couldn't let that blade touch her.

He moved quickly, aiming for the bare parts of her flesh that he could see. The forearms, the face, the throat, trying to nick her in any way. She dodged and rolled, but she was running out of energy, with every offense he attempted, she was losing strength. She had to do something, but he was keeping her away from his sword with ease.

She had not been up against as many skilled fighters as he.

Niamh was scared.

I don't know that I can make it out of this one alive, Goddess. I don't know that I have the skill or the strength for it. But if I do die in this battle, don't let him find Excalibur. Let it sink into the earth, never to be found again. It is too important.

Her prayer muttered, Niamh tried for one last offensive.

When he came for her again, she spun behind him and grabbed him by the back of the neck, sinking the crook of her elbow around his throat and tightening with all the might left inside her. She screamed with the effort as she dragged him down to earth. Everything living in the forest could hear them as they fought. There was blood everywhere.

He fought her with every breath. And just before his eyes closed and he lost consciousness, Niamh whispered to him. "Tell your masters that no matter who I work for, I work against them. Tell them they have made an enemy, and that I will fight to keep their power weak. Tell them, most of all, that the sword is not theirs. Descendant or Ancient, the sword is not theirs."

With that, she dropped his limp body to the ground. By the time he awoke, she would be long gone. Exhausted, but still running on the thrill of the fight, she dug through his clothes, and came up with a letter written in a language she knew how to read. The instructions were clear, direct, and they were about her. It took her breath away. She had not known that the Hidden Ones were being watched so closely, nor that the Order of the Ancients had learned so much about her. Hytham must have been hiding as much from her and she was from him.

The woman you're looking for is named Niamh. She wears a cloak with ravens embroidered on the shoulders, and carries the sword known as Excalibur from the northlands of Caledonia. Whatever you must do to take the sword from her is within your power. She may still be working with the Hidden Ones, so I directed an attack on their little bureau in Lunden at the same time.

– The Adder's Son, serving the Ancients.

"In other words," Niamh said, glancing down at the man she may or may not have killed, "you were meant to kill me and leave my body as a sacrifice for the wolves in your wake."

She glanced up, listening carefully for the sound of other predators that she knew were somewhere in the forest, waiting for a free meal. She had known Mordred's followers would be coming for her, but this was information she could use. The Order of the Ancients – the very people that Hytham and Marcella were fighting against – were the same ones that wanted her dead and now the Descendants of the Round Table were orchestrating an attack on Lunden as well.

She had to warn them. She couldn't let Hytham return to the bureau only to meet his death. And, as much as she despised Marcella, it was better to have her alive to strengthen the initiative of the Hidden Ones, rather than to lose her as an ally.

Niamh felt weak. A little woozy. She glanced down at her forearm and saw that she had not entirely escaped the Order of the Ancients. Her heart fell as she saw the deep gash.

Based on the amount of poison, she wasn't sure if she would die, but she certainly wouldn't make it back to Lunden. Not to help Hytham, in any case. She might not make it to Avalon alive at this rate. She searched her hip for the herbs that she carried, only to find that she had lost her kit in the fight. To go back and search for it in the dark would waste valuable time.

She crawled over to where Excalibur was hidden and sheathed it back on her hip. She was too far away to warn the Hidden Ones, too outside their circle of trust to do it safely, but there was one person who might be able to help her get word to the people she cared about, even if they were on opposing sides of the same conflict. She could go to Valka. She could ask Valka to heal her, if the Norse seer so chose. And she could ask Valka to carry a message or complete her quest, if Niamh did perish. Valka would understand the cost of leaving Excalibur in the hands of the unworthy. After all, the Norse had to have artifacts such as these, artifacts of power that could only be kept by those who were worthy enough to hold them.

Niamh knew, as she hoisted herself up onto her horse once more, that she was not worthy to wield Excalibur except in the service of Avalon. But, as she turned herself towards the south once more, she hoped to be able to pass her quest on to someone she could trust before it was her time.

NINETEEN

The midlands were boggy from the endless rain. The wet and damp soaked through Niamh's layers until they reached the bone. Her horse whinnied often in protest, stopping in front of large puddles of water and refusing to walk through them.

"I know, I know. You want a stable and to be dry. So do I," she said, patting the horse's rain-spattered mane with her free hand. The poor creature wouldn't hold out for much longer under these conditions, and she'd promised to Epona, the goddess and protector of horses, that she would be kind to the animals that ferried her to and fro. The cold was getting to his joints, Niamh thought.

If she took the horse to a glade or meadow, and slept in the open air for another night, the horse might not make it to the next stop, or the one after. And Niamh could not afford to lose a horse in the middle of this journey, not now, especially at this last push.

"At the next inn, no matter who is there, we'll stop," she

promised. After all, slogging through the mud and the wet, she wasn't moving quickly enough for her own liking. If she kept riding like this, she'd be liable to catch cold on top of the poison running through her body, and being ill would not help her fulfill her promises to Avalon.

Soon enough, after following a long muck-strewn road and past pastures full of creatures that were well fed, they came upon a small village, quiet and peaceful in the drizzle. One building, close to the river she had been following toward Lunden, had its doors open rather than shut, and familiar songs flowed out the door like a longed-for greeting. An inn. Without a second thought, she put her horse inside the establishment's warm stable.

Before she could care for herself, she wiped the horse down, drying the deep brown coat so that the horse would also stay healthy and warm overnight.

Before heading through the door of the tavern, Niamh checked to be sure that Excalibur was unidentifiable. She wrapped cloth around the pommel more tightly, unsure if she would be seeing friends or foes inside. She wasn't even sure who constituted friends or foes anymore. After all, an anonymous Pict-appearing woman traveling by herself southward was not exactly the safest thing that she could have been. It was much safer than being herself though, with two to three separate secretive organizations following her for the thing that her people held most dear.

Inside, the tavern smelled of sweat, vomit, damp wool, and ale. It was the best thing Niamh had smelled in a long time. The men and women gathered at the long tables in front of the fire slammed their mugs and drinking horns down, all singing the same drinking song. She didn't know the tune, but she knew how to fake it, joining in by banging the table at the appropriate beats and listening carefully to pick up the words if she could.

A tankard of weak ale was passed into her hands after the song was done, and curious eyes turned toward her. She had hoped she could ignore them, just say she was passing through, but she was too unique to pull that off, and so instead she had to think. Thinking was hard. The cold had made her shiver down to her spine, and her muscles ached from being so long on the road with little rest.

"Where did you come from, girl?" a man with a gruff voice asked. He seemed taller than most of the others in the inn. His hair was silvered and his eyes were deep brown and full of suspicion.

"North," she replied, not wanting to specify further unless required. She touched her kerchief, hoping it remained in place. "Headed south to see family."

She didn't want to expend energy on speaking. The poison was making its way through her system, and she could only hope that it was something she could overcome. Her veins felt like they had mud flowing through them. It wasn't enough to kill her immediately, but she needed treatment. She thought food and warmth might be the first step to such recovery.

"A girl like you off on her own?" he asked, giving her a once over. "You sure you can handle yourself?"

"I do fine with a sword," she said, wishing this man would stop looking at her like she was something to be carried off into the night. She sipped her ale and contemplated what her next move would be even as she soaked up the heat of the room. If the tavern broke into chaos, she'd have to leave this town and find another – which wouldn't do well by her or by the horse. "But I really just want a rest," she finished and even she could hear the weariness in her tone.

The man's eyes filled more with concern than suspicion. Niamh was relieved that he turned away, deeming with his body language that he didn't see her as a threat. It was the first time that had been the case in ages.

"The girl deserves to rest, old man," a woman chided. Niamh turned her head and saw the voice came from the server standing by the casks of ale and mead. She nodded gratefully to the woman.

"A girl on her own on the road deserves some peace of mind, and we can give it to her, no matter who she is." The server came over and placed a meal in front of her. Nothing fancy, but warm and filling after days on the road with only spit-roasted rabbits to eat. Niamh dug in with a ferocity.

"I don't need a room. I'll sleep with my horse," Niamh said after she had eaten her fill. "I haven't any coin to pay for a bed. I barely have enough to cover this." She laid what meagre coin she had on the table.

The woman nodded, and didn't argue, but silently handed her some furs to sleep under. Niamh carried them out to the stable, and curling up beside her horse she fell asleep quickly, smelling the hay and the rain as it fell on the earth.

When she awoke, it was with a dagger at her throat.

"Give it to me," a low, angry voice said. Niamh didn't know who had her at a disadvantage, but instead of wasting her breath on a response, she quickly punched out and a yelp of pain rewarded her. Her assailant dodged backward, the sharp point of a knife no longer at her throat.

On the ground lay her saddle bag, tossed. She leapt over the remains of its insides, pawing through her ruined warrior clothes, and then kicked at her assailant's knee, making him scream in pain.

"You try to move again, I'll just kill you," she said, stomping on his wrist to make him drop his weapon, then kicking it far away from them both. "I'm going to be on my way, and you're going to think more carefully about attacking sleeping women next time."

She swiftly got all her belongings back into the bag, feeling like every second was dragging out longer and longer, as if at any minute she was going to lose speed and collapse, leaving her open for this attacker to catch her off guard.

Slinging the bag over her shoulder she glanced down at her assailant one final time as he rolled on the ground in pain.

"I don't know if you were sent to kill me by someone, or if you just thought you'd take advantage of a woman alone on the road, but either way your choices have led you to this: if you follow me, I'll kill you. It won't be a pretty death, and it won't be what you deserve."

The young man swallowed, eyes growing larger as he realized that whatever he thought he was getting into, this was several times worse than anything he could have imagined.

"Now, tell me, which one of them sent you?" She knelt

slowly, and placed her small dagger neatly at the base of his pulsing throat.

"The Descendants of the Round Table," he whined. Niamh was not used to them breaking so easily, but he was clearly terrified. "My great grandfather served the true king and my family has a claim to the sword that you carry."

At that, Niamh laughed. This scrawny boy who could not hold a dagger well, who broke at the slightest threat of violence, believed that he could hold Excalibur? The sword's energy would destroy him.

"No. The sword belongs to Avalon. You can tell them that. I am letting you live so that you can carry that message to them. Stop trying to convince us that we should give it up," she said.

"Your allies won't help you," he replied, spitting at her. "They can't. We burned their hideout in Lunden to the ground."

The poison in her veins was one thing, but the fear was another. As much as she hated Marcella – and they had parted on bad terms – she didn't want her to die. And there were others who came and went through the bureau. She had never seen them, but she had known they were there.

She couldn't think of anything else to say, no words to threaten them, no questions to ask. All she knew was that she had been too late to help them. Too late to reach Valka in time to spread a warning.

She rose, knowing she did not need to use her dagger to keep him in check any longer.

"They are no allies of mine. I will know if you're following me," Niamh said, keeping her voice low and fierce even though her whole body was shaking with the lies she spoke and her grief over the Hidden Ones. "I am a daughter of Avalon and I will not be stopped by any man in the service of my quest."

With those words, she mounted her horse and sped off, leaving the boy lying in the dust with the shame he would feel when he had to report that he failed to kill her while she was sleeping.

She knew one thing: she wouldn't be safe as long as she was on the road, not from anyone. The Order of the Ancients, the Descendants of the Round Table, and the Hidden Ones had enough contacts across this island, and enough coin to tempt anyone who was desperate to help them.

The moon was high in the sky when she made it out of the town. She hadn't slept long, but it had been enough. Recklessly, she thought she could make it all the way to Avalon, but from the waves of nausea coursing through her, she had to stay on track to find the one person who might be able to help her if she arrived at their door. She turned her horse towards Ravensthorpe.

Perhaps Valka wasn't her friend anymore, but Valka would understand her need to protect the sword. And, if there was a chance that Hytham wasn't back at the bureau, Niamh needed to send him warning. Had he tried to follow her, or had he gone back to Marcella to admit that he had misjudged Niamh? She shuddered to think of Marcella's response before the Descendants arrived, determined to burn the place to the ground. The guilt weighed on her heart.

It would not do to dwell upon the choices she had made – all that Niamh could do was move forward and accept the consequences. Either way, she had to warn whoever was left of the Hidden Ones. Valka's home was, surprisingly, the last place she could try and find sanctuary, even as the poison worked its way further into her veins.

The landscape changed as she continued to ride to the south and west. The trees became taller, and she spotted flowers filling the hills and valleys. If she turned further south, she would find a swamp, full of adders and frogs and probably more small towns populated with Britons starving for a bit of coin. The monasteries wouldn't help her if she couldn't reach Ravensthorpe – their residents didn't approve of her practices – and they would ask her to pledge allegiance to another god in order to receive safety from them.

As she rode, keeping her eyes glued on the far distance, she found the poison continuing to work against her, removing memories and replacing them with fatigue. Even though she knew the way to Ravensthorpe, for some reason everything looked wrong, and she had to rely on her instincts. With a shudder, Niamh realized if she did not find Valka soon, she might not make it.

When Niamh finally spotted the cottage, located slightly outside of the protections of the village, she nearly collapsed with relief. In a way, Niamh felt that the land had accepted Valka and had allowed her a sacred place to work her Norse magics.

With great effort, she dismounted and hid her horse in the woods, in the event Ravensthorpe scouts were searching for her too. Each step felt heavy and difficult, and she could feel how ill she truly was. She could not imagine how much worse it would be if she had taken a deeper wound somewhere critical, one that would have increased the dosage of the poison into her body. Likely, she wouldn't have made it here. Even so, she felt like this was the end of her journey. She gripped Excalibur tight and approached the cottage.

Come on, Valka. Be home, she thought.

The house was small, but the smoke that came out of the chimney was not pure gray like all the other homes in Ravensthorpe. It had an edge of purple to it. Niamh knew that there were herbs that tinted the flame and were used in rituals in Avalon as much as where Valka originated from. Another commonality for them both.

Good. You're here. Niamh sagged as the skies darkened with the coming night and she briefly looked up to see crows settling all around her. Ambassadors of the Goddess, come to bear witness to Niamh. Or were they here as omens of her death? More than likely.

Niamh made her way slowly to the back entrance of the cottage. A strange numbing cold filled her. Her hands shook as she raised her right fist and banged on the door. She hoped that Valka wouldn't kill her on sight.

Valka's face was full of surprise when she opened the door. Niamh was grateful to see that anger was absent from the seeress' expression. Perhaps the news of Niamh's betrayal had not reached her yet. But then Valka's face suddenly transformed.

"You," she snarled, reaching out to grab Niamh by the throat.

Niamh used the last remnants of her energy to duck and step backwards before Valka could make contact. "I'm not here to hurt you. I'm here to give you information," Niamh yelped, adding as an afterthought, "and I need your help!"

"Do you have the sword?" Valka asked with such harshness in her voice. "Do you have Eivor's Excalibur?"

"I won't be able to answer any of your questions until you help me," Niamh said. If Valka didn't help her soon... her knees gave out from underneath her. "You're a healer. Heal me. There was poison. One of the Order of the Ancients got to me. I'm not one of them. Valka, I swear on the Goddess that I do not work for them." She pulled back her sleeve to show Valka the festering wound on her arm.

"I should scream and have Ravensthorpe's warriors deal with you," Valka said, raising her hand as though to strike Niamh. The hand remained suspended, and Niamh waited for the blow.

"But you did everything you could to help the women at that nunnery," Valka said, her hand lowering. "And because of that, I will at least give you the chance to tell me what happened. I might still kill you myself later."

Niamh could have cried with relief. Valka bent down and helped Niamh stand before ushering her over the threshold and settling her into a chair in the kitchen.

"What did the poison look like?" Valka asked, inspecting the wound.

"Black? Thick? I feel like I'm too heavy. I'm getting cold." Niamh shivered.

Valka tsked and began bustling about the kitchen, pulling herbs and various tools from assorted trunks and shelves around the room. Niamh blinked heavily, determined to watch and terrified of falling asleep. Her eyes kept lidding over. There was something important she had to tell Valka … if only she could remember how to speak …

"One of my attackers … a boy … he said the Lunden Bureau has been attacked," she finally managed to say. "He was part of the Descendants of the Round Table. It all blurs together for me now. But it wasn't me. Or the Women of the Mist. Valka, Avalon is a good place. We … they … aren't the enemy."

The walls between her lies and her truth were coming down. The poison was taking her closer to the veil.

Valka thrust something under her nose. It smelled awful. Like bog water, pitch and manure.

"Drink this. I'll talk now. You already had the sword by the time the attack happened, didn't you?" Valka replied, brow furrowing, without waiting for a response. "I saw … that you were not there. I saw that the sword would leave Eivor's side, but I didn't see who had taken it. I think there was more than one outcome to this vision of mine."

Niamh sipped. She nearly gagged, but she forced herself to drink the whole cup. "There usually is when you cannot see through the mists of time in that way," she agreed. "Yes, you are correct. I am a witch-warrior of Avalon. I serve the gods and the goddesses just like you – though different gods and goddesses."

Valka's eyes narrowed at that. "So, you were sent to spy. Marcella was right."

Niamh could feel the medicine that Valka had given her doing its work. Valka was as talented as the Avalon healers.

If she could salvage their relationship, perhaps they could learn from each other.

"I was sent to claim the property of my people. Excalibur never should have left Stonehenge. Eivor shouldn't have freed it or taken it." Niamh struggled to sit up further in the chair to resist falling asleep. This was too important a conversation. "But I did take the identity of the woman, Nimue, that the Hidden Ones were trying to recruit. I intercepted the letter addressed to her and took her place."

"What does this sword mean to you?" Valka said after a long moment.

"It is … like your hammer of Thor," Niamh said, her eyes brightening when she realized there was a commonality, a theme between their two practices. "It is a gift from the gods to our people. But it is only meant to be wielded by those that the gods see fit to send us as protectors. The blade will not light up for me. It does not light up for many. But the legends say that when Arthur picked up the sword, the blade glowed gold with an inner power."

Valka nodded. "An object of power. We do not have Thor's hammer hidden away somewhere for someone to hold, but if we did, we would guard it with the most powerful magics that we could, the strongest warriors that would volunteer. You are the warrior sent to collect it for your people. I do understand."

Niamh sagged with relief. She had been aching for someone to understand her and why she had done what she had. She hadn't wanted to harm the Hidden Ones or their allies. She had only wanted to do what was right by the people whom she served. Valka validated her choice to serve the gods first, rather than the people she had only recently met, despite the relationships they had all built with each other.

"Enough talking now. You must rest." Valka guided Niamh to a room she had not seen on her first visit, a place for convalescence. She lay down in the bed of furs and nestled into their softness and resulting warmth. In the back of her mind, she worried she should be feeling unsafe, that the Danish seeress might betray her in some way, but instead, she allowed the medicines to take over. When she awoke, she knew that she would have more strength than she did now. She trusted in the healing powers of Valka.

TWENTY

When Niamh woke, she felt like she was on fire. Not only was she warm for the first time since she had been attacked in the woods, but her veins were full of energy instead of poisoned mud. Wriggling out of the furs, she put a hand to her forehead, fearing a fever, only to discover she felt rejuvenated. Her mind was as sharp as it had always been.

Yet, when she sat up – still a bit achy and with a head rush – she heard a voice that made her freeze. She had been betrayed. Or at least, that's what it sounded like.

"You let her stay? You didn't kill her?"

Hytham. His voice was not full of warmth and thoughtfulness like she'd grown accustomed to, but instead simmered with anger. At Valka. At her.

"Hytham, I think we've been going about this all wrong. Eivor didn't have a right to that sword. It would be as if Niamh and her leaders had taken Thor's hammer," Valka said.

Niamh strained to hear Hytham's answer, but she

couldn't make out his response. She would have to get closer, but her feet refuse to move.

How had Hytham found her? Had Valka gone straight to him while she slept, with Niamh's story on her tongue? For that matter, how long had Niamh slept for? There was no one to ask but Valka... and Valka was occupied with someone who hated Niamh, but who would at least hesitate before slaughtering her outright, unlike Eivor or Marcella. Niamh sent up a thanks to Valka's forethought.

Finding her courage, Niamh crept out of the room where she had slept and into the hallway, where she could get a clear view of Hytham and Valka in the main common area of the hut without being seen herself.

Hytham's face was etched with rage. He had clearly been wounded by Niamh's betrayal in the highlands. Niamh slunk back into the shadows, hoping Valka and Hytham would not notice her while they talked.

"I should never have grown fond of her," Hytham said, his rage giving way to great regret. His mix of emotions pained Niamh to see.

"She came to me dying, Hytham. She explained everything, even about how she took Nimue's identity to insert herself into the Hidden Ones. She was willing to sacrifice anything to get that sword back for her people. I don't think she meant to harm you, not in the way you perceive, but I do think we weren't meant to have that blade."

Niamh let out a slow breath of relief. Knowing that Valka understood her actions meant the world. She ached to hear Hytham speak about forgiveness, even though she knew she had no right to ask for it. She couldn't look at him due to her shame and glanced out the window for a reprieve. The thicket outside was thick and green ... until she realized the movement among the leaves was no squirrel or rodent, but men dressed in black, armed to the teeth. They seemed to be waiting for someone to give a signal.

Fear raced through Niamh. Had they come to storm Ravensthorpe? No ... there weren't enough of them to take down a whole village. What could they possibly ... ?

With dread, Niamh quickly realized that these men had been following her for a good while. From their dress, they were clearly not members of the Hidden Ones. No, these men were armed like Britons, which meant they were Descendants of the Round Table. They must have followed her after she had spared the boy from the inn.

Niamh, you fool! There was no more time for thought, only to act.

"We don't have time to fight," Niamh announced as she strode into the common room, meeting Hytham's gaze. "Not each other, anyway. Pretend as though you don't see them." She gestured outside at the men and Hytham and Valka's eyes followed. Hytham turned to glare at her, and took two steps forward, but Valka grabbed his shoulder, holding him back.

"Who did you bring here?" he hissed.

"They must have followed me. I was attacked by both the Order of the Ancients and the Descendants of the Round Table. But they're going to kill all three of us if we don't act now!" Niamh snapped. "If I wanted you dead, I could have stayed quiet and let them slay the both of you for me. But I don't!"

With that, Niamh shoved past both Valka and Hytham, and grabbed Excalibur from its resting spot against the wall. She carefully eased the front door open, knowing subtlety would be of no use to her, and charged the first man. Stabbing him with all her might, she bared her teeth at the others, who eagerly stepped into the fight.

It was her that they were hunting, not Hytham or even Marcella. It was the woman with Excalibur that they had come for. She saw the delight on their faces and knew they would kill her if they could and take the sacred sword she wielded.

She would fight them with what they most desired.

Pulling Excalibur into a defensive posture, she waited, and sure enough the first enemy sword blow rained down on her own blade. She felt the parry with her whole body, pushing back with all her might to stay upright. Her legs ached with the force of the attack, making her cry out.

While there weren't enough of them to take out the whole village, there were too many for her to fight on her own. At best count, she estimated eight. In the deepening twilight their black uniforms made it hard to tell who was who, and what was just a tree standing sentry in the darkness.

Another sword came for her, and she blocked it, bringing Excalibur from her front to raise behind her head. Her shoulders and wrists took the brunt of that attack. Glancing to the side, she could see that Valka and Hytham had decided to help her fight off the intruders, but she couldn't ascertain more than that due to another blade crashing down next to her. She dodged, lost her footing, and rolled out of the way into some bushes, concealing her momentarily from view.

Behind her, Valka's shout cut through the battle. "Hytham, you can either be angry and let these men kill her, or—"

Niamh's attacker advanced with two others, and Niamh struggled back to her feet to raise the great sword when Hytham appeared, drawing his own weapon at one of her attackers.

Niamh swung Excalibur at the open side of another attacker, connecting with his leather armor and slicing through it, knocking him backwards into another one of his fellow fighters. A series of curse words flew from his lips.

"Once I help you rid yourself of these vermin we're going to talk," Hytham said, glowering at her before smacking one of her attackers in the face with his sword. The man went down without a sound.

Niamh smiled in agreement. Hytham brought his back to hers and they fought in a circle, taking each attacker as they came. One man charged her like a bull, screaming from the depths of his lungs. She met his attack swiftly, dodging the sword that he tried to drop on her head. As soon as Excalibur made its way into the man's gut his sword fell, useless, with a clatter.

Niamh looked behind her and saw Hytham deflecting a blow from one of the last Descendants. They had gone from eight to one in what felt like a blur. Hytham knocked the man out and his body crumpled in a heap at Hytham's feet. Soon, the only sound was their heavy and exhausted breathing. Both of them had fought hard and well as they defeated their foes.

"You..." Hytham finally said as he turned on Niamh, "... you betrayed me."

"But I also helped you," Niamh countered. "I killed Deoric, I furthered your mission, I went on errands for you, I healed you..."

"And I invited you into my community. I trusted you, and you took something from one of our most trusted allies!"

"It wasn't hers to begin with!"

Both of them stopped shouting at once. Stared at each other.

"I expected that you would be loyal to us if we took you in," Hytham said. "And instead, you stole Eivor's sword. You betrayed her hospitality and soiled the name of the Hidden Ones."

"Excalibur wasn't yours or hers. It's ours. My people's. I'm meant to take it back," she said, sounding tired. She was tired of being hunted, tired of being chased, tired of having to hide who she was and what she was doing from everyone around her. Most of all she was tired of being cold.

"So, you admit that you were planning to steal it from the very first," Hytham said, softer now but still ripe with anger. Yet, he didn't attack her or reach to take the sword.

"It doesn't belong to us," Valka said quietly, approaching them from behind.

"The seer has an opinion," Hytham replied bitterly. "Who are your people, then, Niamh? The Order of the Ancients? Another group believing they have a destiny to crush this country under their heel? Tell me, Valka. What do you see? Because I only see a traitor."

Hytham's criticism of the seer surprised Niamh, but Valka stepped around her, facing Hytham directly. "I'll tell you and you'll listen to it if you want to be a part of this village. I may not know everything about these Women of the Mist, but Niamh has made it clear that this is what her people – Avalon – need. Excalibur is theirs and we must honor that. Now, we all know that both the Order of the Ancients and the Descendants of the Round Table are after this sword. Hytham, you can either help her deal with all these enemies – or you can send her out to an almost certain death on the road without our help. But that's a choice that you have to make."

Niamh turned her eyes up to Hytham, desperate to appeal to him so that he would reconsider being her ally rather than her enemy. "Please. I know you're angry, but I'm not trying to harm you, or destroy the Hidden Ones. I'm trying to make sure that my people are safe and follow the mission I've been given. I'm a priestess with the Women of the Mist and after working with the Hidden Ones, I know we are all on the same side. Avalon's flaw is their secrecy, but if we can get them back Excalibur, I know there is a possibility for a lasting truce between us both."

Hytham held her gaze. Niamh could tell that he was struggling with both his pride and rage, but Hytham would always put the needs of the Hidden Ones above any personal matter.

"Fine," he snarled, sheathing his blade. "What do you propose, Valka, to keep the priestess safe?"

"I suggest that we make things harder for the Order of the Ancients and make them think the sword is gone for good," Valka said, folding her hands together. "The sword is the hinge that makes the Order of the Ancients' plans come together. They need the sword to unite the beliefs of this land and without it, they have nothing but myth. Thus, we must destroy it."

Niamh's mouth dropped in shock. Words dried up. *Destroy Excalibur?*

"No, priestess, I won't destroy the real thing." Valka's amusement was clear.

"It needs to be returned to the isle of Avalon," Niamh sputtered.

"And so it will be. But first, we will create a copy of the sword," Valka said.

"And then what? Eivor carries this false Excalibur until the Order of the Ancients, or the Descendants of the Round Table, take it? We can't afford to even have a false Excalibur floating around," Niamh insisted.

"Why not?" Hytham asked, his hostility seeming to slowly disappear the more they spoke.

"Because even a copy allows people to believe that the bearer has been chosen by the sword. It grants power. If Eivor had carried Excalibur long enough, it wouldn't be outside the realm of possibility that she would have been asked to become queen of Mercia." Niamh studied the great sword and continued softly, "Ultimately, Excalibur's most important function is as a symbol. It rests as part of the Sacred Table. If the Descendants or the Order of the Ancients proclaimed themselves the true king, it could spell disaster."

"Listen to me, Niamh," Valka urged. "By creating and

then destroying a copy of Excalibur, the Order of the Ancients will believe the sword is gone for good, and the Descendants of the Round Table will believe the Northmen responsible for such a desecration, and thus, won't come looking for it on your secret isle." Valka looked pleased with her plan. "They all know you are in possession of the sword, but what if it was seen as if you had lost it back into the hands of the Danes? And us Danes, knowing how powerful the object is, decided to, say, sacrifice it to our gods?"

A startled but understanding smile tugged at Niamh's lips. "You're suggesting you destroy the copy somewhere obvious, somewhere the Order of the Ancients will be watching. It will stop all their machinations in their tracks."

"Exactly. Perhaps we can invoke a ceremony on one of Avalon's sacred sites in our own version of a sacrifice."

"You do know we only light bonfires to celebrate the turning of the seasons and for handfasting and at Beltane, but we don't burn people. Yet, if we take advantage of the belief that we do..." Niamh smiled, "... all the better."

"We will offer a *blót*," Valka murmured. "An altered sacrifice where we offer up the great Excalibur to our gods in exchange for even greater good fortune upon us. The Order of the Ancients will believe this of us, just as we believed in the possibility of your human sacrifice, Niamh. But where shall we do this?"

"One of our sacred sites is the White Horse," Niamh offered. "It is a huge horse carved in the hillside in white chalk."

Hytham and Valka conferred without words and then, as one, nodded in agreement.

"But Marcella cannot know, not until we're done," Hytham said.

Sudden fear for the bureau filled Niamh. "The bureau! Hytham, there was an attack planned. I heard it was burned to the ground. I didn't think... I should have said something earlier..."

Hytham gave her a small smile. "Never fear. I received word from her before I arrived here. Things are not quite as dire as you might have heard. You forget – us Hidden Ones are quite resourceful."

"I think it would be best if Marcella was left entirely in the dark. Perhaps permanently," Valka added. "She will be unhappy to know, but also unhappy not to be involved."

"She will be unhappier when she learns that you were incorrect to trust me, and that you decided to work with a pagan spy anyway," Niamh said.

At that, Hytham laughed and clapped her on the shoulder. "Let's get you some food, priestess. You still seem weak from the poison Valka told me about. You'll need clothes to disguise yourself and more rest. Valka and I will investigate a trusted source to craft Excalibur's twin. Then, we'll set out in the morning."

"I should come with you," Niamh argued.

"I can't invite you into Ravensthorpe. Someone will ask questions. Someone will think that you're not who we say you are – at worst case a scout who was in Caledonia with us will show up and recognize you. You'll be safe here, though."

Niamh sighed. The fight had drained her of any rejuvenated strength, and she could feel the weariness creeping in. "As you will it. I would rather stay in the shadows, anyway."

"Spoken like a true Hidden One," Hytham replied.

Together, they moved the bodies of the fallen and then Hytham and Valka left Niamh in the quiet of the forest. Her whole body ached with the tiredness of fighting on an empty stomach, and healing from the poison.

She lay down on the furs. Looking out of the window she could see the shapes of the stars as night coalesced. The darkness fell so sharply that she imagined if she went out into the forest on her own, she wouldn't be able to see at all and she would have to work on instinct until she found her way back to Valka's hut. She dozed until new movement in the hut startled her awake.

Valka came bearing a warm stew, hearty and thick and full of meat. It was served with a fresh bread, recently out of the fires, and an herbal drink that smelled like something the Lady would concoct for brave warriors who came home tired and wished for their own beds.

"Thank you," Niamh said, accepting the offering. "Is...?"

"All is well," Valka said. "Hytham knows what he is doing and his network on this land is stronger than you think."

Niamh nodded and took a bite, delighting in the food. As she ate, Valka began to speak.

"When I first heard of the Women of the Mist I assumed because you followed different gods, you would be like the Christians, always trying to force us Danes to follow your people, rather than leaving us to follow our own. But it seems that you are perfectly happy to let me follow Odin while you follow your Morrigan." She paused. "Or whoever else blesses you, I should say."

Niamh nodded. "I don't expect you to leave your gods and goddesses behind. Just to respect that we have our own." She glanced up at the stars, feeling at peace and safe. "We believe that we are women meant to protect our people. We are called to serve them, in childbirth, in war, in matters of illness and in heartache. We are witches, but not because we want to bring harm to people – the exact opposite. We want to bring safety. That's why Excalibur is so important to us. Because it is an artifact of magic."

Niamh glanced down at the sword and smiled.

"I'm proud of myself for finding it. For being able to take it home."

"You truly don't believe you're meant to wield it?" Valka asked, taking Niamh's empty bowl.

"I must take it to whomever is meant to bear it." Niamh reached out and picked the sword up, feeling the leather wrapping around the pommel. A fit disguise that she would not dismantle until it was back on Avalon safely.

"You know your own heart," Valka said, nodding. "And, if you speak true, perhaps there is a truce to be forged between Avalon and the Hidden Ones. But until then, I'll leave you to your rest. Tomorrow will be a day of tricks and deceit. We will need all our wits to pull it off."

TWENTY-ONE

Niamh woke to the sun, and she knew without a doubt that she was not alone. Turning slowly inside her furs, she glanced to the door, where she saw a fox staring at her. It did not stir when she made eye contact with it, and she smiled.

"Hello, little friend. Are you here to bless me with your cleverness?"

The fox yelped, neither in agreement or denial, and ran away, escaping back into the forest from whence it came. She felt the blessing of the gods in that moment. She had been clever enough to do what they had asked of her.

Niamh got up and looked out the door. The forest was peaceful, as if the skirmish that had occurred there only the night before had never happened.

Far in the distance she could see Hytham and Valka walking her way. They had kept their word. They were going to help her. Hope filled Niamh, something she had not felt in a long time.

"Good morning!" she called across the clearing. Valka carried a long, wrapped package in her arms, looking smug.

"Good morning. We have a replica for you," Valka said. "And we have a thought of what to do to make our plan foolproof."

Hytham sat down across from Niamh after handing her some bread to eat. "What I am going to suggest is that we disguise you ... not as a Pict woman – they'll be looking for that – but as a Norsewoman. You can carry your sword all the way back to wherever it belongs, but you'll have to go alone. Then, if you're caught, it will still be assumed that Excalibur remains in Danish hands. But first, you'll ride with us as yourself – to that white horse you mentioned."

Niamh caught onto his intentions quickly. "If I ride with you as a priestess, the Descendants or the Order of the Ancients can assume I'm either your prisoner, or that I'm unable to stop you from the ritual."

"The blót," Valka supplied and handed Niamh the package.

Niamh opened the wrappings around the false sword and compared it to the one that she bore on her own hip. It was very close. "This is a remarkable fake. You would believe it was the real thing."

Hytham nodded, pleased. "When the time is right, you'll ride back to Avalon. I assume it's a close enough ride that you can make the disappearance work ... and get there quickly in the event something goes wrong."

Niamh sensed the query, the attempt to gain just a little bit of information about where she was going. She didn't take the bait. "I will be fine with wherever makes the most sense. A horseback ride, long or short, will not impede the plan."

Hytham looked put out with her lack of shared information, but he didn't comment on it further.

Valka looked amused. "I see you're well matched."

Niamh let out a sigh and then looked back at Hytham. She would miss working with him and felt their inevitable parting as a source of sadness. "Will this provide trouble for you with Marcella or the other Hidden Ones?" she asked.

"Perhaps in that I am willingly destroying an item of great power that could aid the Hidden Ones," Hytham mused. "But it is more important that I remove such a powerful tool from the hands of the Order of the Ancients. If Excalibur could be used in a way to control people and make them bow before someone claiming to be a true king, it is something that must be tucked safely away from the greed of those seeking rulership or power. True or not."

Valka stood and put her hands on her hips. "Niamh, you should wear priestess garb or what Women of the Mist wear, if you can. You should look as much like the Caledonian that you are. It's about time that the people of Ravensthorpe began to treat pagans of this land with respect and recognize them as such."

Niamh gave Valka a hug. "What will your Eivor say when she learns the truth?" she asked. "Will she participate in an alliance, if one can be brokered, after all I've done?"

"She will if I tell her that it is the only way forward," Valka said.

Niamh glanced down at the two swords. She wrapped a leather strap around the pommel of the real Excalibur and slid it into the sheath at her hip. Then she looked at Hytham and Valka and smiled.

"I think it's time for us to put on a show, don't you?"

TWENTY-TWO

Niamh took the lead, riding on a white horse that wasn't hers. She dressed as much as possible in a way that would mark her as a Woman of the Mist, and bound Excalibur to her hip. She draped herself in a warm fur and padded herself with armor, because no priestess would take on a trip like this without it. The raven symbol shone on her cloaked shoulder. It felt strange to be out in public as a priestess, but she hoped she would draw many eyes.

Hytham rode behind her, exuding a deadly ambiance as if he was not to be trifled with.

Valka rode last, somber and covered in feathers. She looked otherworldly, and even though Niamh knew that Valka wasn't a frightening woman, if she had seen this procession she would have been afraid. If she had been one of the Order of the Ancients, she would have been suspicious and worried.

Drawing the Order of the Ancients out was the first step in their plan. They had to create a scene that would spread across the land like wildfire. In essence, they had to create a myth of their own – the Avalon representative either leading – or imprisoned by – these Danes and their friends. A following began to track them as they rode. Young women who had pledged themselves to Avalon dropped in behind their processional, making it known that they too were going to whatever ceremony was taking place, or intending to protect the priestess of the white horse. A few Northwomen dropped in as well, their hands gently resting on their swords, identifying Valka as a sacred seer. It was an excellent disguise. Everyone made their own assumption, allowing for truth and story to wind alongside each other.

Hytham glanced to either side as if in surprise. He was not used to being in plain view of anyone, Niamh thought. This went outside of everything he usually did, and she realized how much he had put forth to help her and help Avalon.

"I believe we have enough witnesses," Niamh whispered behind her to Hytham. "Up at this crossroads over the hill, we will fight for possession of Excalibur. It will be taken that the Women of the Mist disapprove of the Hidden Ones having the sword. Everyone will believe that."

Niamh knew that with a crowd this size, they could spread the word that Excalibur had been destroyed with efficiency, but it also meant she would have to ride to Avalon swiftly, lest the Lady think that she had failed at her quest – and that the Hidden Ones were a true enemy.

Her heart pounded in her chest as they crested the next hill, followed by Avalonians and Danes alike.

A few Britons started to step in behind them, and from what Niamh could see at the front of their procession, they were now followed by many onlookers curious about what was happening between these three people who did not belong together. Perhaps some of them were associated with the Descendants of the Round Table and the Order of the Ancients. They did, apparently, have eyes and ears everywhere.

Hytham edged his horse closer to her, so that they could speak with enough discretion.

"I think it's working," he said. "Soon, you should make your escape."

"But you don't know where the White Horse is," Niamh replied with sudden fear, giving him a look of concern. She hadn't thought to give him a map.

"It's a large horse on a hillside," Hytham said. "Might be hard to miss."

Niamh snorted. "Take the right fork and follow it until you see white streaks in the hills. The head of the horse is facing toward Lunden. You'll want to use the first hill that you'll see and it will lead you right up to the nose."

Niamh had gone to the White Horse for dozens of rituals, and she remembered the walk was always awe inspiring, watching as the bright white chalk came into view, and the face of the horse gazed at her. Once a year, the villagers of Uffington came around it and scoured it, singing and chanting as they made sure that their horse still watched over them.

The crossroads arrived in her vision. Niamh regretted that she could not look upon the horse for courage on this difficult day. Instead, she would have to part ways with her friends, and make her way to Avalon to complete what had been asked of her. To complete this quest for the Lady.

"I cannot agree to what you are asking!" Niamh cried out, turning her horse suddenly to face Hytham and Valka. She reared the steed up. "Avalon does not approve! You must give back what you have stolen! If you do not, I will return to the Women of the Mist and report your sacrilege."

"If you insist that the power belongs to only your people, then it should belong to no one," Valka cried, charging her horse toward Niamh. Her own mount reared back, making her cloak billow in the wind. "Excalibur will be sacrificed to Thor and Odin and it will bring power to us Danes. Avalon has failed to protect it, and now the sword belongs to us!"

"Give Excalibur back to me, traitors!" Niamh yelled as she reared a second time and started to gallop for the crossroads. She turned once more to shout, "You will regret betraying the Women of the Mist."

"Then our gods will fight to the death," Valka replied. "And you will no longer have your sacred artifact – Excalibur will be no more."

Hytham raised his bow and aimed at Niamh, loosing an arrow that narrowly missed her. Hytham then charged toward her, and unsheathed Excalibur's twin, letting it shine in the sunlight, as if chasing her away. Niamh turned her horse in response and kicked it hard in the flank. The horse took off at a gallop, leaving Hytham and Valka in the dust.

The real Excalibur was tucked tight against her, safe and headed for its true home.

She hoped this worked.

TWENTY-THREE

Valka brought up the rear of the assembled crowd, determining that they had about thirty people on foot following them. Some split off, running to spread the word of the event that had transpired. She knew that if they had to, or if someone attacked them, she and Hytham would do everything to be victorious. She had her stores of herbs and poisons to use if they needed them. Of course she and Hytham would also be seeing Asgard if she had to drop the hallucinogens on the ground to distract everyone, but Valka knew it would embolden them.

Hytham and she galloped quickly in the other direction from Niamh until they saw a green hill that made her heart soar. Her homelands had endless snows, and such greenery had been a sight only glimpsed when summers came. But here, the green never faltered except far, far to the north.

Past that green hill she saw lines of white and finally the shape of a horse deliberately carved out of the green hill.

She had never seen anything like it, and her breath caught in her throat. Her horse paused, they both took in this moment, the calm of the energy that surrounded this place. It was as sacred as any place beloved of her own gods.

Hytham pushed them forward at a ruthless pace until his horse arrived at the head of the petroglyph, shouting about how the Danes had the source of power that must be broken or given up so that no one could hold the power of Excalibur. That such power should be in the hands of the gods, rather than of men. Some of the assembled people who had followed mumbled about how it wasn't his place, or his choice – ones that Valka pinpointed as followers of the Women of the Mist.

"That sword is the source of Arthur's power," one man snarled, shouting for the sword to be destroyed. "Throw it in a lake for all I care! It brings nothing but trouble for us, only ridiculous stories of knights that drive our boys from the fields."

A woman on the edge of the crowd whispered a prayer in a language that Valka did not know. When she glanced at the woman, she received a stare that meant the woman was against whatever they had planned for Excalibur.

Valka kicked her horse into a gallop, meeting Hytham at the appointed spot. She knew he had used his network to have those belonging to the Hidden Ones leave the makings of a bonfire available, and he quickly stoked a roaring blaze with the pile of branches and logs. He pulled the faux Excalibur out of the sheath and raised it before handing it to Valka.

"How did you get the sacred sword?" the woman from

earlier shouted, watching Valka with anger. "It doesn't belong to you, Dane!"

"Today we are here to witness the destruction and sacrifice of an artifact of power," Valka called across the hill to the assembled company that seemed to keep growing. She hoped and prayed that no one would try to stop her. If any did, now they might not be able to make it out alive.

She and Hytham would die here, she realized, if anyone in the crowd now tried to take the sword. If the Order of the Ancients were fast enough to rally their people, Hytham and Valka would be doomed.

Valka raised the sword up, holding the blade in one hand and the hilt in another. "Here is Excalibur. We have taken it from those who would use it for ill means. Too many claim it as theirs, but we know it belongs with the gods. We shall sacrifice it to Odin and Thor, in the ways of my people!"

Behind her, Hytham shifted and swiftly moved through the crowd, as if he'd spotted something he didn't like. He vanished behind three more, and all Valka could do was continue, her heart in her throat, imagining an arrow being nocked and aimed straight at her.

"I call upon the heat of Loki's flame to destroy this sword. I call upon the strength of Thor to destroy this sword. I ask my gods to make this sword no longer a tool of power. Strip the power of magic from this blade and make it no more useful than a child's toy. Take that power and heap upon us your favor."

She plunged the sword into the flame, letting the white-hot heat engulf it. The newly forged twin began to melt, made for show rather than use. As she threw another log onto the fire, a man clad in black stepped out of the crowd and charged.

"For Mordred!" he screamed. "The heir to the sword! To the true king! Save the sword!"

Valka saw her death coming upon her. She pulled out what poisons she had, but knew they would not work fast enough. She gripped a dagger, and hoped it would serve her well.

But Hytham stepped forward, grabbing the man and diverting him away from Valka and saving her life. Their swords met with a sharp clang.

"That sword belongs to us!" the man screamed, trying to dart around Hytham to grab Excalibur's twin out of the flames. Hytham met him blade-to-blade as Valka opened her mouth and screamed as if she were a Valkyrie. She watched in triumph as the false sword continued to melt into slag.

"You cannot take it now!" she cried, pointing at the fire with joy.

The attacker stared at the melting sword in horror. His distraction became his undoing, allowing Hytham to stab him in the side, throwing him down the sacred hill to die. Chaos thundered in the crowd, spreading like a madness. Valka had not realized how many people truly had feelings about the sword that Eivor had taken out from underneath Stonehenge.

Some screamed. Others cried. Some helped build the bonfire further, adding what they could to the roaring blaze. The woman who had been speaking in prayer ran toward the sword, looking to see if she could rescue it, but there was no way for her to do so. The sword melted so fast that it would be unsalvageable and had pooled over a large stone in the middle of the fire, the sword's remnants sticking out at an awkward angle. Once that witness realized there was nothing she could do, she charged off. Valka hoped that Niamh had reached the Women of the Mist fast enough to stop any retaliation on the Danes.

In the chaos, Valka turned to Hytham, and gestured for them to leave. They mounted their horses and rode as quickly as they could back to Lunden to report to Marcella and send a missive to Eivor about the fate of Excalibur. They would report its destruction, and aside from the Women of the Mist, Valka and Hytham would be the only ones to know its true fate.

The news of their ritual would spread quickly, and thus a legend would be born.

TWENTY-FOUR

Niamh headed for Avalon as fast as she could beg Epona to let her steed go. She tore across bridges, past fields she had known for years and through towns where the residents attended rituals like Beltane and Yule. These were her people, and each time someone saw her pass, they turned their back, acknowledging that they had never seen her, that she was on a mission that no one but the initiated could witness.

As she rode, she could feel herself being pushed along by the winds of the gods until she reached the shores of Avalon, and she prayed she would not meet a foe or friend. Time was of the essence, to deliver Excalibur and spread the word that her friends, Valka and Hytham, were not to be harmed for what they had done at the White Horse.

She rode, and the gods watched.

When Niamh reached the shores of Avalon she was covered in sweat. Her hands shook as she lifted the sword off her hip and uncovered it from any sort of wrappings keeping it hidden.

"I come to the shores of Avalon to return her sword to her people," she said, facing the water and holding the sword with both hands, pointing the tip toward the sky. She began to walk into the water, each step carrying her closer to the end of her quest. "Lady, hurry! I am here on your behalf."

The rowboat came out to her, and she approached it, stepping into the bow. She did not stop holding onto Excalibur, even as her skirts and her boots soaked through with water and the mists parted to bring her to shore.

The vision that greeted her was the Lady, and all the priestesses and other witches assembled to greet her. They stood silently, bearing witness to her approach.

When the rowboat docked, she stepped off, and raised the sword in her right hand.

It was only then that she saw that the blade glowed gold. She tilted the sword and brought the blade to rest flat side down on her left palm, preparing to hand it off to the Lady and present the sacred sword back to its owner.

Yet, her heart pounded. What could it mean, to have the sword glowing for her? What kind of power was it offering?

"I don't understand..." she whispered as she knelt in front of the Lady, but the Lady only smiled.

Avalon was in control of her sword once again.

And they had a new Lady to wield it.

TWENTY-FIVE

A few weeks later, Hytham and Valka approached the shores of Avalon with an invitation of their own and were greeted by a familiar face when they arrived.

Niamh met them in the rowboat with a smile. The sun shone bright upon Glastonbury, and she was able to give them a clear ride through the lake.

"Have they determined what truly happened?" Niamh asked. "Did the Order of the Ancients continue to search, or have they left well enough alone?"

"There are murmurings…" Hytham replied. "But I hear the Descendants of the Round Table have fallen into disarray and are no longer certain of their goals. It may be possible the death of Excalibur killed any link holding them together."

"And Marcella?" Niamh asked, archly. The Roman had not been invited to Avalon, but Niamh had a terrible curiosity about her fate. Marcella was unwilling to face

Niamh again unless it was on the other side of a sword, according to Hytham's last letter.

"She is as she was. Angry." Niamh almost laughed and shook her head. She realized she had a strange kind of respect for Marcella, but knew the two of them would never see eye to eye.

Once the rowboat stopped on the other side of the lake, the three of them stepped onshore only to be met by a full complement of guards: six young women dressed in deep moss green robes, wearing circlets that included the symbol of the goddess over their brows.

The guard dropped in to surround their guests, and they began the walk up the Tor from this side of the veil. Niamh led her Hidden One companions, dressed in the white gown that she had become accustomed to in her new role. She was not sure how she felt about becoming a Lady, and she wondered if she would prefer a more active life than the one that she was signing up for, but as she led Hytham and Valka up the mossy path to the top of the Tor, she at least knew that this was the right thing for the moment. This was where she belonged, despite her longings for home. A new witch-warrior had been sent in her stead, after all.

"Niamh, why are you carrying Excalibur?" Hytham asked as they paused for a moment for him to catch his breath.

"Everything will be explained when you meet the Lady," she replied, a sly grin crossing her face. "I'm the one with the secrets, after all."

All three of them laughed then, aware of the reality.

They continued to climb the Tor, which had become

part of Niamh's day and no longer strenuous after weeks of morning rituals and evening bonfires. She had been learning how to lead this community, and it had taken many steps to get to where she was headed. However, she kept a close eye on Hytham's progress, only stopping for a breath if he seemed to slow and only when he wouldn't notice.

"What exactly are we here for?" Valka asked as they neared the crest.

"The Lady will fill you in on everything," Niamh responded and stepped through the sacred circle at the top of the Tor.

It was a beautiful glade, paved with white chalk like the White Horse, with a spiral drawn to the center of the circle. It was meant to give the priestesses a walking path during meditation. The edge of the circle was built in stone, a smaller stone circle than the one at Stonehenge or even Avebury, but a circle, nonetheless. The mists began to roll in over the hills to the east. Far in the distance, Niamh imagined she could see the White Horse, watching over the countryside.

Waiting at the center was the Lady herself. She motioned for Niamh to stand next to her. Niamh did so, looking behind her to watch her two friends' approach with awe on their faces. They did not bow or kneel but nodded with respect to the woman who led this island.

"Thank you for coming," the Lady said. "I understand from Niamh that you all are very skilled in the arts that you practice. That you helped her when she was at her darkest hour and that you put the needs of Avalon above your own, at least in your own way. I hope that we can be friends rather than enemies."

Hytham stepped forward. "I am not entirely sure what it is that Avalon does, but I know that we are here to learn about each other and, I hope, to forge a new alliance. While my relationship with Niamh became somewhat hurt in the events of her quest on your behalf, I hope you understand that the Hidden Ones would be happy to work with her again." Hytham spoke politely but with a firm tone.

"Niamh is deciding what her calling is to be, and that is none of your concern," the Lady said sharply, "but whether or not you ally with us is. The Order of the Ancients, as you call them, aren't going to be satisfied just because Excalibur was seemingly destroyed. They seek power. I think that you and I can agree that the way they use that power is not something we agree with, even if we are not entirely on the same side on every decision."

Hytham nodded in agreement, and the Lady's voice softened.

"Niamh has a choice to make – she can either become the liaison to your people – if you're willing to work with her, that is... or she can stay here to become my Lady in Waiting. She'll become the next Lady either way. The sword has chosen her to be my successor, that much is clear. But she can choose what kind of Lady she wants to be. One who wields the sword, and works from the shadows, or one who works as I have done, in the rituals of our people."

Niamh had not known the Lady was going to be quite so plain, but she had mentioned that secrecy was part of Avalon's flaws, after all. Knowing she was going to be the next Lady had been a shock to her, and she was still adjusting to the idea that she had worth to her people beyond being a witch who loved and was dedicated to the Women of the Mist. But she hoped one of the things she could usher through was a strong relationship between the two groups so that prosperity could thrive on the isles.

"The next Lady?" Valka said, the weight of the title heavy in her voice, as she finished wryly, "Well, we've certainly got an interesting ally."

Hytham smiled broadly. "I agree. I look forward to Niamh's choice in the future, but for now, it seems we have some work to do, don't we?" He spread his arms wide, a gesture for everyone to gather together.

Hope filled Niamh. The immediate crisis was over. And now they could build bridges.

ABOUT THE AUTHOR

ELSA SJUNNESON is a Hugo, Aurora and British Fantasy Award winning editor. A deafblind hurricane in a vintage dress, her work has appeared in Serial Box/ Realm's: *Marvel's Jessica Jones: Playing with Fire, Uncanny Magazine*, and *Fireside*. Her debut memoir *Being Seen: One Deafblind Woman's Fight to End Ableism* was published in 2021.

snarkbat.com
twitter.com/snarkbat

WORLD EXPANDING FICTION

Have you read them all?